BEST OF
FRIENDS

BEST OF FRIENDS

KAMILA SHAMSIE

BLOOMSBURY CIRCUS
LONDON • OXFORD • NEW YORK • NEW DELHI • SYDNEY

BLOOMSBURY CIRCUS
Bloomsbury Publishing Plc
50 Bedford Square, London, WC1B 3DP, UK
29 Earlsfort Terrace, Dublin 2, Ireland

BLOOMSBURY, BLOOMSBURY CIRCUS and the Diana logo are
trademarks of Bloomsbury Publishing Plc

First published in Great Britain 2022

A catalogue record for this book is available from the British Library

ISBN: HB: 978-1-5266-4770-2;
Waterstones special edition: 978-1-5266-5786-2; TPB: 978-1-5266-4769-6;
ePub: 978-1-5266-4773-3; ePDF: 978-1-5266-4768-9

2 4 6 8 10 9 7 5 3 1

Typeset by Integra Software Services Pvt. Ltd.
Printed and bound in Great Britain by CPI Group (UK) Ltd,
Croydon CR0 4YY

MIX
Paper from
responsible sources
FSC® C171272

To find out more about our authors and books visit www.bloomsbury.com
and sign up for our newsletters

For Sarah

KARACHI
1988

SUMMER

First day back at school. The sky heavy with monsoon clouds, the schoolyard clustered with students within striding distance of shelter: the kikar trees planted along the boundary wall or the neem tree partway up the path from gate to school building; the many bougainvillaea-framed doorways carved into the building's yellow-stone facade; the area of the playing field beneath the jutting balconies on the first and second floors. Only a few boys, with daring to prove, roamed the most exposed parts of the yard, shirtsleeves rolled up, hands in pockets. Zahra, standing beside the archway that housed the brass bell, was using her height to look over the heads of all the girls and most of the boys, searching.

The school day hadn't officially started yet, but students in grey and white uniforms were already resettling into their formations from the previous term. The cool kids. The thuggish boys. The couples. The judgemental girls. The invisible boys. Zahra had invented these categories after watching a string of teen-centred Hollywood movies on pirated videos, but it did little to make up for the inadequacy of Karachi school life. Without detention, how could there be *The Breakfast*

Club? Without a school prom, how could there be *Pretty in Pink*? Without the freedom required to make truancy possible, how could there be *Ferris Bueller's Day Off*? But the one area where the failure was that of the movies, not of Karachi, was when it came to friendship – it was almost always a subplot to romance, never the heart of a story. Except *The Outsiders*, but that was boys, which meant it was really about how girls caused trouble and led to fights and burning buildings and death.

From where she stood, Zahra had a clear view of the school gate. For most of the day, buses and rickshaws and vans and other ageing vehicles clogged up the streets of Saddar, perhaps heading to Empress Market or the electronics stores that populated the area, but twice a weekday, sleek air-conditioned cars joined in the melee to ferry students to and from the most prestigious of Karachi's schools.

There she was. The Mercedes, sleekest of sleeks, drove right up to the gate and Maryam stepped out and walked into the school grounds. A different Maryam, a different walk. The plumpness that had been on her face seemed to have descended elsewhere over the course of the summer, though it was hard to know exactly what was going on beneath the sack-like grey kameez she was wearing. Maryam stopped to say something to one of the older boys, and as they were talking tugged at her kameez with what was clearly meant to be an absent-minded air. The fabric pulled taut over new breasts, a new waist. The older boy kept on speaking to her as though nothing had happened but when she walked past him, heading to Zahra, he turned to observe her all the way down the length of the path.

Other things had changed too. The wavy shoulder-length hair was artfully tousled rather than wild, the messy eyebrows reshaped into two curved lines. But the smile was the same old Maryam smile that greeted Zahra every time Maryam returned from her family's summer trips to London. And her outstretched hand held a cassette that was always her belated birthday present to her best friend – a mix tape that she had recorded off the radio, with the best of the London charts.

'Do you see what's happened to me?' she said.

'Is it your mother or your tailor who's having difficulty accepting it?' Zahra said, gesturing to the kameez.

'Hard to say. Master Sahib stitches what he thinks my mother wants. Mother says he's easily offended; we can't go back and say it's all wrong or he'll stop doing our clothes and he's the only one to get my sari blouses right.'

'Adulthood is so complicated.'

They smiled at each other, confident of the futures ahead of them in which they'd never face such petty dilemmas. They had barely moved on to swapping notes about the summer apart when Saba approached, with that smile of hers as if she was holding some forbidden delight in her mouth that she was willing neither to swallow nor to reveal. They knew all of each other's smiles, the three girls; at fourteen, they were ten years into what might loosely be called friendship, though Zahra had once looked up from a dictionary to inform Maryam that what the two of them had with each other was friendship, and what they had with the other six girls and twenty-two boys in class was merely 'propinquity' – a relationship based on physical proximity. 'If you moved to Alaska tomorrow, we'd still be best friends for the rest of our lives,' she had told Maryam, who was the only person in the world towards whom Zahra displayed extravagant feelings.

Now there was Saba, standing in front of them, allowing them to cajole her into giving up the secret which she had just heard from her aunt – Mrs Hilal, the biology teacher, to the rest of them. The school's bomb alarm was going to be complemented with a riot alarm. There would be drills throughout the term to ensure the students didn't confuse the first with the second. You wouldn't want 700 students evacuating the building when they were supposed to be inside with doors and windows firmly shut. The school had never known either bombs or riots, but Saba conveyed the news of the anticipated disaster, and the possible mix-up over alarms, with relish.

'My parents are going to get even more hysterical if they hear that,' Maryam said, dragging out the word 'even'. 'The day we got back from London they hired armed guards for our house because all these expats over there kept telling them how dangerous Karachi is. Give me dangerous and keep your boiled cabbage, Londoners. Now no one can come indoors without having to go through some ridiculous procedure of guards calling up the house to make sure they're acceptable, and if someone's on the phone and they can't get through then one of the guards has to run inside – not that they ever run, it's the slowest crawl. You don't worry, Zahra. I gave them a picture of you and said if anyone tries to stop you from entering I'll have them fired.'

'Lucky,' Zahra said, and Maryam grinned. She liked nothing better than to be compared to Lucky Santangelo, heroine of the Jackie Collins novels, composed in equal parts of courage, ruthlessness and loyalty. Saba made a little face and Zahra recognised this expression too: it was the one that said Saba didn't see why Maryam continued to be best friends with Zahra and share private jokes with her when Saba, like Maryam, belonged to that subgroup of students whose parents were part of the 'social set' and who went abroad for their summer holidays and swam at the same private members' club.

'Maybe it's a good idea for the school to have some kind of plan in case the worst happens,' Zahra said, glancing towards the high boundary walls, shards of glass embedded at the top to prevent anyone from climbing over. Last summer, car bombs had killed more than seventy people in Saddar – not far from this school, one of the explosions shattering all the windows of the shop where Zahra and her mother had been buying new school uniforms the previous week. For days after, she'd imagined pieces of glass piercing her throat and eyes. Maryam had been in London and when she'd returned she'd said, 'That was awful; thank god it was during the school holidays,' as if to suggest that no one they knew could have been anywhere around Saddar at such a time of year.

The school bell rang, sending them to the playing field, where ragged columns of students had started to form. The soil was damp from yesterday's rain, and there was one large puddle in the middle of the field, into which some of the rowdier Class 9 boys were stomping to try to splash any girls walking past.

Maryam wasn't the only one in their class to have changed over the summer. There were boys who were taller, other girls who were curvier; this boy had finally shaved off the nest of caterpillars above his lip, that girl had replaced glasses with contact lenses. The only change in Zahra was an added inch of height; beyond that, she was still skinny with poker-straight hair, which her mother cut to just above her shoulders. But something felt different in everyone in their year, however much their outward appearances might have remained unchanged. There was more step in their step than before. They were conscious they were in Class 10 now, old enough for the younger students to look up to them, and also at that stage where familiarity could start to replace deference in their relationship with the A-level students.

School assembly had been cancelled to get everyone indoors as fast as possible as the clouds turned even darker, so they made their way straight up to their new classroom with its thick walls of seaweed green and its wooden desks freshly painted a revolting pink-brown. Maryam and Zahra found two seats together, separated from other desks in the row by an aisle, and Zahra told Maryam about the highlight of her summer, which had been a sighting of all the members of Vital Signs walking out of a house in Phase 5, near that intersection where the man with bougainvillaea behind his ears used to direct traffic. Her father was driving and refused to slow down, let alone stop so she could look at them a little longer. *Just because some boys record a pop song doesn't mean you have the right to start treating them like zoo animals*, he'd said.

'But still. You saw them. That's so cool. It might even be cooler than seeing a pop star in London,' Maryam said, having seen Paul Young strolling through Hyde Park one summer. This was clearly a serious topic that they would return to later, when they had the time to pick through it forensically – did an internationally famous pop star in the city where you spent your holiday outweigh homegrown national sensations hanging out not far from your own neighbourhood?

'I learnt a new Italian word this summer,' Maryam said, resting her elbow on the top of Zahra's chair and leaning towards her. 'Zia. It means "aunt". Also slang for –' she lowered her voice, as she should have done before making light of the name of the dictator '– homosexual. Can you imagine, every time the Italian ambassador meets General Zia he must be thinking –'

'Maryam!'

Zahra glanced around to see if anyone showed signs of having heard. She didn't think that any of their class-mates were from families that supported the president, but it was an unspoken matter, and assumptions were dangerous.

'Don't be paranoid,' Maryam said. She lowered her face towards the hole cut into the desk which served as a pen holder, as if speaking into a mic. 'GHQ, do you want to know what we all think of Wordsworth's "Daffodils"? Off with their sprightly heads!'

The boy sitting behind them – Babar – strode to the front of the class. Picking up a piece of chalk, he scrawled on the blackboard DON'T WORRY IT'S ONLY EVERYTHIN

A teacher's voice sliced off the 'G' he was about to write. 'Mr Razzaq, it's best you sit at your desk and don't parade trousers from a bygone era, don't you think?'

Babar was still for a moment, then reached up and ran his fingers through his thick hair, squared his shoul-ders and turned with a cocky smile. If he'd had a leather jacket, he would have flipped up the collar. He sauntered back to his chair, sat down.

'*My* older brother's school uniform goes to our cook's children,' Saba said loudly.

Zahra pivoted to face Saba, who had found a seat across the aisle from Babar. 'Saba, he's not going to like you if you insult him any more than he did when you wrote him love poems.'

An *Ohhhhhhh!*, building in volume, went round the class until the teacher cut it short by starting to take

11

attendance. Saba wept into her exercise book. Zahra reached into her schoolbag for a tissue, leaned back in her chair, rapped on Babar's knee and passed him the tissue under the desk.

'Is there supposed to be something written on this?' he whispered a few moments later.

Zahra turned around. He'd unfolded the tissue and was holding it like a letter, thumb and forefinger gripping either side. 'She shouldn't have said that, but you can be the nice guy,' she said.

'Miss, do you want me to take my trousers off?' Babar called out, which made all the students laugh, including Saba, and rendered the tissue unnecessary.

*

DON'T WORRY IT'S ONLY EVERYTHIN

Zahra approached the words on the board when everyone had left the classroom. There was a dot of chalk where Babar had intended to start the 'G' before the teacher had interrupted. Until now they had all been students together, taking the same classes, learning or failing to learn the same things, easily able to recover from a bad set of exams brought on by a bout of illness or a cricket series that ate into revision time. But today was the start of the O-level course, and how well or badly you fared in the exams that waited two years down the line would determine the life-altering matter of which American or British university would want you another two years after that. In Zahra's case, it wouldn't be enough to be wanted; she'd have to be wanted enough to qualify for a scholarship in Britain or financial aid in America. She was equally drawn to both countries – the grandeur of Oxbridge, the glamour of

Ivy League – but knew she'd prefer the word 'scholar-ship' attached to her than 'financial aid'.

'How important are the O-level marks, really?' Babar had asked a young teacher – freshly graduated from Columbia in New York – at the end of the previous year, and the teacher had replied, *Don't worry, it's only everything.*

Zahra found a piece of chalk and wrote in the 'G', trying to make it slope forward just as Babar's letters did so it wouldn't look out of place. At a laugh behind her, she turned. Maryam, leaning against the doorframe.

'Always tidying up for everyone,' Maryam said.

'Thought you'd gone to the computer lab already.' Zahra tossed the chalk on to the teacher's desk and deliberately allowed it to roll off the edge.

'We go together as far as we can,' said Maryam, link-ing her arm through Zahra's as they left the classroom.

Maryam was going to Computer Science; Zahra to Chemistry. With the start of the O-level course they'd all had to choose which subjects to take, and so the sep-aration of paths had begun. Zahra would have preferred Computer Science to Chemistry, but the former was a newly introduced subject and there was some taint of a fad to it; universities might not take it as seriously as the more established subjects, one of her teachers had warned. Maryam didn't stop to consider what univer-sities took seriously or even how well she did in her O-level exams because she knew her parents' money would pave the way into some university or other and she didn't care too much which one it was. It was this casual attitude to academics that separated Maryam from most of her classmates, more than the money and social status that eclipsed almost all of them, even in this school known for its connection to the elite. Everyone else – whether Babar or Saba or Zahra – could recite like cricket stats which students in past years had been to Harvard, to Princeton, to Yale, and what their O-level results and SAT scores had been. But for Maryam, university was just an interruption before she could take over the family business. The only future that mattered to her was the one that would unfold in Karachi, a city to which Zahra had no intention of returning once she'd left it. But that was a separation of paths beyond any Zahra was willing to contemplate right now as they walked, arms still linked, down the stairs and along the corridor, greeting other students they hadn't seen all summer.

'So, now people are going to think you're the one who likes Babar,' Maryam said.

'Do you think Babar thinks it?'

'Probably. You touched his knee.'

'So knobbly.'

An A-level boy walked towards them saying, 'Look who's grown this summer.' Zahra was accustomed to comments about her height, and it took a moment to see where the boy's eyes had actually landed. His name was Hammad; he was one of the 'thuggish boys', known to have friends beyond the school walls who were either criminals or headed in that direction. Rumour placed a gun in the glove compartment of his car.

Zahra made a noise of disgust and walked on, pulling Maryam along with her, hoping she'd done so in a manner that would make an observer say they both 'swept past him'. But there were only a few feet to sweep before she reached the Chemistry classroom and had to say goodbye to Maryam. As she made her way towards an empty desk, ignoring Babar waving his hand to indicate the place next to him, she heard one pair of footsteps in the corridor slow down and another speed up.

*

It had been happening since last year without anyone but Maryam and her tailor taking much notice, but London had accelerated it. All that chocolate and ice cream and fast food had settled in unexpected places, and brought with it the discomfort of underwired bras and a body that felt unknown. For a while, in London, she thought she had lost the ability to judge her own dimensions, which was why her breasts kept bumping into strangers, until she realised it was almost never women with whom she was making the unexpected contact. Once understood, she didn't know how she felt about it. Sometimes she wanted to cry, other times she was triumphant.

It was purely humiliating, though, to overhear her father tell her mother that she needed to go to Oxford Street and buy their daughter an entirely new wardrobe because all her clothes looked 'indecent'. So out went her favourite shirts – the Madonna one, the tiger with diamanté eyes one, the nautical striped one. The new shirts were looser fitting and without images or ornamentation that might draw people's eyes to her chest. It made little difference to the men bumping into her on the Tube, or to that friend of her parents who'd started squeezing her shoulders affectionately and pulling her close the way her 'uncles' had always done, but never him.

The previous summer in London, she had imagined visibility was what she wanted. In Karachi, men stared if you were a girl; it was something to which she was accustomed and shared with every other girl in the city.

15

In London, people looked through you. The contrast was disquieting. *Notice me, notice me, notice me*, she'd chanted internally when walking down the streets. And now, wish granted, she had passed into a new category of person, her relationship to the world around her altered. At the same time, everything seemed to carry on as it always had.

There was no one in London she could talk to about this. A significant number of her parents' Karachi friends decamped to flats in Mayfair and Kensington and Knightsbridge for the summer with their children, none of whom were old enough for Maryam to want to spend time with. She was entrusted with babysitting when all the parents went out for dinner or to a movie and had used the increased responsibility to argue her way into greater independence. During the plentiful daytime hours she was allowed to head out of the Mayfair flat with her Walkman, drifting in the direction of Hyde Park or towards the music store in Piccadilly Circus. Sometimes she made it as far as Trafalgar Square, where she watched boys and girls her own age laughing together while trying unsuccessfully to climb on to the backs of the bronze lions that surrounded Nelson's Column.

As the summer wore on, she increasingly fell into the routine of walking to the Trocadero by Leicester Square, where she'd learnt to ignore the dispiriting air of a place where teenagers should be having fun but no one was, and instead focused on the turning racks near the entrance, which displayed postcards of Hollywood actors and Top Ten singers. Here, Tom Cruise in a white vest and blue jeans looking the kind of sad that only needed a girl's smile to make him happy; there, the women of Bananarama staring straight into the camera

16

as if to say, 'Impress us if you can.' Then back down Piccadilly, where the cost of everything made no sense when you translated it into rupees, which didn't stop her parents and their friends from buying biscuits from Fortnum & Mason, coffee-table books about Islamic architecture and vintage cars from Hatchards. Maryam rarely entered any of the shops, and when she did, it was only briefly. The previous summer she'd mentioned to her parents how helpful shop assistants in London were, repeatedly asking, 'Can I help you with anything?' Her parents informed her that was the English way of saying, 'Buy something or leave.' She had been embarrassed not to have realised that. Back in Karachi, she'd prided herself on her skill at reading subtexts.

From Piccadilly she made her way into Green Park, where she sat beneath a favourite tree and spent a very long time writing a postcard to Zahra, thinking through each sentence carefully so that everything that had been most important in the preceding twenty-four hours could fit on to the back of the card. She used the entire space, including the lines reserved for the address, knowing that Pakistan's postal system made it useless to actually mail the letters, so she would simply take them to Karachi at the end of the summer and hand them over to Zahra all in one go.

But on the last day in London, she picked up one of the postcards and read the lines *I was wearing a denim shirt and I undid the top two buttons when I saw a group of boys, a couple of them really cute. I could feel them looking at me after I walked past but I didn't look back because I want them to look at me but I don't know what I want after that.* She put all the postcards into a black rubbish bag, pulled empty juice cartons and packaging for fish fingers out of the kitchen bin and threw them on top of the postcards, tied the bag securely and took it out to the large bins on the landing.

Only on that first day of school, during break time, watching Zahra reach over the heads of students standing in front of her to pay the man in the tuck shop for two bottles of Coke and two packets of chilli chips, did it all make sense. There had always been a joke at the heart of their friendship, a gag that appeared first at the visual level before revealing itself to run through many layers. Now there was Zahra all straight lines and Maryam all curves, adding another element to their study in contrasts.

'Thanks, Stan,' she said, taking her Coke and chilli-chip packet from Zahra.

'Welcome, Ollie.'

She wondered if Zahra shared this feeling of completeness when they were together that could surely only be possible when you'd been best friends with someone since the age of four and your character had been defined by the other. She suspected not. There were things Zahra wanted from the world that Maryam didn't understand – things she found in books and in her own mind which sometimes wandered far away from Maryam into places she rarely talked about because she knew Maryam couldn't follow her there. When Zahra did say things like, 'Do you think everyone has a purpose in life or do we invent purpose to stop feeling irrelevant?' Maryam never knew how to answer. She didn't know which part of the question made less sense to her – 'purpose' or 'irrelevant'. She had tried to come up with an answer, something to do with wanting to expand her family's business into the international market, and Zahra had frowned and said, 'That's ambition, not purpose.'

They wandered into the front yard, noticing how the departure of the previous year's second-year A-level students had altered the configuration of things. The area around the flagpole where the most dazzling of the second-year students had lounged during break last year was now occupied by two smaller groups of Class 11 students; the new group of dazzling second-years had marked the stone archway under the bell as their territory for the year. Maryam heard her name called out and took Zahra's elbow to steer her towards the flower beds near the music-room entrance, where several of their friends had claimed a spot, some sitting on the low whitewashed borders of the flower beds while others stood, half in conversation with their seated friends and half bantering with whoever was walking past. It was humid and close, the rain clouds no longer a threat but a tease.

Zahra sat, Maryam stood. A standing Zahra towered over everyone else; seated, she was half a head taller than the girls beside her, though some of the boys were finally catching up. She'd once said to Maryam, in her matter-of-fact way, that she thought her personality would have been different if she were a few inches shorter. She simply didn't fit among the girls who leaned their heads together to gossip among themselves. But really there was no question of not fitting; they'd all been friends so long. After her two months in London, caught between children and adults, Maryam wanted to embrace everyone around her for how easily conversation flowed, how lightly they teased one another, how entirely at home she felt. Babar came to join the group and Maryam said, 'Parade clothes from a bygone era! Parade!' and Babar marched back and forth, turning the march into a gyrating dance, the girls clapping out a

19

beat and the boys calling out 'Oye oye oye' in time, so that the joke was entirely on the teacher for her choice of expression. Babar inclined his head in Maryam's direction, thanking her for finding a way between the awkwardness of pretending that classroom exchange hadn't happened and the embarrassment of saying something sympathetic. She didn't require any thanks or even acknowledgement; she was filled with the satisfaction of being with a group of people and knowing the words and tone that would produce exactly the effect you wanted. This is what was meant by 'belonging' and 'home', words she understood in the way that Zahra understood 'purpose' and 'irrelevant'.

Hammad walked across her line of sight, and her thoughts shifted to what other effects she could produce.

*

On Wednesdays, Zahra came home with Maryam and her two younger sisters. 'Home' to Maryam was a single-storeyed house in Old Clifton, set behind high boundary walls and now with armed guards stationed at the gate. It lacked all the potential for playing with the downstairs neighbours' dog and sneaking down to the sea, which existed in Zahra's flat in Sea View, though Zahra showed little interest in either. This routine had started when Zahra's father took on a TV role as anchor of a cricket show – he had to be at the studio on Wednesday afternoons, so he couldn't pick Zahra up as he otherwise had been doing since her mother was elevated from class teacher at Zahra's school to principal of a newly opened school.

Maryam still missed Mrs Ali, as she was in school – Aunty Shehnaz outside of it. There had always been a brightness to those few seconds of the day when the understated elegance of Mrs Ali crossed paths with Maryam and greeted her with the smile of Aunty Shehnaz. Every other teacher regarded Maryam as brilliant Zahra's slightly inexplicable best friend, a middling student whose parents bought her cashmere sweaters in London for the winter uniform when everyone else, including those who drove around in Pajeros, did just fine with the local cotton-polyester ones. She knew they scorned her for this because Saba had informed her that her aunt, Mrs Hilal, said the staffroom had been wondering if Maryam was allergic to polyester. Maryam, like every other student in school, allowed her mother to choose her school clothes without thinking too much about it, but that conversation with Saba made clear that even the smallest of decisions shouldn't be left to either of her parents.

On this particular Wednesday, a social crisis had detonated in Maryam's household, and the girls arrived home to find Maryam's mother on the phone instructing her husband to come home from the office right away because there were things to discuss.

Things to discuss meant it was too sensitive for a phone call, not so much because everyone knew that the intelligence services were always listening in but because crossed lines meant that someone you knew might end up eavesdropping on your call though they'd intended only to call their mother to ask her to remind them how so-and-so was related to so-and-so. Ever since Maryam's mother had found herself on a crossed line with her cousin's husband speaking to his previously unsuspected mistress, she'd refused to say anything on the phone that she wouldn't happily shout across the aisles of Agha's Supermarket.

Maryam's father pretended there was work keeping him in the office, but really it was Maryam's grandfather who ran the family business, which provided luxury leather products to the rich of Pakistan. Maryam's father merely had an office with his name on it in which he spent his days solving crosswords, approving products that had already met his father's exacting standards, and occasionally having meetings with someone important to the company who needed to feel appreciated. Maryam's father made everyone feel appreciated, and knowing the ubiquity of his appreciation didn't stop anyone – other than his immediate family – from being won over by his ability in this regard.

So, lunch was delayed until Maryam's father returned home. Zahra and Maryam made their way through the long, painting-lined hallway where a clumsy sketch of a cow, drawn by Maryam's father when he was at Oxford, hung among Sadequain and Chughtai and Gulgee and Naqsh. The paintings gave way to a cluster of photographs of Maryam's mother's antecedents in all their aristocratic pomp; their unimpeachable class allowed the cow drawing to be amusing rather than a crass symbol of the wealth that had made the art collection possible. Maryam found it mortifying.

The hallway led to Maryam's bedroom, where Maryam shooed out her sisters, closing the door behind her. The central air conditioning made the faintest of hums, the marble floor cool beneath thin socks when they kicked off their shoes. Maryam told Zahra to choose the music, and got on to her knees on her double bed to plant a kiss on the mouth of George Michael, who was hanging on her wall in his 'Last Christmas' incarnation.

'Your turn,' she said.

Zahra remained where she was, walking her fingers through Maryam's CD collection on the white shelf with blue trim. Just beneath it was the bookshelf lined with Judith Krantz, Sidney Sheldon, Jackie Collins – on the inside of each book's back cover were numbers, written in a code known only to Maryam and Zahra, listing which pages had the 'good bits'. And beneath that was a desk with the computer – Maryam's own home computer, the Apple IIGS, her pride and joy – which had allowed her to start the O-level Computer Science class miles ahead of everyone else in programming knowledge.

'Why do you speak to Hammad when you think I'm not looking?' Zahra said, back turned towards Maryam. 'I saw you again today, when I came out of History.'

'You don't approve of him.'

'What difference does that make? We tell each other everything.'

They both understood *everything* to mean everything that happened within school. Their family lives were a different matter. So, for instance, Maryam never discussed how embarrassed she was by the indolence of her parents' lives, the superficiality of their concerns, so at odds with the kind of adult behaviour she saw in Zahra's home. Even the names by which her parents were known to their friends – Toufiq and Zenobia shortened to Toff and Zeno – were caricatures compared to the solidity of the Alis, Habib and Shehnaz.

In the first week of O-level Economics, Maryam had learnt about Division of Labour and understood that her family's version of this was for her grandfather to run the business while her father procreated, so there'd be someone competent to whom the business could be handed down. Her father had managed three daughters and no sons before her mother said that was quite enough, this was the twentieth century, his daughters would inherit the company. But it was obvious early on that the younger two had taken after their father in replacing competence with charm, and so it was understood that all actual responsibility must fall to Maryam. Sometimes her grandfather teased her and said perhaps once she went to university in England or America she would never want to come back. She only rolled her eyes at that. He knew perfectly well that the summers in London were enough to excise any desire to live Elsewhere. Elsewhere was where you were no one. To be honest, she wasn't at all sure why she had to go to university, but her grandfather seemed to think it was necessary.

'OK, but first, your turn.' Maryam gestured again to the poster, and Zahra went to stand next to the bed. Maryam saw her draw back a little at the sight of the fleck of spit that Maryam hadn't realised she'd left on George Michael's mouth, and that made her wipe her lips and feel aware of her body – the saliva in her mouth, the blood of her period, the weight of her breasts. Zahra hastily kissed the corner of George Michael's mouth, and went to sit down at the foot of Maryam's bed rather than in their usual pose – shoulder to shoulder and propped up against the headboard.

'So yes, he stops to talk to me whenever he sees me. What am I supposed to do – pretend I haven't heard him?'

'Have you ever spoken to him on the phone?'

'He asked for my number and I didn't give it. Happy?'

There was the slightest shift in the air with that, the first lie between them.

'Even being seen talking to him could be bad for your reputation.'

This word – 'reputation' – carried such weight in Zahra's life. Maryam knew it had something to do with the uncertainty of her social position, and that made it unkind to laugh. 'She's smart and well-mannered and thoughtful and any good family would welcome her in,' Maryam's mother had said once, anticipating a bright future for Zahra in which marriage would unyoke her from the background of her parents who were 'decent, hard-working people', a phrase that was clear in its conde-scension towards those who couldn't simply assume a position in the world, regardless of character or action. Maryam gestured to the space next to her, and Zahra placed herself where indicated, slouching down and lean-ing slightly into Maryam, who had pulled herself upright, bringing their heads level.

'Don't you ever want to do anything that you shouldn't, Za?'

'Of course I do.'

'Like what?'

'Kiss a boy.'

'Zahra Ali!'

'Shut up.'

'I'm teasing. Which boy?'

'Any boy. It's the kissing I want.' She went very red as she said it. 'But you'd have to trust the boy not to talk about it. And it would be stupid to trust anyone that way, except you.'

Maryam nodded. That last part was certainly true. 'Do you think it would be that different, if you closed your eyes . . .'

'What?'

'To kiss a girl.' A new kind of possibility, suggested by a movie she'd watched late one night in London.

'You mean each other?'

Maryam scrunched up her face at the sheer wrongness of that thought. 'Never. Not even for practice. OK. That's decided. Straight on to Babar for you and Hammad for me.'

'I don't know which half of that sentence is worse. Does he call you?'

'You think I've started lying to you over Hammad? Please.' She stood up on the bed and peeled off her sock. 'You've sinned against the friendship and now you have to face your punishment.'

'Oh god, no, not that.'

'Yes that. Sniff the sock! Sniff it!' She waved her sock in the direction of her friend's face, and Zahra rolled off the bed to escape. Seconds later, Maryam was chasing Zahra down the corridor, waving the sock, and around the dining table and into the study, where Maryam's mother yelled at them for being a pair of hooligans with no regard for the terrible day anyone else was having.

Zahra said some words of apology and exited the room. Maryam joined her in the bedroom a few minutes later, gleeful at the dilemma her parents had been placed in. They were hosting a large party later in the month and one of their guests, her father's old university friend, had called to ask if he could bring along his brother, who was going through a hard time and needed cheering up. It was the kind of request no one could ever think to turn down, but this brother had recently been arrested for drug trafficking and everyone knew that his release had been due to a bribable judge. 'Why should I be the first step in his rehab programme?' her mother said to Maryam, meaning social rehabilitation. She had pretended there was a crisis in the kitchen that meant she had to swiftly hang up on the university friend,

26

but she or her husband would have to call back with an answer before long, and there was no pathway to a 'no' that she could find.

'So will they cancel the party?' Zahra said.

'It's my father's fortieth birthday,' Maryam said, joining Zahra by the CD collection. 'They're not going to cancel that.'

'But they're not going to have a drug smuggler in their house, are they?' Zahra had pulled the *Dirty Dancing* soundtrack out of the rack and was reading the song list with great concentration, as if she didn't already know it by heart.

'He's fine in a social gathering,' Maryam said, having met the man several times and retaining no clear memory of him beyond a soft-spoken politeness. 'The main thing is, his brother's a friend asking for a favour, so what are you going to do?'

'I didn't think of it that way,' Zahra said, finally looking up at Maryam.

'Very diplomatic response.'

Zahra placed the CD into the player. There was the clattering sound of a spinning disc that hadn't been pressed down firmly enough, and Zahra shook her head, always impatient with her own imperfections, before fixing the problem. The opening bars of 'Time of My Life' erased any differing opinions they might have about the adult world as they sang along together.

'I suppose if your sisters became criminal overlords and you asked if you could bring them along to my fortieth birthday party I'd say yes,' Zahra conceded, halfway through the song.

'Please. I'd never make you invite those irritating creatures to any party. Forty! What do you think we'll be doing at forty?'

This was the kind of conversation they loved to have, and they reduced the volume slightly and returned to their side-by-side spot on Maryam's bed to consider it.

'I suppose we'll be married, with children,' Maryam said. 'That's sort of inevitable, isn't it?'

'Is it?' Zahra said.

'Well, I'll have to have children so there's someone to inherit Khan Leather,' Maryam said. 'The difficult part will be finding a husband who doesn't mind that I'm running my own company and letting him have no say in it at all. But he can't be weak.'

'I suppose we'll want those kind of things one day,' Zahra said, a little gloomily. 'But we'll still be us when we're together, won't we?'

'We'll always be us,' Maryam said firmly. 'Even if you're living in Alaska. This is friendship, not Propane Kitty.'

'Propinquity!'

'My version's better.'

'True.'

There was a slight thumping sound against the window. One of the garden cats had jumped from the chikoo tree on to the windowsill. 'Propane Kitty!' they called out together.

Their laughter built, moving beyond the immediate joke into a deep laugh of joy for friendship, for each other, for the certainty that whatever happened in the world you would always have this one person, this North Star, this rock, this alter ego who knew your every flaw down to your atoms and who still, despite it all, chose to stand with you and by you through everything that the world had yet to throw at you, every heartache, every disappointment, every moment of darkness. Always this friendship, always its light.

*

When Zahra's mother came to pick her up later that afternoon, Maryam's father was on the phone telling his university friend that of course his brother was welcome at the party, which meant one of the gun-toting guards at the gate had to go round to the kitchen entrance and call for the cook because he wasn't allowed to enter the house – but the cook was indoors talking to Maryam's mother about dinner, so the guard walked over to the servants' quarters and called out until the driver, Abu Bakr, woke up from his afternoon nap and went to tap on one of the windows, which alerted Maryam's sisters' ayah, who couldn't understand what Abu Bakr was saying through the glass because Maryam's sisters were playing their music too loudly, so she shuffled outside to see what he wanted and then shuffled back in and found Zahra. By this time, Zahra's mother had been sitting in her car for several minutes in the oppressive August heat.

'I'm sorry,' Maryam said, coming outside with Zahra to apologise.

'Does he make you feel any safer?' Zahra's mother said, indicating the man who had opened the gate for Maryam and stood there watching her, Kalashnikov dangling from his hand.

'Ma!' Zahra said, hurrying into the car to prevent a prolonging of the conversation.

'No, he just annoys me,' Maryam replied. She turned to the guard. 'This is another person who is always allowed in, understand?'

Zahra saw the disapproval in her mother's expression at the tone of Maryam's voice. The first burning embarrassment of Zahra's friendship with Maryam had been when her five-year-old self had addressed the driver as 'Abu Bakr Bhai' and Maryam, looking horrified, had said, 'He's not related to us!' Zahra soon learnt that almost everyone she went to school with referred to the people who drove them around, cooked their meals and made their beds without attaching either honorifics or familial relations to their names, class positions overriding deference between generations. In Zahra's house, the couple who came to clean and cook were 'Zahoor Bhai' and 'Shameema Apa' to her and to her parents.

A Pajero, large and gleaming, turned the corner and pulled up right behind Zahra's mother's car.

'First I couldn't enter and now I can't leave,' Zahra's mother said.

The back window of the four-wheel-drive slid down and Maryam's grandfather leaned out. 'Is this car coming or going?' he said.

'Going. It's Zahra and her mother,' Maryam said.

The Pajero door opened and a silver-topped walking stick emerged, followed by Maryam's grandfather. The Patriarch, as he was known in Zahra's family, was impeccably dressed as ever in a pinstriped Savile Row suit. Zahra didn't know what a Savile Row suit was, but it had somehow long ago entered her consciousness that this was the only kind of suit the Patriarch ever wore.

Zahra's mother sighed at the unnecessary dance of etiquette but turned off the engine and motioned to Zahra to join her in getting out of the car.

'Isn't this ridiculous,' the Patriarch said. 'I've blocked your exit and now I'm delaying you further in order to apologise.'

'I haven't seen you in so long,' Zahra's mother said, which managed to imply this was a source of regret without her actually saying anything insincere. They spoke for a few minutes – the Patriarch showing a deep interest that couldn't possibly be genuine in Zahra's mother's new school – while humidity tightened its wet grip on everyone. But at last Zahra's mother switched on the car engine, the Pajero backed up, and Zahra waved goodbye to Maryam while the Patriarch shook out the handkerchief from his pocket and wiped his whole face.

'God, he makes my skin crawl,' Zahra's mother said. It was the kind of thing her parents often said about the Patriarch, though they always refused to explain what they meant by it. 'Anyway, how was your afternoon?'

Zahra made the mistake of telling her about the drug trafficker.

'These people, they always protect their own,' her mother said.

Zahra looked away, aware of the talcum powder rather than perfume scent of her mother. It was the one thing for which she could confidently reach when she needed a reason to justify what she recognised as unwarranted rage towards a woman adored by every other fourteen-year-old who knew her. Talcum powder and the fact that she thought of her new position as an elevation even though the school she now ran, named Andalusia, was referred to in Zahra's school as And-a-loser for its comparatively low academic standards.

Adults were unbearable, she thought, looking out of the car window. All of them, all. This was a feeling that came and went often these days, and it was almost always accompanied by the thought that the one person in the world she wanted to spend all her time with was Maryam. But something was different between her and Maryam now, something summed up by her memory of Maryam pulling the fabric of her kameez taut around her body and pretending it wasn't intentional.

Zahra did want to kiss a boy, it was true. And it didn't just stop at kissing. She wanted to understand better the

31

things happening in her body that made her wrap her legs around her pillow in bed and direct water from the shower to her nipples. Wanted someone else to make her feel the way she made herself feel late at night when she slipped her hand between her legs and thought of walking masked through a room of older boys, letting them do things to her, doing things in return, without anyone knowing it was her. But no mask could disguise her; everyone she grew up with recognised her by the length of her shadow, so she wouldn't do any of this, not for a long time, maybe not until she went to university, away from the prying eyes in this tiny world in which they lived within a city of millions. There was no horror she could imagine greater than people whispering about her, saying she had behaved in ways that no girl from a good family should behave. 'Zahra's very sensible and I trust her,' she'd heard her father recently say to a cousin of his on the phone. She didn't know exactly what that comment was about, but suspected it had to do with the cousin's disapproval of a co-educational school with a reputation for 'fast' girls. Her father's response had made her feel proud and also crushed her with the terrible weight of living up to all that trust.

And then there was Maryam, who didn't see why her parents' opinion – or the world's opinion – had anything to do with what she wanted or what she did about it. Zahra didn't know if Hammad was what Maryam wanted. Maryam said he wasn't, but sometimes she lied. Zahra had seen her do it with her parents, with teachers, with other students; but she'd never learnt how to recognise it – there was no giveaway blush or averting of the eye or saying too much or change in the tone of her voice. Zahra knew when Maryam lied because, until now, Zahra had always known the truths of Maryam's life. But she couldn't be sure of that any more. A drift had begun, which would only grow as the years went on. Deep down they both knew that no one had the kind of friendship when they were forty that the two of them had at fourteen.

*

The rains came at last, ferocious. Tree branches ripped from trunks, streets became lakes, electricity meters sparked and smoked. The downpour left the city in darkness. No one knew if the power outage was a preventive shutdown or a collapse since the electricity company wasn't answering its complaints line. School would certainly be closed the next day; the flooded streets would be impassable. Given the predictability of the August monsoons it was ridiculous that the holidays didn't start and end later each summer, but the school's response to this suggestion – made by more than one parent – was that it was the roads that needed to be fixed, not the school year. 'The beauty of Pakistan is that there's always someone else to blame for a problem,' Zahra's father had said.

The best place to be in Karachi that night was precisely where Zahra was: on the balcony of one of the Sea View flats overlooking Clifton Beach, with a mosquito coil at her feet and a candle on the table at her elbow, its flame flickering in the warm breeze coming off the water. The slapping sound emerging from the darkness was the rain-swollen waves crashing into the sea wall. A burst of music and headlights was a car cruising down the street and parking right in front of one of the painted signboards staked into the ground that announced Section 144 was in place, prohibiting activity that was a threat to safety and public order. In her History class Zahra had learnt about the use of Section 144 during the Raj to prevent gatherings of anti-colonial demonstrators; now she felt embarrassed on behalf of her nation that it was used to keep people from swimming in the monsoonal sea with its murderous undertow.

How tedious it was to live now, in this place, with its repellant dictator and its censored television and the everyday violence that had shrunk all their lives into private spaces. When they moved here, her parents had been clear that she wasn't ever to go across to the beach without an adult, but Maryam had come over a few days later and convinced her they should sneak off when her parents weren't at home. Together they'd walked across the silver-grey sand to one of the vendors with a wooden cart, on which he was roasting corn on glowing coals. Maryam sauntered, whistling a tune Zahra didn't recognise, but Zahra only felt vulnerable, her mind going to the stories of kidnappings that circulated in the schoolyard. One of the girls in Class 8 had missed three days of school the previous year and though she'd returned claiming she'd had a stomach bug, the whisper went around that she'd been kidnapped and ransomed but her parents didn't want anyone to know because people would wonder what had been done to the girl in those three days among criminal men. Zahra had insisted they take the corn home and eat it in her room rather than staying out any longer. And at the end of it all, the chilli-lemon-flavoured kernels were hard with over-roasting.

She slapped at a mosquito that had made its way on to her arm despite the coil, and wiped the smear on to the pages of her History book. Closed the book, slipped headphones on, and pressed Play on her Walkman. Bruce Springsteen sounded mournful about how tough he was on the mix tape Maryam had recorded off Capital Radio in London. The song ended and the DJ's voice – filled with the fresh possibilities of somewhere-not-here – said, 'And that's what he—' before Maryam cut off the recording and restarted somewhere during the opening bars of Tracy Chapman singing a song made for Karachi nights in which being driven around in a fast car with your friends, listening to a mix tape, was as good as life got – particularly if someone's older brother was doing the driving.

Bunching up her hair, she pulled it away from her neck to allow the breeze on to her skin. Even when it wasn't hot there was still this incessant stickiness. She looked up at the sky, dense with stars now that the rain clouds had emptied and blown away, and allowed herself to slip further into a satisfying dissatisfaction which she knew she would look back on in a few years, when living in New York or London, with an amused fondness for her younger self who only half-believed in the future that awaited her. The details of that future were hazy but glittering. The sliding door opened and her father walked out, holding his nightly glass of whisky. Zahra slipped off her headphones and looped them over his head, creating a trough in his wiry grey hair, held the rewind button for what she estimated the correct length of time, and pressed Play. Enough of the music seeped out for her to know she'd judged well. 'This Tracy has a voice, not like all those others who have a look,' he'd said the first time he heard 'Fast Car'.

'It's nice, isn't it? Living here?' He gestured in a way that took in the sea breeze, the star-filled sky, the location.

Zahra wished she wasn't too tall to rest her head against his shoulder. Instead, she made do with linking her arm with his and leaning into his comforting stockiness. Some years ago, annoyed at having to drive out from KDA to Clifton in the middle of watching a cricket match to drop her at Maryam's house, he'd asked why for once Maryam couldn't come to see Zahra. 'Why would anyone come here when they live there?' Zahra had said, meaning both the upstairs portion of the gloomy house that she and her parents occupied and the neighbourhood, far away from Defence and Clifton where all her friends lived. He'd received this with a silence that had stretched out through the rest of the day. Last year, when his salary as cricket correspondent for the country's leading Urdu-language paper was vastly augmented by his role as anchor for a cricket talk show, he brought Zahra and her mother to a three-storey block of flats by the sea, led them up two flights of stairs, opened the front door with a key he produced with a flourish and said to his daughter, 'Good enough for Maryam?'

His lips moved, not along with the music, and she knew he was replaying lines he'd used in the soon-to-be-aired episode of his show, *Three Slips and an Ali*. The show's huge success had been a surprise to everyone, turning Habib Ali into a celebrity. He couldn't walk through the school gates to pick up Zahra the day after an episode aired without students gathering around to discuss it. Whatever social stigma had once been attached to the fact that he wrote for the Urdu rather than English press had been entirely washed away by his TV role, which was peppered with enough English to let anyone know that he was fluent in both languages and choosing to communicate primarily in the one that more viewers could follow. In school it had only recently become possible to speak Urdu outside the day's half-hour language lesson without some teacher telling you off.

'Yes,' she said, returning her thoughts to the sky, the breeze, the sea-across-the-street. 'It's very nice.'

The carpets were still thin underfoot, the furniture scratched, and a CD player was a distant fantasy. But up on this balcony you could stand with your father and watch his spine lengthen as he contemplated all he had achieved for himself and his family, and in a moment such as tonight that was even more rewarding than when you stood here with your best friend, watching her breathe in the sea air and knew that, for once, you had something that she wished were hers.

The world blazed around them. Zahra shielded her eyes against the brightness of the light bulb on the balcony, which surged to a terrifying brilliance that would overload the power supply and burn out all electronics if it continued. The light dimmed to its usual wattage, and Zahra's father tapped his watch face and said, 'Just in time.'

Zahra blew out the candle and followed her father indoors to watch *Three Slips and an Ali*. Her mother was already sitting in the living room, reading Bapsi Sidhwa's new novel, *Ice-Candy Man*, and as her husband and daughter entered she flipped back a few pages to read out a paragraph that had particularly pleased her.

Zahra's father made noises of appreciation, and he and Zahra staged a mini-argument about who would read the book next. 'You take so long to read anything,' Zahra said; 'I didn't know you were interested in books without gold-embossed letters on the cover,' he said, his only words of criticism about the blockbuster novels she'd recently started to devour.

Then *Three Slips and an Ali* started, and everyone quietened. It was still strange to see her father on the screen – everything about him so familiar but made strange by the knowledge that all across the country people were watching him. Today's episode was primarily about the West Indies' recent Test victory over England, which he discussed with the satisfied air of a man who thought of colonial rule as a memory rather than history, though he'd only been five years old when it ended. While his TV self was expansive and confident, his at-home self kept glancing over to his wife, checking her expression for an approval that was never withheld but still mattered more to him than even cricket itself. A trio of guests always accompanied him on-screen – purely to justify the pun in the show's title, Zahra's mother said – but the final segment, called *Howzzat*, was Habib Ali alone, reminding his audience, with the aid of TV footage or radio commentary, of a significant moment in Pakistan's cricketing history. He often reached back into past decades, but today the West Indies victory had spurred him to relive a Test match from just a few months ago, Pakistan vs the West Indies in Bridgetown and surely, surely, if the home umpires hadn't made a series of unfair decisions Pakistan would have won the match and with it the series.

Habib Ali was in his element as he built up context and significance, and though Zahra – and everyone watching – knew exactly how the match had unfolded, her father still knew how to make the audience lean towards their TV screens in anticipation as he led them through the final overs of play. By the time he'd finished, Zahra knew more unshakably than ever that Pakistan had outplayed the most worthy of all rivals but couldn't outplay the umpires and so their loss was injustice rather than defeat.

'Why does that feel even worse?' she said to her father.

'When you live in an unjust world you want sports to be a refuge, not a reminder.'

His eyes had that sheen that the combination of cricket and whisky could bring on. Talking and writing about the game wasn't merely his profession, but also his calling. In a nation of oppression and losses cricket was a blazing light, an arena where you could feel proud of your country and united with your compatriots. Cricket told you that talent and grit and character would win out, that giants could be felled, that today's defeat could always be followed by tomorrow's victory. Yes, there were errors and injustices, cruelty even. But beyond that was the game itself, radiant and untainted. She was old enough now to know that when her father communicated this to his viewers he was trying to communicate something larger about life itself and how to live it, always with integrity, always with hope.

Although there was no one in the world she loved more, sometimes she caught herself thinking he was a foolish man, ill-prepared for the world in which he found himself living.

*

Most Saturday mornings, Maryam could be found on the cricket pitch laid behind the office block of Khan Leather, bowling her off-spin or opening the batting. The other players rotated as they came off shifts in the warehouse or artisans' block, though sometimes, if a player was having a particularly good game, she'd send a message up to her grandfather to ask if Haris or Lamboo or Kashif could stay out on the field a little longer.

From a very early age, she'd enjoyed picking up a cricket bat and joining the workers on the pitch – at the start, the bowlers gently lobbed balls in her direction, the fielders dropped all catches that came off her bat

39

with exaggerated cries of disappointment. But once her abilities became clear, her grandfather had sent her off to be coached by a former international player, and now there was no question of anyone treating her like the sahib's granddaughter rather than the best all-rounder on the pitch. Elsewhere on the factory grounds she was Maryam Bibi, but here she was 'Skipper'. Her grandfather had never said that the cricket pitch was where she would undercut the disadvantage of her femaleness and teach the men to see her as a leader, but she knew that was why he'd been so insistent on the coaching.

This Saturday, eager to get back to the game after her summer in London, she'd asked Abu Bakr to drive her to the factory in Federal 'B' Area earlier than usual. When they'd left behind those parts of the city where they were likely to be seen by people who knew them, Abu Bakr pulled over to the side of the road and moved into the passenger seat.

A decade earlier, four-year-old Maryam, on her way home from kindergarten, had commanded the family driver to stop beside a large house with a falsa tree growing in its garden and had him hoist her on to the boundary wall so she could pluck the purple-black berries from its branches. The family who lived in the house had driven up in time to see this act of theft and trespassing. Maryam's parents had been appalled, her grandfather delighted. It was the driver's fault, he said; she needs someone both strong-willed and trustworthy to ferry her around. He offered up his own driver, Abu Bakr, for the job, the first sign of his favour to Maryam. Over the years, Maryam and Abu Bakr had worked out an accommodation between her nature and his duty; he was willing to be her accomplice in breaking certain rules but not if he thought it would put her in danger.

Now, she took the wheel and drove confidently through the melee of brightly decorated buses and yellow minibuses, vans and motorbikes, and the occasional pedestrian dashing between traffic. The blocks of flats and offices on either side of the road were all greyed with exhaust fumes. At one point a motorcyclist drove close alongside her car window for a little too long, and Abu Bakr rolled down his window and raised his kameez to show the man the pistol holstered in his waistband. The motorbike veered away and Maryam continued on, only allowing Abu Bakr to return to the wheel when they were a few minutes away from Khan Leather.

The guard at the gate saluted with a particularly snappy wrist that acknowledged how many weeks she'd been away in London and how welcome her return was. Abu Bakr parked in front of the office block and she stepped out, aware of the ground that her foot alighted on, aware that this vast factory ground was her inheritance, her fiefdom.

Her skin turned clammy as she walked towards the tree-shaded gardens laid out behind the office building where she would wait for the cricketers to gather. The leaves were usually thick with dust, but the rains earlier in the week had turned everything bright and new. She stood under a tree, eating a yellow-green guava from its branches, watching sunlight filter through the leaves, listening to the tempo of the cutting and stitching machines. The fresh-from-the-tannery scent of leather sheets was a mere suggestion, perhaps the work of memory, since there were never deliveries this early. Lamboo and Haris walked on to the pitch, tossing a red ball between them. Everything in the world was exactly as it should be, the anonymous endless days of London distant.

But in the pre-match practice things started to go awry. Maryam ran in to bowl her first delivery, and with every pumping action of her legs her breasts moved up and down. Jiggling, that was the only word. She slowed her pace and that threw off her bowling action, so she had to turn around and start again. The cricketers showed no sign of noticing, but what else could they do? Again, she ran in, but it was all wrong. Her body no longer moved as she wanted – fast, unobtrusive. She threw the ball to Lamboo and said she'd bat.

Here, things were better. The sound of the ball smacking off the middle of her bat was one of life's deep pleasures. Warm-up ended and the match started with Maryam and Kashif opening the batting. She was able to hunch a little when running between the wickets, which made those flapping breasts less ridiculous. But just a few overs in, she looked down at her shirt. Sweat had adhered the fabric to her skin and there, unmistakably, the outline of her nipples strained against the cotton.

'It's too hot,' she said, tucking her bat under her arm. 'That's enough for today.'

Usually the players would have teased her with the informality that only existed on the field – 'too used to life in air conditioning, Skipper' – but today they said nothing. Kashif looked relieved. She pulled the shirt away from her skin and held it there as she walked to the office block.

Up the stairs she went to her grandfather's office and opened the door. Her grandfather was sitting behind his desk in his great winged chair, handing something to the man who was facing him. Both men looked towards the opened door – she caught a glimpse of the stranger's broken-nosed face as he turned – and her grandfather yelled 'Get out!' in a tone he never used with her.

She closed the door hurriedly and went next door to her father's office, which was always unoccupied on a Saturday. Ignoring the leather sofas and armchair that made up a seating arrangement at one end she walked across to the desk and sat behind it. The desk had been her great-grandfather's; the pen holder and document tray and tissue-box holder were all Khan Leather products. She rested her head on the table, cradled by her arms, unable to put a name to this feeling of awfulness.

Eventually, her grandfather came to find her.

'Why aren't you on the pitch?' he said.

She shrugged, made a face of indifference.

'No, you don't behave in that insolent way around me,' he said, coming round to her chair and tapping on the back to indicate she should let him have this prime spot and find herself some other pew. She stood up, not looking at him.

'You know you should knock before entering,' he said. 'But I'm sorry I spoke to you so sharply.'

'Don't you think you should introduce me to him? He'll have to deal with me eventually.'

Her grandfather leaned back, tapping his fingers on the edge of the desk. 'Do you know who he is?'

'You pay him protection money every month. But really the person you're buying protection from is the people he works for.' She knew this from Abu Bakr. The rest of it was just forming in her mind. 'And you also pay him something extra, on the side. He's the phone call, isn't he?'

When people in her parents' circle wanted something done, they called her grandfather. They might want to bring suitcases filled with alcohol into the country past customs; they might want a business-class seat on an overbooked PIA flight; they might want a No Objection

Certificate to allow their foreign guests into restricted areas. Whatever they wanted, her grandfather would say, 'Let me make a phone call,' and then he'd arrange it.

'"The phone call" isn't just one person,' her grandfather said. 'Always diversify your assets. But yes, Billoo's one of the people who is willing to be useful for a price.'

'How will he feel about dealing with a girl one day?' she said.

'How does the girl feel about it?'

She walked to the mini-fridge in the corner of the office and took out a packet of fruit juice. Punctured the packet with the end of the straw and pretended to take a moment to think about it, even though she knew clearly her opinions. 'I don't mind paying him to be helpful to us, and our friends,' she said. 'But I hate you paying him because otherwise his real boss will send some thugs to burn down the office.'

'Of course you hate that. But always respect where power lies – and then work out how you can use it to your advantage.' He held out his hand and she passed him the fruit juice. 'Your father doesn't see any of this. Little princeling wants a crown on his head and his hands lily-white. He can't have both. Why do you have to be so young?'

'I'm fourteen,' she said.

'I'm seventy-one.' He sipped noisily through the straw. 'If you want me to introduce you to people who'll one day have to take you seriously, don't walk into my office looking like you've been in one of those Indian movies where rain drenches the woman in a white sari.'

Maryam crossed her arms in front of her chest, felt again that strange new awfulness.

*

In the back seat Zahra's lips were fiery, tingling from Silver Spoon's gol guppas. Her father loved to spring the delight of an outing to Silver Spoon on her, as he'd done this evening – always after ascertaining there was no test the next day that would force Zahra to make the intolerable choice between an extra round of revision and the world's best gol guppas. Now the Alis were stuck in Shahrah-e-Faisal's rush-hour traffic and wouldn't be home for another half hour at least, which meant they'd miss *Neelam Ghar* – which was fine, really, she spent most of the quiz show with her face in a book anyway; it was her father who loved watching Tariq Aziz play quizmaster, even though he occasionally hurled insults at him for having betrayed his politics and bowed to General Zia in order to stay on the air. But think of all the people who'd be denied their Rahbar Water Cooler prizes if the show had ended, Zahra's mother would tease him in response, and sometimes Zahra would enjoy the familiar back-and-forth and other times she'd be so bored with the endless recycling of conversation that seemed to be married life.

A car pulled up at the traffic light next to the Alis' car. Zahra had noticed it earlier – a red Suzuki FX, which was a model her mother had driven until quite recently, but the tinted windows gave it an air of mystery, turning it into the kind of car with a rear windscreen plastered with a decal of Sylvester Stallone as Rambo or the Ferrari logo or a heavily made-up pair of women's eyes. Sometimes there was that momentary thrill when the boys driving alongside rolled down their tinted windows and gave you that if-your-parents-weren't-here look. Zahra knew you were supposed to look away immediately when they did that, but sometimes she didn't, safe in the knowledge that her father's presence in the front seat would prevent the boys from giving chase.

The FX reversed a few feet so that the driver's side window was alongside her own. In the front seats her parents were absorbed in discussing what to order from the new butcher they'd been advised to try out in Defence Market. The driver lowered his window and puckered his lips at Zahra. The lips were red and full under a moustache, like Tom Selleck's in *Magnum*. He was older than most of the young men who liked to drive alongside girls or follow them through traffic, but not old enough to be disgusting. Zahra looked straight ahead at her parents, then back at the man. She touched the place where the neck of her T-shirt rested on her collarbone and dragged her fingers a few inches. The T-shirt was pulled along, revealing most of her shoulder and the white of her bra strap.

The man took one hand off the wheel and dropped it into his lap. In novels, words like 'furtively' attached themselves to what she understood the man to be doing, but he wanted her to know what was going on, his arm pistoning, his eyes intense on her face. She glanced to the front again. Her parents were still talking, unaware. The light turned orange. She slipped a finger under her bra strap and pushed it down the curve of her shoulder. The man mouthed the word 'rundi' at her. Her father accelerated away. The man, his attention elsewhere, was left behind.

Zahra returned her bra, her T-shirt to its normal position, her heart leaping wild. She recognised immediately the feeling of shame that had come upon her the moment the man called her a prostitute, but beneath that, beyond that, breaking through that was something else, something gorgeous that moved the tingling of her lips to all the way inside her, deeper than she'd ever felt. She'd carried a book into the car with her as she always did, and now she placed it on her lap, her hand beneath the book, legs slightly parted, fingers pressing down. She closed her eyes but turned her face away, allowing her hair to veil her expression. If her parents looked back all they'd see was the same Zahra who had been sitting in the car five minutes ago and that – their unknowing – was part of the evening's deliciousness. She could be wanted as much as any other girl, she could respond to the wanting, and no one would have to know. The pleasure of the thought rippled through her, her hand pushing more firmly against herself.

*

Sunday afternoon, and a tall, straight-backed man rang the doorbell. Zahra was the one to greet him through the bolted screen door with an enquiring 'Hello?' He responded with a pointed 'Asalaam-a-laikum' that made her apologetically retreat into a 'Walaikum-asalaam'. By now her father had walked into the corridor and the man looked through the screen and called out 'Haboo!' which was a nickname only his old schoolfriends used. Her father called out enthusiastically enough in response and embraced the man when Zahra unbolted the screen door and let him in, but then he said, more loudly than necessary, 'Last I heard, you were a colonel. Where have you got to now?' and Zahra knew this was a warning to Zahra and her mother of what shouldn't be said, what couldn't be assumed, in this man's presence.

The man was a brigadier. Zahra's mother had a cousin in the navy and her father had a nephew in the air force, but a brigadier in the army was something else entirely. 'Why is he here?' Zahra said, following her mother into the kitchen. Shameema Apa was having her mid-afternoon rest, so Zahra arranged the tea trolley while her mother poured oil into the karhai for the pakoras.

'You heard what he said,' her mother said. The man had said he was driving by and thought why shouldn't he stop in and see his old friend Habib, whom he watched on TV every week but hadn't seen in person for too long. But he hadn't said how he knew where his old friend lived, given the decades they'd been out of touch.

'How does it feel to have a celebrity husband?' the Brigadier said when Zahra's mother, followed by Zahra, returned to the living room, wheeling the trolley ahead of her. 'Everyone watches his show, everyone. You know, the President himself is a fan.'

'I didn't know that,' Zahra's mother said, and her father said, 'Is he really?'

Zahra's parents smiled, looked appreciative but unconcerned, her father gestured to Zahra to hand the Brigadier a plate and some pakoras, her mother asked him how he liked his tea.

'Well, you know General Zia is a great cricket fan,' the Brigadier said, taking the plate, showing no sign of noticing that Zahra was extending her arm as far as it could reach so that she didn't have to stand any nearer the man than necessary. Her father gave her a warning look and she moved closer. 'He was the one who convinced Imran Khan to come out of retirement and lead the team to the West Indies. You know that, don't you, Haboo?'

'Of course,' her father said, 'of course.'

The Brigadier took a bite of the pakora. 'Baita, any ketchup?' he said to Zahra.

An image came to Zahra's mind of the empty ketchup bottle in the kitchen, which should have been replaced earlier in the week. She'd gone into Deltons to buy a few things while her father was buying vegetables across the road, but when she placed the shopping basket next to the cashier, he'd snapped at her for keeping the sanitary pads on top. Such things must always be kept out of sight, he'd said, while swiftly engulfing the pads in a brown-paper bag, which he placed in a polythene bag, the handles of which he tied firmly into a knot that left no opening for anyone to peer inside. She'd exited, flustered, forgetting to take the second polythene bag that the man had placed the rest of her shopping in, and then was too embarrassed to explain to her parents what had happened and said she'd simply forgotten to buy the ketchup and orange squash. Yesterday she'd turned the old ketchup bottle upside down to get out whatever remnants possible to eat with her chips, and now there was nothing left in it and the Brigadier would have to eat his pakoras dry.

'There's chutney,' her mother said, holding out a bowl.

'Much better,' said the Brigadier, and Zahra felt a slight loosening in the constriction of her chest.

'I wondered,' the Brigadier said, dipping the pakora, 'I wondered if somehow, Haboo, you were the only person in the country who didn't know that the President's intervention was the reason that Imran led the team so spectacularly in the West Indies – of course we would have won the series if it wasn't for the umpires. Everyone is so angry at those umpires, even you the other day on TV, but I say, they are patriots, they didn't want their players to lose to a foreign team. I can understand that. I can even appreciate it.'

Zahra was standing, plate of pakoras in hand. Her mother had poured the tea but wasn't handing out the cups. Her father's smile had turned wide and thin.

'We all recognise the President's role,' her father said. There was a long pause, during which the Brigadier held out a hand, and Zahra's mother apologised and handed him his cup of tea.

'And are grateful,' her father said, his voice very small.

'I'm pleased to hear you say that,' the Brigadier said. 'These pakoras are really excellent, and just the right amount of mint in the chutney. Because you know, last night I was thinking that even when the series was on-going and you used to talk about it every week and then last night again you've never mentioned General Zia. As I said, he's a fan of the show so he would have been watching. He's not a man who asks for praise or thanks, but even so, he's a human being. My guess is – and I'm only guessing here – that he's a little hurt.'

Zahra's mother came to stand next to her husband with a cup of tea for him. He looked up at her, and then at Zahra, before turning back to the Brigadier with that smile of a stranger.

'Next time I mention the series, I'll remember to give him credit.'

'Perhaps in next week's episode,' the Brigadier said. 'A few words of gratitude on behalf of the nation.'

'Oh, it's no use trying to get my husband to reveal what he'll say in next week's episode,' Zahra's mother said lightly. 'He treats it like a state secret.'

The Brigadier laughed, a deep laugh from the belly. 'He never liked giving anything away, even in school. Has he told you about that time he pulled that prank with the teacher's bicycle? How old were we? Ten?'

He didn't stay long after that. A few anecdotes, some reminiscing, polite questions about Zahra's mother's school and Zahra's own education. He knew where Zahra went to school, and he knew where her mother was principal. When he stood up to leave, he embraced Zahra's father again and said, 'We are friends, Haboo, despite all the years.'

'I'm very grateful for it,' Zahra's father said, and for the first time she thought of the other ways in which this message could have been delivered and it occurred to her not to hate this straight-backed man but to want to kiss his hands.

The Brigadier left and Zahra's mother bolted the screen door and both locks on the main door. Her father walked on to the balcony and stood there a while; when he finally turned and nodded to her mother Zahra knew the man had driven away.

'What's going to happen?' Zahra said.

Her parents sat down on the sofa, close together, and her father patted the cushion beside him. But Zahra stood where she was, raising one leg off the floor, flamingo-like for no reason except that the act of balancing gave her something to concentrate on beyond this caving-in feeling.

'You could say something factual,' her mother said.

'The success of the series would not have been possible without the captaincy of Imran, who as we all know came out of retirement at the request of the President,' her father said.

'Is that a little ... pointed?' her mother said, reaching for the pakoras, which she hadn't touched while the Brigadier was there. '*We all know*. Is that saying, why are you making me state the obvious?'

'They want you to thank the President,' Zahra said. 'You have to thank him.'

'I'm not thanking that man, jaani. I have to be able to look Iqbal in the eye.'

Iqbal, her father's friend and one-time colleague, had been one of the journalists who staged a hunger strike to protest the press censorship enacted in the first years of military rule. Along with three other journalists, he was arrested and flogged. Ten lashes each. Zahra was four years old at the time. She remembered walking into her father's room and seeing him lying in bed, staring up at the ceiling, an odd texture to his face which turned out to be tears. It was one of her earliest memories, though it wasn't until years later that her parents gave her the information to understand what the memory was about.

'Please, Aba, please,' Zahra said.

'What is this?' her father said, coming to her, arms holding her close. 'What are these tears?'

'They'll hurt you,' she said. They'd tied Iqbal's hands and feet to a wooden frame and used a belt to secure his torso in place.

'Oho,' her father said, kissing her hair. 'For this kind of thing they don't do that kind of thing. At worst, they'll ban me from the airwaves, like they did to Iqbal Bano for singing a Faiz poem. It's OK. I'll still have the newspaper column.'

'They'll have to change the name of the show or find another cricket expert called Ali,' her mother said.

'Much easier to find another Ali,' her father said.

They were being flippant for Zahra's sake but she could see the fear in them. As long as she could remember, there had been this feeling of threat stalking her, everywhere. Say the wrong thing, turn down the wrong street, allow yourself the mildest transgression, and some creature awful and unknown would swoop down on you, talons tearing into your flesh. And now it was here, in their midst, and it had entered in the guise of an old friend just to drive home the point that nothing, no one, nowhere was safe. She held on to her father, feeling the softness of his flesh, the breakability of his bones.

'It'll be OK,' he told her, more foolish now than he'd ever been.

*

Another Wednesday, and Zahra and Maryam lay on the floor of Maryam's bedroom, the marble cooler than any other surface as the third hour of a power breakdown rolled along. They had agreed, minutes ago, that all effects of the central air conditioning had dissipated and it was time to open the windows to let in what breeze there was, but neither of them could bear the exertion of standing up.

Maryam was on her stomach looking at the printout of possible new logos for Khan Leather that she'd designed using MacPaint. The blocky ornate capital 'K' and 'L' of the existing logo looked old-fashioned rather than classical, but she suspected her grandfather wouldn't be convinced by the lower-case letters that she was advancing as an alternative, the stalks of the 'k' and 'l' mirroring each other with identical loops. Zahra was using Maryam's back as a pillow, reading a magazine article about Nelson Mandela, or pretending to, though Maryam hadn't heard her turn the page in a very long time and her usual reading speed was lightning fast.

'Are you annoyed with me?' Maryam said at last. She knew Zahra had heard Hammad say 'Call you tonight' as they passed by each other in the schoolyard at home time, and had expected an interrogation to follow. But Zahra hadn't said anything about it. In fact, she'd hardly said anything at all through the day.

'No,' Zahra said, in a strange voice.

'What is it, then?'

'Nothing,' Zahra said. Then, after a pause, 'Family stuff.'

'Oh. OK. Well, if you feel like discussing anything.'

'I know. Thanks.'

The door opened and Maryam's father looked in. 'There's ice,' he said. 'Outside.'

The girls peeled themselves off the floor and followed him into the garden where one of the guards was using the butt of his Kalashnikov to hammer a slab of ice into chunks, splinters sparkling in the air. It was ice from the bazaar, which meant it couldn't be consumed but it could be placed in wide plastic basins, with water from the garden hose streamed on top.

'Ahhhh,' said Maryam and Zahra, sitting side by side on the grass, their feet sharing a single basin of iced water. Maryam's parents sat on cane chairs with a basin each. The gulmohar trees, their flowers flame red, provided essential shade. The youngest two of the family took a basin and walked off to the other end of the garden, where they could giggle together about whatever secret they were sharing these days.

Maryam's father had carried a peach out of the house and he cut that in half, the scent of it perfuming the air. The guard walked back towards the driveway, wiping his hand against the butt of his Kalashnikov and smearing the cold water on his neck.

'What do you think?' Maryam said, holding up the piece of paper she'd brought out with her. 'A new logo design.'

Her father leaned forward. 'Is this for your computer class?'

'No, it's for the company,' she said.

Her father made a noise, both indulgent and dismissive, as he prised the corrugated pit out of the yellow-gold peach flesh.

'You really like doing things with computers, don't you,' said her mother. 'Do you think there might be a future in that?'

'Do I think there's a future for computers?'

'No, for you to do something with computers.'

'At Khan Leather? Yes, of course. We'll soon be using computers for everything.'

'No, I meant ... If you had to imagine some other kind of future, somewhere else.'

'Why would I do that?'

'Zahra, you're planning to go to university abroad, aren't you?' Maryam's father said. 'Do you think you might stay there?'

'I don't have a family business here.' Zahra touched her fingers against Maryam to say that whatever her parents were trying to do here, she was on Maryam's side.

'There are so many opportunities out there,' Maryam's mother said, coming to sit next to her daughter. But as she lowered herself down, her palm touched the damp soil where the water had spilled out of the basin, and she ended up hovering awkwardly in a squat to keep her clothes off the ground. 'Many opportunities and no bomb alarms in school and guards at the gate.'

'You don't need the guards. They're just a status symbol because all your friends have them,' Maryam said.

'Do you know how many of our friends have been held at gunpoint in their own homes?' her mother said.

What Maryam knew was that all the tales of armed robberies in the middle of the night had made Zeno insist that her daughters sleep in 'modest' clothing rather than the long T-shirts to which they were all accustomed, and that everyone who had been held up had emerged unscathed, with increasingly competitive stories to tell at parties for weeks after.

'Anyway, Dada and I have decided,' Maryam said. 'I'm going to university abroad and then I'll come back and start work at the company.'

'We are your parents,' her mother said, standing up. 'Even if both you and your grandfather seem to forget it.'

'Zeno!' her father said in a warning tone.

Maryam's mother raised her hands in the air. 'What is it going to take?' she said.

'That's enough for now,' her father said, handing a slice of peach to his wife and holding the plate out to his daughter and Zahra.

Maryam reached forward to take the peace offering, glad that whatever this unnecessary conversation was all about, invoking her grandfather's authority had brought it to a close.

*

After that initial conversation following the Brigadier's visit, Zahra's parents had refused to discuss the matter in her presence. Her father had been to see friends for advice – schoolfriends who knew the Brigadier, journalist friends who had spent years navigating a path between conscience and consequence. But all he said to Zahra was, 'Stop worrying, it'll be all right.' If he was so sure it would be all right why had he taken the whole family to their favourite restaurant, Yuan Tung, on a school night? Why had he been so insistent Zahra put aside her schoolwork and come for a long walk along the sea wall during which he told her stories from his childhood? Why did he hold his wife's hand when they watched video rentals at night?

'What did he say?' Zahra said to her mother when she came to pick Zahra up from Maryam's, while her father was still at the TV studio pre-recording the show for the evening broadcast.

'I don't know,' her mother said. 'He still hadn't decided this morning.'

Zahra usually retreated to her bedroom with its boombox when she came home from Maryam's, but that afternoon she sat in the living room so that she'd see her father as soon as he opened the front door. Her mother came to sit on the sofa with her, a pack of playing cards in her hands. They played Snap, over and over, throwing cards down fast on the cushion between them.

Halfway through a game, Zahra felt all the strength leave her limbs. She put her cards down, looking at the King of Clubs staring up at her, a sword in each hand, a face of indifference. Why didn't whatever was going to happen just happen? She couldn't bear another day of normal life in which nothing was normal. The most unexceptional acts – passing the salt shaker to your father – could suddenly feel weighted with significance. What if they took him away and you never passed him a salt shaker again? And everything was made stranger because her parents had said she couldn't tell anyone what had happened, which meant Maryam didn't know and couldn't make everything better simply by knowing.

She could hear her father singing as he came up the stairs. 'Oh no,' Zahra said. He was singing 'Hum Daikhain Gay', the banned Faiz poem that Iqbal Bano had performed at the Alhambra in Lahore two years earlier, driving her audience into a frenzy that culminated in cries for revolution. One of the nation's most beloved singers, she would never perform on TV or at official functions again.

'This man,' her mother said, shaking her head but smiling.

Her father walked in and spread his arms wide. 'My loves,' he said, all the weight of the last few days lifted off him.

'What did you say?' Zahra said, standing up.

'Nothing,' he said, swiping his hand diagonally through the air as though it were a rapier. 'Not one mention of the President, as has been the case every week, as will be the case every week. Let them come and arrest me for saying nothing. Let them reveal their trembling desperation.'

'All right, all right, hero,' her mother said. 'No one's going to arrest anyone. Stop frightening your daughter.'

'What's wrong with both of you?' Zahra shouted, and ran into her room.

Her father came in after her. He wasn't being foolish, he tried to explain. He had talked to many people, taken sound advice. Governments didn't want to look weak and what is it but weakness to arrest a man or push him off the airwaves because he didn't say thank you. They would ignore him, that is all that would happen.

'You're guessing,' she said. 'You're hoping. And for what? There's nothing to gain, not one single thing.'

'It was the only thing I could do,' he said. 'One day I hope you'll understand.'

He left the room and Zahra locked her bedroom door, rotating the lock this way and that twice to make sure he heard it. Turned Bruce Springsteen on as loud as her boombox could manage before its speakers started whistling. She started to dance, fast, wild, trying to shake off everything but the music. She was still dancing when the phone rang. It was the Brigadier, she knew it. Now consequences had arrived. The Pet Shop Boys sang 'It's a Sin'.

Her mother shouted for her father. Zahra ran out of her room in time to hear 'He's dead! He's dead!', her mother's voice giddy. 'Someone finally killed him.'

'What?' her father said, and her mother said, 'His plane exploded.' Her father: 'A rumour?' Her mother: 'No, it's confirmed.'

They hadn't said his name, but there was only one person they could be talking about, holding on to each other's hands. Zahra said, 'He can't be dead.' Her parents turned to her, each of them letting go of a hand and extending their arms towards her so she could walk into their embrace.

'My god,' her father said. 'Today of all days. Thank you, Allah, I'm a believer again.'

'But what will happen now?' She didn't know why they didn't seem scared. Without the dictator who had ruled almost all her life, who could know what would happen?

'Now you'll see,' her father said. 'Now you'll see what this country can be.'

Her mother said the unimaginable words: 'Elections. Benazir.'

Her father began to cry in a way that told her that all the tears he wept when Pakistan beat England were just practice for this moment, this turning of history towards the light. Zahra held her parents close, not wanting to be the one to tell them that they were wrong. None of this would happen, how could it? There would be another dictator and he might be worse.

Her father switched on the television. The screen was taken up by a message saying normal transmission would resume shortly. Zahra and her parents stood and looked at it, and then her father opened a cabinet drawer, brought out a camera and took a picture.

'Will they broadcast *Three Slips and an Ali*?' Zahra said.

'I doubt it, jaani. We may be looking at this screen for a while.'

'Thank god,' she said.

Her father smiled at her. 'I think you may be fixating on the wrong details here.'

The phone rang again, and it was Maryam.

'Did you hear?'

'Yes, just now.'

Speaking about it to Maryam made it feel true. And their unspoken agreement to discuss it on the phone without naming it let her know that Maryam, like her, understood that the rules of the world hadn't changed, and probably wouldn't.

'Sad for his family,' Maryam said.

'Hmmm, yes.' Her tone trying to suggest she had been thinking this too.

'I hope things don't get too unstable.'

'Is that what your parents are saying?'

'My father and grandfather. My mother – she's thinking about her old schoolfriend. But no one really believes that's going to happen.'

Maryam's mother had known Benazir Bhutto at school, but Zahra had never heard the term 'friend' applied to her before.

'My father's upset that he may have to cancel his fortieth party.'

'That's too bad. But at least they won't have to have the drug overlord in their house.'

Zahra's father slid open the glass door that led to the balcony and the sound that came rushing in was a wedding song playing loudly through a car speaker – no, two car speakers, three, their synchronisation just slightly off. Her father clapped his hands and snapped his fingers, her mother responded in kind, and then they were dancing, laughing together.

'What's that noise?' Maryam said.

'That isn't noise. It's music.'

*

There was no way of counting the hundreds of thousands of mourners on the streets of Islamabad the day the President was buried. Men, all men, dressed in white, surged towards the white marble edifice of the Shah Faisal mosque. Heat shimmered across the television screen, making everything feel illusory. And perhaps it was. What reality corresponded to all these mourners, or to the newscaster whose soaring eulogy went on and on until he broke into tears, convinced by his own sorrow even if no one else was? In Karachi, the troops were on high alert, but that was just a piece of propaganda or perhaps a show of respect by the armed forces for their Commander-in-Chief, pretending there was some possibility that the city would be convulsed by a grief that would turn to violence.

'Say what you will about the man, and I've said enough over the years, but you have to give him his due,' Maryam's grandfather said, shelling a peanut with one hand while holding the telephone receiver to his ear with the other. He'd commanded her and her parents to come and watch the funeral with him, but as the coverage entered its second hour with the body nowhere near the burial site he had turned his attention to telephone calls with friends, while Maryam's father made his way through the evening-paper crosswords. Her mother had long since departed the room and was probably speaking to one of her friends on the second phone line.

All the leaders of what was called the Free World had come in person or sent their emissaries to the funeral of the dictator who had played a key role in driving the Soviets out of Afghanistan. 'He put this country on the geopolitical map,' her grandfather was saying now, as the newscaster identified George Schulz of America and Geoffrey Howe of Britain among the dignitaries at the funeral. 'All this democracy people are getting so excited about. Power respects power, whether it comes from ballot boxes or bullets.'

Maryam stood up and walked out of the study, bored by it all. Her grandfather's house in Bath Island was a 1930s double-storeyed structure of stone walls and high ceilings and black-and-white handmade floor tiles; when her grandmother was alive it had been famed for the frequency and glamour of its parties. 'Invited or uninvited, you were always welcome,' one of her grandmother's friends had once said. Now the parties had been reduced to two a year – her grandmother's birthday, though she'd been dead nearly a decade, and New Year's Eve. Her grandmother's birthday was when her grandfather invited people he liked; the New Year's Eve party was far larger and included guests who were 'useful to know'. *When you see the chance to increase your proximity to power, take it*, he'd told Maryam, and waved his hand dismissively when she asked if it wasn't better to be the power than the proximity.

In the garden she whistled for her grandfather's German shepherd, Dash, who came charging at her, nearly knocking her over in his joy. They wrestled together for a while, played Fetch for a bit, and then Dash followed her indoors to the bedroom that her father had grown up in, larger by far than the bedrooms of his two older sisters. She sank into a beanbag, Dash's head resting on her feet, and started to read through the stack of Archie comics that she kept there for these dull stretches of time. She heard someone calling for Abu Bakr, wondered what that was about, but only vaguely.

Eventually, her grandfather's bearer, Shah Nawaz, came to tell her she was being called for. She said a regretful goodbye to Dash – banned from the study since the exuberant wagging of his tail had knocked over two bowls in her grandfather's Gardner collection – and returned to the adults.

'Shut the door, we don't need the servants hearing this,' her grandfather said when she entered the room. Someone – he didn't say who – had seen her driving the Mercedes on Shahrah-e-Faisal.

'Lots of kids my age drive,' she said. 'Saba's brother has been dropping us home from parties and school events since he was fourteen and no one's ever minded.' She gestured to her parents. 'They know he has.'

'Yes, we know he has,' her mother said. 'And his parents know he has. You've been sneaking around and making Abu Bakr cover for you.'

'It's not his fault,' she said.

'No, it's your fault,' her grandfather said. 'But Abu Bakr is the one who's lost his job over it.'

'You can't fire him.'

'You think anyone wanted to?' her father said, angry as he rarely was. 'But what choice have you left us? Should all the servants think it's forgivable to aid our children in breaking our rules?'

'And the law,' her mother said, with so little conviction no one had to respond to it.

'Shahrah-e-Faisal,' her grandfather said. 'That was stupid. How did you think you wouldn't be seen by someone who knows us? It's the only Mercedes of this model in all of Karachi.'

'I usually only drive nearer the office,' she said, stung by the charge of stupidity. 'Dada, please don't fire Abu Bakr.'

'You're spoilt,' he said, his nostrils wrinkling as if she were a putrefying fruit set in front of him. 'I want you to be fearless, not like every other soft, silly girl. But instead you're turning out spoilt and reckless.'

Her mother's indrawn breath was a surprise, but it turned out it wasn't in response to the charges being levelled against Maryam. On the screen, something draped in green was being lowered into the ground. Her grandfather turned up the volume.

'My god,' her mother said. 'My god. He's really dead.'

Maryam's disgrace was pushed into a tiny corner of the world. A man who had bent the country to his will was being buried, and even her grandfather leaned forward in his chair as if he wanted to be closer to an event that seemed as unreal as anything they'd ever seen on television, including Vulcans and Klingons.

Maryam ran outside, calling for Abu Bakr, but he wasn't there among the drivers and cook and bearer sitting around a radio, listening to the sound of shovels.

'He's gone,' Shah Nawaz said, looking up.

'General Zia's gone,' the cook said, and everyone laughed and returned their attention to the radio.

Dash rubbed himself against her legs, sensing her disquiet, and she squatted down on the ground and rested her head against his warm animal neck. She recognised, but couldn't change, the awfulness of being less upset about Abu Bakr's fate than she was by the tone of disgust in her grandfather's voice when he told her she had ceased to be exceptional.

*

Every video shop in Clifton and Defence offered the same mix of Indian movies, Hollywood movies and American TV shows, and yet shifting your loyalty from one to the other was a serious matter, not lightly undertaken.

64

Maryam had been going to Star Video for years, but last week when she'd asked for *Bull Durham*, the man who had handed her every movie she'd asked for without comment for years said it wasn't appropriate, there were too many 'dirty' parts; even though she'd ignored the advice, that was the end of that relationship. Zahra said she should go to Crystal Palace, Saba said Everest was the best option, Babar said you couldn't beat Video Tech.

Now she stood in Ocean Video on Boat Basin, looking up and down the tall shelves of videos as if she might be interested in any of them, even though she knew every video store kept its newest releases under the counter for prized customers, and she had no intention of settling for anything less than *Gorillas in the Mist*, which had just arrived in Karachi in a master print after several weeks of no option but a juddering version of it with people talking in the background. She heard the door open and someone came in singing Nazia and Zoheb's 'Telephone Pyar'. He walked over to the wall of videos and stood close enough that they could talk in whispers but not so close that anyone walking in would think they were together.

'Our first date,' Hammad said.

She glanced at him. She'd never seen him out of school uniform before. Blue jeans and a white tennis shirt with a gold chain like Andre Agassi. She knew the only game he'd been playing was video games at Sagar, where he spent every evening with his friends from outside school before returning home and phoning her. The calls were boring; his part of the conversation largely consisted of 'And? Tell me something else', but he was good-looking and older and even though he only sounded ridiculous when he dropped his voice to a whisper and said things like 'I want to touch your breasts', she was curious to know if she'd like it when it actually happened or if she'd like any of the other things he said he wanted. Though how she'd ever be able to find out, she didn't know. The guards outside her gate meant she couldn't sneak out of the house unseen and get into his car at a pre-appointed time, and Zahra would turn prissy and disapproving if she suggested using her flat as a pick-up point. So instead she had to make do with following his instructions about which video store the new driver should bring her to and at what time so he could stroll across from Sagar and meet her.

He placed a cassette from Offbeat on the shelf with American soap operas – *Dynasty, Dallas, Falcon Crest.* 'I had that made for you,' he said. She picked up the mix tape, looked at the typewritten list of songs visible through the cassette cover. 'Get Outta My Dreams, Get Into My Car' was the first song on side A.

'Thanks. Can you tell him I want *Gorillas in the Mist* in master print?' She indicated the man behind the counter, whom she could feel watching her.

'Boss!' Hammad said, stepping away from the shelf and walking to the counter. She liked him more now that he was speaking with authority, telling the video-wallah to show her all his newest movies but only in master print, and then she was annoyed by the way he was standing – legs apart, hands on his hips, chest out – a posture allowed to him because he was a boy but which she couldn't replicate anywhere, not even on the cricket pitch.

The videowallah reached beneath the counter for a pile of videocassettes and told her the limit was usually one video per day from the coveted stash, but she could have two. She took *Gorillas in the Mist* and *Mystic Pizza.* Hammad asked if there was anything new in WWF for him. He'd told her one evening on the phone that this was code for porn movies.

'I have to go,' she said. 'My driver will come looking for me if I stay longer.'

And that ended her first date.

WINTER

At first, hope approached falteringly: now tangible, now a mirage. There would be genuine party-based democratic elections; there would not, yes there would. The elections would be timed to ensure the pregnant Benazir Bhutto was giving birth, unable to campaign – no, Benazir outwitted them all by wearing voluminous clothing that made it impossible to know if she was in her second or third trimester and then had her baby in September, well in time to take active part in the November elections. There would be orchestrated violence that would require the military to step in for the public good; no, instead there was a giant party that transformed Karachi into a city of galloping hope and frenzied nightlife.

The frenzy started every evening along the beachfront outside Zahra's flat and continued into the early hours of the morning. Its soundtrack was composed of election songs and car horns and voices learning their own power for the first time, calling out 'Jeeay Bhutto', 'Jeeay Altaf' – it didn't much seem to matter, in that moment, which party you supported. Zahra and Maryam had been caught up in two public rallies while in Zahra's car with her father – one for Benazir's PPP, one for Altaf

Hussain's MQM – and both times they were swept along in the music and jubilation of it all, taking hold of party flags that shining young men on motorbikes handed to them through the rolled-down car windows, singing the party's election song, calling out the slogans as though they had never believed anything more profoundly or unshakably. And Zahra's father, who would in any other circumstances have issued a look of warning to young men on motorcycles approaching the adolescent girls, added his own cry, 'Pakistan Zindabad,' which was taken up by the shining boys and raced through the rallies.

At parties, Madonna's primacy in drawing people to the dance floor was replaced by Shabana Noshi, the singer from a part of Karachi that neither Zahra nor Maryam nor any of their friends had ever ventured into, who sang Benazir's catchy, joyous campaign song 'Dila Teer Bija'. A young Englishman at one such party was heard saying, 'Can't imagine teenagers in London going crazy to a "Long Live Maggie Thatcher" song,' and this confirmed what all of them already knew: everywhere else was to be pitied for not being Pakistan in the winter of 1988.

The November night when everyone waited for the election results that would tell them if they'd merely been living in a dream-state, Maryam was staying over at Zahra's. In Maryam's house, tucked away in a quiet street, you couldn't hear the heartbeat of the city as you could in Zahra's flat by the sea. And also, once her mother's attempt at rekindling a schoolday friendship that never was with Benazir had proved fruitless, the enthusiasm for democracy had waned in Maryam's household for everyone but Maryam herself, who saw in Benazir an idol she hadn't known she'd been waiting for. Even her younger sisters, eight and ten years old, were given to saying things like, 'How can that girl hope to rule?' which they'd heard from their father. Maryam understood that the word 'girl' had nothing to do with Benazir's age, which, at thirty-five, was only five years short of her father's.

'Is that what you're going to say when it's time for me to take over the company?' Maryam had said, and her father spread his hands in a way that said the situation there was far from ideal. Her grandfather, walking in just then, said, 'You're not a girl, you're a force of nature,' which was half a compliment, half admonishment for the stupidity of driving where she would be caught, which he hadn't yet completely forgiven. Her grandfather had little time for democracy, which brought too many variables into play, but he was certain that the people Billoo the Phone Call worked for would be significant in the new democratic set-up and it would prove more invaluable than ever to have Billoo on the unofficial payroll.

When the round-the-clock coverage of election night began, Maryam and Zahra were together in Zahra's living room, legs drawn up to their chests, gripping each other's knees. Zahra's parents were across the landing watching the news with their neighbours, so the two friends had the flat to themselves. They devised an election scorecard with a complicated colour-coding scheme; played Snap in the coverage longueurs; sang 'Dila Teer Bija' when the first win for the PPP was announced. The night stretched on past the point when cards or ice cream could keep them going, so they took it in turns to fall asleep and wake each other up on the sofa in front of the TV. That way, there was no moment of history that at least one of them didn't witness. In the early morning, Zahra's parents came home and said the results were clear and it was time for everyone to sleep. Maryam and Zahra said no, there was something important for which they still needed to stay up. The adults, smiling and indulgent in a way that was new, didn't argue. At dawn the two girls stepped out on to the balcony to watch the sun rise on a democratic Pakistan which would soon have Benazir as its Prime Minister.

'How can you think about living anywhere else, Za?' Maryam said. 'This is where we belong.'

The world had new role models now, rendering those of a few months ago irrelevant: Benazir herself, Shabana Noshi, everyone who had faced down teargas and batons and prison sentences and exile for the sake of a democratic future that Zahra hadn't believed possible. It was to them that this day truly belonged, the ones who hadn't given up when the world told them they were fighting a losing battle, when their daughters told them there was nothing to gain from courage. Next time, she promised herself, she would be among their number.

*

Maryam knew it wasn't the new driver's fault that he wasn't Abu Bakr, but even so she referred to him only as 'Driver' so that her parents and grandfather would know she hadn't forgiven them for treating as replaceable someone who'd been so loyal to her. No one noticed – all of Khan Leather's many drivers were simply known as 'Driver' – but by the time she realised this she felt awkward about switching to his first name in case he wondered what had brought on this familiarity.

Driver took her to Khan Leather that Saturday two weeks after the elections when the euphoria had already started to be tempered by questions around the power-sharing deals that would be hammered out and what it might mean for Karachi's fractured population. In October there'd been blood, retaliatory violence for a massacre in Hyderabad along ethnic lines. Curfew had fallen, the army was called out. Her grandfather told her that democracy would only make this sort of thing worse as political parties formed along ethnic lines tried to assert their street power – she'd been grateful when he said that because speaking to her about the ways in which the world worked was his way of saying she was being restored to his favour. And that Saturday, a further sign of restoration: when Driver drove through the front gates the guard stopped the car to say her grandfather wanted her to meet someone and asked that she come straight to his office rather than the cricket pitch.

She walked up the stairs, looking down at her chest more than once, grateful for the item that her mother had left on her bed soon after her grandfather's white-sari-in-the-rain comment, though she still didn't know who among her mother's network had handed down this miracle called a jog-bra. It wasn't exactly comfortable, but it allowed her to run and sweat on the cricket pitch without forcing the men to keep their eyes fixed on her face or her feet.

When she entered the office, broken-nosed Billoo was there. He stood up, placed a hand over his heart and bowed his head slightly.

'I was just telling our guest that you'll be running the company after I've gone,' her grandfather said. He'd never said this to anyone other than Maryam herself. She was unprepared for how enormous the public anointment would feel, how it would straighten her spine, push her shoulders back, allow a feeling to settle on her that she couldn't name but could visualise very clearly – a robe of silk-lined leather, weighty and beautiful. 'And he was about to ask me a question about that when you walked in.'

Billoo spread his hands philosophically. 'Girls taking over is the new fashion,' he said, and she knew the question he'd now decided not to ask concerned her father.

'You've met my son,' was all her grandfather said, or needed to say.

It had never been made clear to Maryam what conversation her grandfather had had with his son about the whole thing – perhaps none. Toff knew, everyone knew, that Maryam would come to work at Khan Leather after university, and when her grandfather died she would be ready to take his place and nothing would change in Toff's ornamental role. She didn't much mind about titles. Her father could have one that superseded hers; she had no wish to embarrass him.

Billoo looked from her grandfather back to her and then to her grandfather again. 'Is she staying?'

'We'll both be here,' her grandfather said, gesturing for some reason at one of the office windows.

There was no mistaking Billoo's surprise but he only said, 'Should I go now?' and her grandfather said yes.

When he'd left her grandfather asked her to sit in the chair Billoo had vacated, the wide expanse of his rosewood desk between them. She sat and quickly stood up again as soon as she felt the warmth of Billoo's backside on the seat. Her grandfather laughed and stood as well, walking over to the window he'd indicated earlier and asking her to join him.

'What are we looking at?' she said. The garden her great-grandfather had planted in the months just after Partition was spread below them, sturdy trees that produced fruit and shade intersected by a pathway lined with flowerpots that changed through the seasons. The approach of winter brought with it a paucity of options, so the flowerpots displayed only dark and light pink sadabahar – periwinkles, as her father insisted on calling them, with the same pretentiousness that made him refer to spices by their English names. Even Zahra's impeccable politeness with regard to Maryam's parents had cracked the day she heard Toff speak of methi as fenugreek.

'Did you know someone's been stealing inventory from the warehouse?' her grandfather said, rubbing his handkerchief on the grimy windowpane even though he must know the accumulation was outside, his office interior buffed to gleaming every morning before he arrived. 'Has your father mentioned it?'

'Someone who works here?'

He nodded, looking as grave as she'd ever seen him. 'We know who it is. So – if you were running the company, what would you do about it?'

'Not the police,' she said automatically. There'd once been a theft in Saba's household – an inside job – and her parents had taken the rare step of calling the police. They'd arrested all the servants and some hours later told Saba's parents they were sure the ayah who'd raised her was innocent because they'd put mice down her shalwar, repeatedly, and though she'd fainted at one point when they revived her and did it again, she still swore she knew nothing about the crime. The ayah had returned to work the next day and no one ever mentioned the arrest or the mice in her presence. Saba had told Maryam all this, a note of scandal entering her voice when she whispered that people of 'that class' wore no underwear. Maryam still couldn't look at the ayah without imagining frantic rodents scrabbling down her thighs, up her thighs, drawn to heat and scent.

'That's the correct first step,' he said, his understated praise more meaningful than anything anyone else could say to her.

'Make him return the inventory or the money he got for it?' she said.

Her grandfather frowned. 'He'll say the money went to his sister's dowry or his mother's medical bill or the cost of a roof that was falling in.'

'Isn't it possible that's true?'

'The men know they can come to me when there's a real need. I've put children through universities, built back collapsed houses, paid so many medical bills I should have used the money to build a hospital on these grounds instead. We do what we can, and what is right, for those who are our responsibility. Not dowries, though. Uncivilised practice. So, no police, no repayment. What, then?'

She rolled her tongue around the inside of her mouth, thinking. 'Fire him?'

'Well, of course fire him. Is that all? Is that the message you're sending to the rest of the workers? Steal from us and all you risk is your future employment?'

'So . . .' There was some kind of commotion downstairs, shouts coming from the direction of the warehouse. 'So, you do call the police after all?'

'They can't be trusted to respond with proportionality.' The shouts had become a single voice calling out, calling for her grandfather, asking for his forgiveness. He sighed. 'It's not a terrible thing that you can't bring yourself to think of the correct answer.'

Billoo strode on to the path, a cricket bat in his hand, its blade propped jauntily on his shoulder. Behind him, Kashif and Lamboo were dragging along a man – thank god thank god not one of her cricket players – who was on his back, screaming. There was a wet patch on his shalwar, near his groin, expanding in a rivulet down his right leg. A group of workers from the warehouse followed, silent. From the other direction, artisans from the workshop were making their way along the path. Kashif looked up to the window and she stepped back.

'Do I have to watch this?'

Her grandfather rested his palm on the top of her head. 'No. Go into your father's office. You won't hear anything there.'

She went directly to the bathroom attached to her father's office and threw up.

When her grandfather came to find her a few minutes later, she was sitting in the desk chair, doodling cartoon figures – Snoopy, Garfield, the Wizard of Id. The radio was playing Noor Jehan because some sounds had carried from outside. He held out his arms, a rare gesture, and she ran into them.

'Sorry,' she said.

His arms tightened around her. 'It should never feel all right to see that. I'm glad you didn't want to watch.'

When she pulled out of the embrace, he rested his hands on her shoulders. 'Billoo knows how to inflict hurt without causing permanent injury. The police wouldn't be so careful. I don't want to deprive a family of a breadwinner. You understand?'

She nodded.

'You can ask me anything,' he said.

'Does my father know?'

'He doesn't try to stop it, but he doesn't want to be here when it happens. That's your father, and most of the world. Justice isn't gentle, but it is necessary. That's also why Abu Bakr had to go – it was necessary for you to learn you can't get away with certain behaviour. Do you see that?'

Again she nodded. He kissed her forehead.

'I intend for it to be a very long time before you have to take on this kind of responsibility yourself.'

Maybe the police will be different by then, she almost said, but she knew she would disappoint him with the refusal to look the world in the eye. Instead she said, 'I think I'll skip cricket today.'

'Of course,' he said. 'Why don't you help me with a design decision I've been trying to make. So many people have foreign citizenship now, we need a passport holder that'll take two passports. I've narrowed it down to my two favourites, and whichever one you choose we'll have in our spring line.'

She smiled, though that had felt impossible just a few seconds ago. When she walked with him to his office she could almost hear the rustle and creak of her silk and leather robe.

*

November drew to a close. On one hand the imminence of Benazir's inauguration made everything extraordinary, on the other hand nothing about being fourteen was made any easier because of it. Zahra had spent the previous evening walking up and down her living room in a sari, making sure she could manage the grown-up garment without tripping over its hem or looking like a child trying on her mother's clothes. Her first outing in it was tonight, at a wedding in the palm-lined garden of Beach Luxury Hotel, to which she was accompanying her father in place of her mother, who had a school function to attend. She was unlikely to run into anyone from school – it was the daughter of one of her father's newspaper colleagues who was getting married – so even if she did look less assured than she should, there'd be no one to see it who mattered.

Or so she had thought, walking in beside her father. She'd been so resentful about having to come she'd forgotten that, although she might think of her father's colleague as just another gasbag uncle, he was also a journalist who had tested the limits of press censorship through all the years of dictatorship, winning international awards for courage in the process. And so Zahra should have known that the hundreds of wedding guests would include politicians who had spent the years of dictatorship in exile, foreign correspondents who used 'uncle' as a source to file reports that said the things no one in Pakistan could say, and human rights champions, including a diminutive lawyer with the heart of a lion and the presence of a Colossus.

Zahra caught her father by the arm and pointed to Fehmida Dawood. The woman's laugh carried across the garden, its earthiness reminding Zahra that when she'd once asked her father about his encounters with this embodiment of justice – an ardent cricket fan who used the privileges of fame to sit in the media section during Test matches and gossip about the players – he had unexpectedly replied, 'She tells the bawdiest jokes; I can't possibly repeat them.'

'You want to meet her?' her father said now, and she nodded, suddenly shy.

'Come,' he said, setting off past trees wrapped in fairy lights and waiters carrying chilled bottles of Coke and Mirinda towards the guests who were standing about, women talking to women, men talking to men – no one showed much interest in the stage at the far end of the garden, where the bride and groom were posing for an endless succession of photographs with friends and family and people of importance who had to be called up to join them so that they could know their presence here was valued enough to be immortalised in the wedding album.

As they approached Fehmida Dawood, Zahra wondered how her father would break through the phalanx of admirers, men and women, surrounding her, but to her surprise it was the lawyer who raised her hand and called out to him with a term of affectionate abuse.

'Another True Believer,' she said, as he drew closer. 'I hear you hurt General Zia's feelings in the last days of his life, Habib. The government of Benazir Bhutto should make it a matter of priority to get you a medal. And who have you brought along?'

Zahra barely had time to take in the glow of being her father's daughter, a hero's daughter, before her father lightly pushed her by the shoulder, urging her forward. 'This is my daughter, Zahra.'

'Zahra. How does it feel to be your age and see the world change?'

Zahra felt she might faint or throw up. But Fehmida Dawood was looking at her, and so was everyone else, as if they really cared what she had to say and weren't simply being polite for her father's sake. She was suddenly very aware that her kitten-heeled shoes were uncomfortable, all the weight landing on the balls of her feet, and this was so distracting she couldn't think of anything but relieving the pain. She shifted her weight; the heels of her shoes stabbed through the grass, unbalancing her, and as she reflexively put out her arms the sari slipped off her shoulder.

As if it was the most natural thing in the world, Fehmida Dawood took hold of her hand and held on, and with the other hand draped the sari back in place. 'I really do want to know how it feels,' the lawyer said, still holding on to her hand.

'It feels amazing,' Zahra said. She was conscious that she was being touched by greatness and that she must say something that didn't sound like any other silly teenager. 'And it feels like more things are possible in the world than I'd believed.' That came out wrong. She sounded like the Queen in *Alice in Wonderland* saying, 'Sometimes I've believed as many as six impossible things before breakfast.'

But Fehmida Dawood stepped back and smiled at her, a warm full-beamed smile, as if Zahra had summed up everything that was wonderful in the world. 'Isn't that an extraordinary thing to learn. Remember it always. How old are you? Sixteen?'

'Fourteen,' she said.

'A sari and an intelligent response at fourteen. My god. What are you going to grow up to be? A journalist like your father?'

'No. A lawyer like you.'

'This is news to me,' she heard her father say.

'I suppose all your generation wants to go off to university in America.'

'No, England. I want to go to Cambridge,' she said.

'My old alma mater,' Fehmida Dawood said, as if she didn't know that was why Zahra had said it. 'Get in touch with me when you're applying and I'll have a few words with a few people.'

And then it was done, her moment at the centre of the universe over. The conversation returned to the grown-ups, and someone's teenaged daughter appeared and she and Zahra were made to talk to each other – one of those conversations no one wanted to be in, but no one knew how to leave, so it continued endlessly until someone else joined in and made extrication possible. Zahra's father was in a haze of cigarette-smoking journalists by then, so Zahra stepped away from the wedding guests and on to the walkway by the creek; the lamps at the garden's edge were reflected in the water as submerged balls of light, and cast enough illumination to make the huddled shapes of the mangrove trees visible on the far bank. She lifted the hem of her sari and tapped her heels on the ground to loosen the soil they'd sunk into.

'Look who's transformed since home time this afternoon.'

Zahra glanced around. 'Hammad.'

'How different things would be if the school uniform was a sari,' he said, looking at her in a way that she knew she shouldn't like. His jacket was slung over his shoulder, held in place by a finger hooked inside the collar; she found herself thinking the word 'taut' in relation to the torso beneath his slim-fitting black button-down shirt – a word she associated with the pages of books marked in secret code on Maryam's shelf.

'Would they?' she said, trying to sound indifferent. That feeling of transformation that had come upon her when she pushed her bra off her shoulder and made a man shudder with desire returned, accentuated – here she was, a grown-up version of Zahra who moved through the world, admired not just by her students and teachers but by women like Fehmida Dawood and boys whose glances had previously flickered past her.

Hammad laughed, reached out and grazed the tips of his fingers against the bare skin of her midriff. She quickly stepped away, not wanting anyone else to see. But no one seemed to be looking in their direction. The buffet dinner had been served at the other end of the garden, and guests had very quickly formed a raggedy line along the white-clothed tables, piling seekh kababs and pulao and korma and deep-fried prawns on to

84

their plates. Zahra could feel the warm imprint of his fingers, and a tingling sensation that came from it. She had never been touched like that before, never thought it could happen so easily and with no need for her to do anything other than stand there.

He stepped forward, closer to the creek. A wooden boat was the only movement on the water, its oars making little sound. A kerosene lamp revealed the rower to be a boy, barely a teenager, smoking a cigarette. Hammad whistled low and the boy rowed closer. 'Sutta?' he said, and the boy tossed a packet at him. He caught it deftly and flipped it open. It had a single cigarette and a box of matches inside. 'We need to give him something in exchange,' Hammad said. He reached out for Zahra's wrist – but this time he didn't touch her skin, only caught hold of the bracelet of jasmine flowers there. As if they were in a PTV drama where physical intimacy was only suggested. He slid the bracelet off her arm, the jasmine cool against her wrist and hands, held it up to his nose for a thrilling moment, and then threw it in the direction of the boat. The boy caught it deftly on the blade of his oar and flicked the oar to send the bracelet into the air and back down on to his outstretched palm. Zahra watched them both, admiring their ease.

Hammad lit the cigarette, offered her a drag, which she refused, and pulled on it for a long time – transformed from PTV drama hero into a worldly man in one of those ads that played during the commercial breaks of cricket matches.

'So,' he said. 'What does she say about me?'

'Who?' She heard the sullenness of her voice, wondered if Hammad could hear it too.

'Come on, don't tease. She's your best friend. I know she tells you everything.'

Zahra shrugged. 'Why should I tell you what she tells me?' She was accustomed now to Hammad walking Maryam to and from the gate at either end of the school day, the fact of their occasional calls – *Who knows how he got my number*, Maryam had said unconvincingly – and it was obvious that while Maryam enjoyed the pursuit, she didn't like him, so Zahra had stopped being bothered by it. How long could a seventeen-year-old boy remain interested in a fourteen-year-old girl who gave him only the dregs of her attention? But now, the musk of his cologne a faint presence that made her want to put her face against his neck to get to the source of it, she couldn't believe that chaste walks and phone calls was all Maryam wanted from Hammad.

'What is it about her?' he said. 'I mean, there's the obvious stuff. But something else. She's so . . . like she could rule the world one day and it wouldn't even surprise her. Do you think Benazir was like that when she was fourteen?'

'No,' she said shortly.

'Put in a good word for me, will you. Or tell me how to move things beyond Ocean Video dates. You're the only person she listens to.'

Now Zahra understood why Maryam had refused Zahra's offer to take her to Crystal Palace and introduce her to the videowallah who'd give her the newest movies in the best prints.

'Unless,' Hammad said, drawing the word out slowly.

'Unless what?'

He smiled, and it went all the way through her, making her legs feel unsteady. 'Want to walk?' he said, flicking his cigarette in the direction away from the lights and the wedding guests. His hand reached out and stroked

86

her bare skin again, and everything in her brain stopped except the word *yes*.

But from her heart came another word. *Maryam*. She stepped back, away from the intoxication of his scent, his proximity.

'You're not at all nice,' she said, and he smiled that smile again that said, no, he wasn't, not nice at all. She had to turn away from him quickly then, almost tripping over the hem of her sari as she walked back into the garden towards the world in which she was worthy of standing with the bravest and wisest of people, no taint in her, no dark desires.

*

The night after Benazir was sworn in as Prime Minister, Zahra and Maryam arrived at a party in Gizri thrown by Saba's older brother, the school's star athlete. Saba had invited a number of her own class-fellows, including Zahra and Maryam, but her brother had come up to Maryam in the schoolyard and made it clear that she was on his guest list too and he really hoped she was planning to be there. He barely glanced at Zahra until Maryam said, 'I'll come if Zahra's coming,' and then he said, 'Zahra, be a sport.'

Maryam's new driver had taken them to the party. 'You know you're not to wait, yes?' Maryam said as they got out of the car.

'There'll be plenty of people here to drop us,' she said to Zahra in explanation, raising her voice over the music coming at them from the dance floor.

There was no need for Zahra to ask if Maryam had lied and told her parents that Zahra's father would be picking them up from the party to take them back to

Zahra's, even though she'd told Zahra that her father shouldn't bother, she'd tell Driver to work late. Zahra had been too pleased when Maryam suggested a sleepover to wonder about her motives. In the car, she had been strangely distracted. Zahra had taken the moment alone together to finally tell her about the Brigadier's visit – it seemed safe at last to assume the military was out of power – and all Maryam had said was, 'Lucky timing,' and made an exploding sound, as if Habib Ali's act of conscience wasn't something she'd even registered. Now Zahra watched with silent disapproval as Maryam pulled off her oversized turquoise blouse and placed it in a polythene bag that was stuffed into the back pocket of her jeans. Beneath the shirt she was wearing a white tank top, clearly inspired by Whitney Houston on the cover of her *Whitney* album. She placed the polythene bag behind a row of flowerpots, ran her fingers through hair that had acquired a feathery fringe and bounce in a salon earlier that day, and said 'Come on' without looking at Zahra, who had been feeling stylish in her unbuttoned denim shirt with rolled-up sleeves over a striped shirt but was now conscious that her red pumps were scuffed at the toe and her legs were too long for her acid-washed jeans.

A group of A-level students called out to Maryam, but when Zahra kept on walking towards the table at the far end of the garden with its steel basin of iced drinks, Maryam followed her. They stood side by side, unspeaking, sipping Pakola from bottles through plastic straws that collapsed in on themselves if you sucked up the liquid with too much vigour. Night-blooming flowers filled the air with heavy perfume. The trees were strung with fairy lights, and the verandah had been transformed into a dance floor where an invisible demarcation line separated the Class 10 students from the A-level ones. There was a chill in the air that made Maryam's tank top even more infuriating. Hammad approached, all leather jacket and gelled hair and that cologne again.

'Dance,' he said, without acknowledging Zahra, and, taking hold of Maryam's hand as if that was the most natural thing in the world, led her on to the dance floor where she walked past her classmates without looking at them.

Zahra stood alone in the garden. She couldn't join her classmates while they were all watching Maryam and whispering to each other, and it would be desperate to attempt to interpose herself into any of the groups of older students. But worse to spend the evening standing here by herself while Maryam danced closer than she should to Hammad. The cold was beginning to raise goosebumps on her skin and she wondered if it would be fatally uncool to roll down her sleeves.

Surely, the world shouldn't still be this? Benazir was Prime Minister; she had taken the oath of office in a bright green shalwar with white dupatta, the colours of the Pakistan flag, and made the men around her look like pygmies. Military men and bureaucrats, the old guard, and now here they were: administering the oath of office to her, saluting her. Military officers saluting Benazir. You could cry remembering it, and perhaps no matter how long you lived on this earth you would always cry remembering it. They'd hanged her father, put her in prison, cast her into exile. And now they saluted her, this woman of only thirty-five, because millions upon millions of people went to the ballot box and said they must. Zahra brushed her hand across her eyes. What did all this matter – the school cliques, Maryam's awfulness, Hammad's inattentiveness, the scuffed toes of her shoes. Why should any of this matter when the world was transformed?

'How does it feel to become unglued?' Babar was walking straight across the garden to her. His blue button-down shirt had a rough patch near his heart where he'd unstitched the fashion label's logo from it. Boys who went abroad and bought expensive shirts could unabashedly also wear the knock-offs sold locally, but if you wore the imitation without being able to afford the real thing you looked like a wannabe, he'd explained to her some weeks earlier when she asked about the red marks on his finger where he'd clumsily pricked it with the needle. She had been both attracted and repulsed by the way he told her this, as if confirming a shared understanding about both their lives.

'Maryam and I aren't glued,' she said. 'I thought you said you weren't coming.'

'I wasn't, but then you said you were.'

She saw his hopeful smile, the way his shoulders filled his shirt, the perfect straight line of his nose. So much more handsome than Hammad, she thought and tried to make that matter. Sipping on her Pakola, she looked across to the dance floor; Maryam and Hammad had disappeared somewhere in the mass of bodies, but she caught Saba's furious stare.

'Go dance with everyone,' she said to Babar.

'You'll have to come with me or I'll go on standing here making you feel awkward.'

He made it easy to join their classmates, who had stopped their whispering even though they clearly remained aware of Maryam and Hammad. Saba was so glad to have Babar dancing in the same mass of bodies as her that her smile reached out to envelop everyone, even Zahra. Soon everything disappeared except the beat of the music, thudding within Zahra's heart, and the occasional not-accidental brush of Babar's arm against hers. She closed her eyes as she danced. It wasn't Babar's arm, it was someone else, unknown. The familiar stirring inside. They danced and danced. Maryam left the floor and sat down on Hammad's lap in one of the plastic chairs in the garden, his jacket draped over her shoulders. Saba gave Zahra a look that said she should drag her best friend away from this scandal that would follow her into the schoolyard tomorrow. But Zahra just closed her eyes again, let the music move her body and obliterate everything else.

People moved on and off the dance floor. Babar asked Zahra if she wanted to go and get something cold to drink but she said no, so he stayed. Saba's brother started to dance behind Zahra – his wooden movements more than offset by the glory of his athlete's physique – and three times she leaned back and her shoulder touched his bicep. The third time he apologised and moved away. The music changed to 'Fast Car' and everyone who wasn't part of a couple made a sound of protest. The dance floor half-emptied, but Saba stayed where she was, dancing slower now next to Babar, who danced slower next to Zahra. Hammad and Maryam came back on to the floor; Hammad had his arms around Maryam's waist and she clasped his back, their bodies swaying together. Tracy Chapman's voice pierced Zahra, cut open her heart and showed her how much longing was in there. Babar moved closer and she closed her eyes again. An arm touching her arm, the back of a hand against the back of her hand, fingers on the verge of entwining with her fingers. Saba caught her by the elbow, pretend-friendly, and pulled her close, arm around Zahra's shoulders so they could move together in time to the music, facing Babar, who looked crushed but gamely danced on. Zahra turned her face to the garden so she wouldn't have to see any of the slow-dancing couples – it wasn't just Hammad and Maryam, every boy holding a girl around her waist made her feel the same. Beneath the frangipani tree a group of boys stood together, a flash of silver that was a hip flask adding something to their bottles of Coke. Everyone wanted something more than school rules allowed, it wasn't just her. It was the slow-dancing couples, the hip-flask boys, it was Saba, it was Babar, everyone, all of them, why did they have to be so constrained, made drab in their school uniforms, forced to walk on the right-hand side of the stairway going up at the start of each day, why couldn't they be allowed to break free, the world was new and different now, how could any of them stay the same?

'Where's Maryam going?' Saba said, a loud whisper close to Zahra's ear.

There she was, hand in hand with Hammad, walking towards the front gate. *Look at me*, Zahra willed, and Maryam turned her head, and let go of Hammad's hand. Zahra stepped off the dance floor and Maryam came towards her.

'You're having fun so you should stay a while,' Maryam said, one hand in a pocket, hip jutting out, as if posing for cameras. 'I'll go for a drive with Hammad and then we'll come back for you.'

'You get into that car and tomorrow the whole school will say you did it with him.'

'Fine, then you come with us, Madam Chastity Belt.'

That was Hammad, who had walked up without Zahra noticing. Maryam's mouth opened in surprise.

'Come on,' he said. 'Whoever's coming, come on. We're leaving.' He turned and strode across the grass. Maryam set off after.

'My brother's picking me up soon. We can drop you home, one or both of you.' Babar's voice was reassuring, but Zahra looked at the dance floor, saw every pair of eyes watching Maryam, and followed her best friend out.

Hammad continued striding out of the gate and down the street past the row of parked cars and the group of drivers perched on the edges of a long flower bed, smoking and huddling together for warmth. Some of the drivers looked up at Maryam and Zahra before looking away again, and Maryam glanced back towards the house – she'd just remembered, as had Zahra, the polythene bag with the turquoise shirt. Further down the street, a car's headlights flashed on and off. Hammad raised his hand and quickened his pace.

'Why is his driver parked so far away?' Zahra said. Maryam shook her head, really properly looking at Zahra for the first time that evening.

It felt strange to be standing out here, on the street, at night. She wasn't cold any more, not after the dancing, but it felt right to roll down her sleeves, button them at the wrist. On the other side of the gate there was a world of light and music where girls and boys could dance together and everything was familiar, from the music to the party-goers to Saba's house itself, which Zahra and Maryam had known since the age of birthday parties with balloon-animal and performing-monkey entertainment. But the street itself was darkness and shadows, a feeling of exposure heightened by the breeze that had got inside her shirt, against her skin. All at once she understood that the world beyond school rules was here, on the wrong side of the gate. She felt drugged or drunk, though she'd never been either, wishing she could move the cup of her bra away from her body so the breeze could get in there and play.

'Let's go back inside,' Maryam said.

Back to closing your eyes and imagining that someone other than Babar wanted to dance with you, back to Maryam sitting on Hammad's lap, back to waiting for something exciting to arrive.

'Don't you want to wait to tell Hammad?'

He'd got into the car, which was now coming towards them. It was a white Suzuki FX, with tinted windows. Hammad stepped out and said, 'Ladies, your chariot awaits.'

He smiled at Maryam, and Zahra felt, as she had by the creek, the power of being the person his attention fell on. Babar was just a boy, but in Hammad's smile, in the strength of his wrist as he extended his hand towards Maryam, there was something else – something heady that made Zahra tingle. She touched her hand to that place on her torso that his fingers had brushed. Maryam said, 'We're not coming. Come on, Zahra.' Zahra pretended to take something out of her shoe to give Hammad a moment to try and change Maryam's mind.

'Bibi, I can drop you both home,' said a voice from near the front gate which she recognised as belonging to Saba's driver, Manzoor.

The driver-side window of the Suzuki rolled down and a man leaned out and said, 'Challo,' as both command and enticement. He was a few years older than Hammad, wearing a shiny shirt and cologne that was pungent but not unpleasant. His hair was cut like Wasim Akram's, so thick and deep on top you could lose a cricket ball in it, and that made the acne-scarred face all right because he shared that with the fast bowler too.

Hammad said, 'Come on, let's go, don't make a scene in front of the drivers.' He gestured to Zahra to go to the front passenger seat and she did, around the back of the car where she saw decals of a pair of boxing gloves and the words 'GOOD 4 U', which could be either boast or praise; she wondered which one the driver of the car intended. Just as she was about to open the car door she heard a 'Za!' from Maryam, who was pointing her thumb towards the gate. The man in the driver's seat leaned over and opened the door. Zahra ducked inside the car. A moment later, Maryam slid into the back seat, Hammad following after.

The man – he really was a man, not a boy – regarded Zahra without much interest, and then tilted his rear-view mirror and looked at Maryam, extending the moment just long enough to become an appraisal.

'Welcome to Jimmy's FX,' he said, gunning the engine to life. He had his car seat pushed back as far as it could go so that he looked almost as he if was reclining. That meant Hammad had an excuse – as if he needed it – to sit pressed up right against Maryam.

'Maryam, Zahra, Jimmy,' Hammad said, as Jimmy accelerated fast to leave the party behind. 'Anything you want done in Karachi, this is the man who'll do it for you.'

'In that case – Jimmy, could you drop us at Zahra's. It's Sea View.' Maryam spoke as though she were talking to Driver. Zahra hated her more then than she had at any other point in the evening.

Jimmy glanced towards the back seat. 'She wants to run away from you already, loverboy,' he said, speaking in Urdu except for that last word, and raised the volume on the car stereo, drowning out any response with 'Beat It'. He turned towards Sunset Boulevard rather than Phase 5. Zahra found herself delighted that for once Maryam's imperiousness had so little effect.

Once they were on the broad expanse of Sunset Boulevard, Jimmy drove billboard-blurringly fast. It was like being on one of the rides at Funland, but sitting next to a university student rather than your class-fellows. Zahra rolled down the window to feel the rush of speed more intensely, the shock of the cold wind strangely pleasurable. Michael Jackson made her drum her hands against her thighs and move her lower body in time to the music. The city lights dazzled, posters of Benazir hung everywhere. Jimmy overtook cars and motorcycles with loud triumphant music blaring. MQM's election song, Benazir's election song, Michael Jackson braided between them as if mixed by a DJ. More music spilt out of roadside kiosks where men bought cigarettes and paan and the chance to loiter; on Clifton Bridge there were donkey-cart races – high spirits everywhere. And beyond all this, the feeling of freedom, of choosing at last to embrace life outside the same circuit of homes and families that had been her entire existence. She slipped her hand under the collar of her shirt, felt her skin, the interruption of her bra, her skin again. Here it was, life itself, at last she was in it, not just watching it from the next car over but actually really in it.

She was aware of bodies moving in the back seat, but the music drowned out all sound. Zahra bit down on the tip of her thumb so she could concentrate on that instead of imagining Hammad's hand under Maryam's shirt, looked at Jimmy and tried to want his attention rather than Hammad's. She didn't like his face much, so she looked at his hands on the wheel instead, dark hair at his knuckles that should have been disgusting but wasn't. How would those hands feel on her? He was driving towards the Pearl Continental Hotel where she knew the older students went late at night to the ground-floor restaurant where you could eat cake and drink coffee under crystal chandeliers. Was that all that would happen tonight?

Jimmy's hand came towards her leg, but he was only pressing in the lighter. From the back seat, Hammad handed him a cigarette and Jimmy placed it between his lips. The lighter popped out, and Jimmy snapped his fingers at Zahra. She pulled it out, with its glowing circular end, and tried to pass it to Jimmy, but he kept his hands on the wheel and leaned his head towards her, his eyes still on the road, his foot pressing down on the accelerator. She had never been in a moment so devastatingly cool. She brought the glowing lighter to the end of Jimmy's cigarette, her fingers inches from his lips, and hoped Hammad was watching. Jimmy took hold of the lit cigarette between index and middle fingers and withdrew it from his mouth. His tongue emerged to lick his chapped lips and then slid wetly back in.

It took just that instant of repulsion to dissolve the feeling of potential and possibility and see him as a man far too old to be behaving this way with fourteen-year-old girls. A creep.

She turned to look at Maryam, seated directly behind her, but Maryam had her head tilted back, eyes closed, arms crossed over her body. Her expression was annoyed, maybe slightly bored. Hammad had the look of a boy who has been denied a birthday present. Jimmy took one hand off the steering wheel to place his fingertips against Zahra's cheek and guide her back forward again. It was the hand holding the cigarette, she could feel its heat against her face. His touch was soft but not gentle, as if he knew she would obey the slightest pressure. As if he was instructing her that she must obey every mildly expressed order if she wanted mildness to continue to be the tone of command.

A snaking terror moved from her stomach up her windpipe. She breathed in deeply through her open mouth, trying to get past the constriction in her chest. The wind was pummelling her, whipping her hair into her face, numbing her lips and nose with cold, but she didn't know if she was allowed to roll up the window.

Jimmy drove past the Pearl Continental. Maryam was saying something in the back seat, but the music was so loud Zahra couldn't hear her and she dared not turn around again. He turned on to Bunder Road, the city's central artery, and a traffic snarl made him press down on his brake as he hadn't done for any red light. Men were sitting at pavement tables outside some place called Cafe VIP, just feet away from her. One nudged another, jerked his head in her direction. Jimmy raised his eyebrows at her, daring her to open the door and get out. There were men, only men, at the cafe tables and in the cars and motorcycles around them. Her father's newspaper office was nearby, she'd often visited him there, but that was during daylight hours – Karachi's nights were not for girls or women.

Even without turning around, she was aware of Maryam's bare arms in the back seat, the brightness of the white shirt moulded close to her chest. Jimmy tossed his cigarette out of the window and rolled it up, gesturing to her to do the same. She didn't know which was worse – being watched by the pavement men or being sealed in here with him – but she knew she had to obey. Her hand was clumsy on the window-crank, but she got the window all the way up and everything turned even darker inside. Jimmy's sweet-and-spice cologne mingled unpleasantly with the lingering cigarette smell, the music jarring through the scratchy speakers with too much bass. The traffic eased, and the car moved past the pavement men.

Maryam so close, so out of reach. Zahra considered slipping her hand in the space between the passenger seat and the vinyl door panel to find Maryam's hand, feel her strength, but that might make Jimmy angry.

Jimmy ejected the tape, flipped it, and turned the volume up again for 'The Girl Is Mine'. He drove past the Port Trust Building and turned on to the road leading towards the beaches – Hawkesbay and Sandspit – at the outer limits of the city. Traffic thinned, then disappeared. Trucks hulked on the sides of the road, parked end to end; polythene bags and other debris filled empty stretches of land. Street dogs prowled; a piercing howl entered the car so close her entire body lifted off the seat for a moment. It was the opening to 'Thriller' – the howling, the creaking door, the footsteps, she'd heard it a thousand times. Jimmy laughed. They had left all habitation behind, only little shacks lined the road – in the daytime they sold cold drinks and fruit and cricket bats to beach-goers but now they all had their shutters down. The road was empty ahead, leading all the way out of Karachi and towards the distant hills. Was this how kidnappings happened? Two girls in a car on a deserted road, held hostage without knowing it. Maryam's family could pay any ransom, but her family couldn't. Maybe he knew this. Maybe he'd take Maryam and drop Zahra on the side of the road in the middle of nowhere – but there were fishing villages nearby all along the coast, she could go there for help. A flicker of hope, awful to recognise. Maryam was in this car because of her.

Jimmy slammed on the brakes, and Zahra's head almost hit the windscreen before she was thrown back again. There was no obstruction, no animal running in front of the car. Jimmy switched off the engine and the headlights. The music was swallowed by an absolute silence. There were no street lights, and the darkness was vast.

'Sometimes trucks come round that bend,' he said, pointing to something Zahra couldn't see just ahead. 'The drivers have such long shifts they stub their cigarettes out on their hands to stay awake.'

'Jimmy, come on man,' Hammad said. 'Take us home.'

'So much for loverboy.' Jimmy turned on the interior light and twisted around to look at Maryam. 'You want me to take you home? Ask nicely, and maybe I will.'

'I want you to die.' Maryam's voice cold, precise.

'Maybe,' he said, flicking the light switch. 'But then we all will.'

Hammad made more sounds of protest, but Jimmy's hand, raised in reprimand, silenced him.

They sat, looking at the road ahead, waiting for a juggernaut of a vehicle to come charging at him. After a little while Zahra could hear waves, faintly.

Jimmy looked at his watch. Then he switched on the ignition, put the headlights on full beam. He turned the car round with a loud screech and headed towards the city, its lights beautiful as they approached. She'd never been so happy to see Karachi's late-night traffic – red brake lights in one direction, white headlights in the other.

They were behind a slow-moving truck, its back overladen with stuffed gunny sacks, held in place by a thick rope. Jimmy weaved into the other side of the road, a bus bearing down on them. He accelerated – bus horn, headlights, the driver's shouting face. At the last possible moment he swerved back into his lane ahead of the truck. Hammad was yelling, Zahra biting her fist, Maryam silent. Across Netty Jetty Bridge, towards the gateway to the port, through which Zahra had driven countless times with her parents on the way to an evening on a fishing boat. She could almost smell the kerosene lamps and damp cushions and spiced crab. The thought of her parents, the safety of their presence, made her want to cry. He would put them on a boat and take them somewhere no one would ever find them. On the fishing boat, crabs scrabbled about in a wooden crate, trying to climb over each other to escape, as if they knew they would soon be lifted out and cracked apart. She was going to be sick. She couldn't be sick in Jimmy's car. She recited 'Daffodils' in her head, but that didn't work, so she tried 'The Charge of the Light Brigade' until she got to 'the valley of death' and then she cried silently.

They were almost at the gateway to the port when Jimmy pulled up on the side of the road. A man who had been squatting on one end of a speed bump, watching traffic, stood, retrieved something from the shadows behind him and walked up to the car, carrying a duffel bag on his shoulder. The contents of the bag shifted against each other, something hard, maybe metallic. Guns everywhere in Karachi, the phrase 'Kalashnikov culture' part of their everyday lives. Jimmy got out of the car, taking the keys with him.

He'd barely closed the door when there was a sharp cry of pain from the back seat. With Jimmy out of the car, Zahra turned to look. Maryam had caught hold of Hammad's little finger and twisted it. 'You get us home now,' she said quietly, 'or I'll have you expelled from school.'

'I swear I didn't know this was going to happen.' Hammad cowered, though whether he was more terrified of Maryam or of Jimmy it was hard to know.

Maryam looked at Zahra. 'I should have listened to you about him.' Nothing about her voice or her expression suggested any emotion beyond irritation. It was only when she took a closer look at Zahra that her expression changed and her voice rose. 'Are you *crying*?'

'You change places with her,' she ordered Hammad.

But as soon as Hammad opened the door, Jimmy said, 'Stay where you are,' and he quickly closed it.

'Don't cause any trouble,' Zahra said to Maryam, and she turned to face forward before Jimmy had to tell her to.

Jimmy opened the hatchback and placed the duffel bag in the boot – the metallic sound of guns unmistakable now, and separated from Hammad and Maryam by little more than the thin vinyl seats. When he got back into the car, he was smiling.

'Please will you take us home,' Zahra managed.

'Home?' he said, starting the car engine. 'I'm not taking you home. You want to get out, get out, but your friend is staying.' Zahra realised only now that he hadn't readjusted his rear-view mirror since Maryam had got into the car, and must have been watching her all along.

*

A few hours earlier, Maryam had stood naked in front of the bathroom mirror, enjoying the sight of herself. She'd felt different since Benazir's inauguration. A woman was in power. Maryam spent a good portion of her days imagining a meeting with Benazir. She'd say she was going to take over the family business and Benazir would put an arm around her shoulder and say, *Welcome to the club.* She felt a charge running through her at the thought of Benazir's hand on her in a way she never did at the thought of Hammad's touch. But even so, something had to change in life; how could everything be as it was before Benazir placed one hand on the Quran and held the other one up and took the oath of office with a voice of complete authority, as though she had always known this moment would come? And so she'd said yes to Hammad, and hoped her older cousin had been right when she said the act of kissing could turns frogs into princes (she'd also said, with a creepy flickering of her tongue, that it could turn princes into frogs, but Maryam tried not to think about that).

When she saw the FX, though, she knew they shouldn't get into it. But Hammad had ushered Zahra towards the car and Jimmy opened the door and for some reason Zahra did what the boys wanted her to do. When Hammad got in next to Maryam, he tried to put his arm on her thigh, and she pushed him off. Why had he asked Zahra to come along, and who was this man with the cheap cologne and cheap clothes and forgodssake 'Beat It' – was he living in 1982?

And what was wrong with Zahra, singing along, swaying her body, window rolled all the way down. What music video did she think she was in? Hammad stretched his arm out across the seat just a few inches above Maryam's shoulders. Maryam turned to look out of the window. A few seconds later his arm dropped on to her shoulder. Maryam shoved him away from her and looked up at the roof of the car, which was the only direction that allowed her to avoid the sight of both Hammad and Jimmy and their reflections. The longer Jimmy drove, the more she was aware of a deep loathing. Loathing for the boy who couldn't manage anything as simple as finding a way for them to be together in private, and loathing for the man who had almost instantly revealed himself to be one of those cheapsters whose fast driving and overpowering cologne were attempts to compensate for being a nobody. She knew he was watching her, but she didn't want him to think she'd noticed or cared.

And so, with her eyes on the roof, she hadn't noticed when the singing, swaying Zahra disappeared and a frightened Zahra took her place. She'd left her on her own in the front seat, and now Zahra was crying; that bastard had made Zahra cry, and he would have to learn that this wasn't allowed.

He slammed down the hatchback. What was in the duffel bag? If she had to guess from the sound of its contents sliding around, she'd say videocassettes – pirated videos, all the latest in WWF, no doubt.

But why did Zahra have to speak to him in that pleading tone of voice, allowing him – that nobody – to speak to her as if she was disposable? 'You want to get out, get out, but your friend is staying,' he said.

Maryam leaned forward between the front seats, one hand on Zahra's shoulder. 'So, here's the situation,' she said, in her most conversational tone of voice, even while her thumb moved in reassuring circles on Zahra's denim shirt. 'It's been about half an hour since we were expected back at Zahra's. By now her parents will have called our hosts who'll speak to their driver and get a description of you and your car, and then her parents will call my parents, and my parents will call the DIG Police, who is an old friend of theirs, and he'll soon have all his officers looking out for us, if they aren't already.' In fact, it was the previous Deputy Inspector General of Police who had been a friend of her grandfather's, but he'd fallen into some kind of professional disgrace and been replaced by someone new whom her grandfather hadn't yet cultivated. 'So why don't you start driving us home now, and maybe the DIG will get a call from my parents to say we're safely home before a police van stops you and has a look in the boot of your car.'

There was a satisfying silence when she'd finished. Hammad shifted further away from her. Jimmy started the engine and drove without a word, not so fast or wild. Maryam kept her hand on Zahra's shoulder, wishing her friend's muscles would start to uncoil now that Maryam had taken charge. They were on the busy, broad avenue of Bunder Road, Hammad's hands folded on his lap, Jimmy still silent.

Jimmy turned on to one of the streets branching off from Bunder Road. 'Do you think the police will come looking for you here?' he said, his tone as conversational as Maryam's had been. He slowed almost to a stop and shifted into first gear, rolling ahead, inch by inch.

'Where are we?' Zahra said.

The buildings here were a mix of old and new, but it was the old ones with their mournful dilapidation that caught the eye. Made of yellow Gizri sandstone, like Maryam's grandfather's house, with carved wood-work balconies jutting out, some enclosed, some not. You might think *Romeo and Juliet* if you wanted to put a gauze filter over what really went on here. The street was criss-crossed with electricity wires, a canopy of snakes, some dangling low, almost touching the roof of the car. A peepul tree grew out of the pavement.

Zahra would know what this street was if anyone had spoken its infamous name, but no one did and there was no sign to identify it. Maryam knew where they were because one evening when Abu Bakr had allowed her behind the wheel in the old part of town he'd refused to let her turn down here. Not a place for you, he'd said, and

105

that told her it could only be Napier Road. She had tried to insist, said she was interested in the architecture of the old theatres and entertainment halls, but he knew her well enough to know why she wanted to drive through the street where the seediness of prostitution commingled with the promise of stardom for the few who made their way from the entertainment halls into the world of cinema. She wanted to look up at the balconies and see if she could glimpse one of the women whose lives were so unimaginable to her. But Abu Bakr was adamant, and there was a part of her that didn't want to see things that she might have to think about afterwards, so she'd relented and driven past the red-light district that was so handily accessible for the port, the business district, the universities, and the high court.

Now, in the darkness, a man was crossing the street with a tray of something that turned out to be laddus when the light from the doorway he was entering shone on it, brightening the golden spheres. Then the door closed behind him, cutting off the music that had rolled down a briefly glimpsed flight of stairs.

'Come on, yaar,' Hammad said. 'Let's take them home. No one's having fun.'

'Or we could start having fun,' Jimmy said. The car was still inching forward, Jimmy looking through the windscreen at the balconies and boarded-up windows on either side of the road as if trying to recognise something or waiting to see someone. There were no women visible; they must be inside, waiting for their pimps to bring men to them. Or else they were all already occupied. The word 'occupied' made Maryam feel strange. Benazir Bhutto taking the oath of office felt very far away. You could do anything to a woman on this street and no one would stop you.

The street was narrowing as they progressed through it. Jimmy looked into the rear-view mirror again. 'Why don't you ask me nicely to take you home. Twice you've asked in the rudest way. Ask nicely and maybe I'll do it.'

She met his gaze in the mirror. His eyes were cold, hard, something ugly in them that she hadn't seen before in anyone's eyes.

And maybe I won't, his eyes said to her, and the tight knot of loathing that had been inside her all this while unspooled into fear. All these months she hadn't wanted Hammad, but she had wanted to be wanted by him. But Jimmy's eyes in the rear-view mirror told her that her wants were irrelevant. He could do whatever he wanted, would do it, was thinking right now of how it would feel, a cold hard smile to match his eyes.

You could do anything to a girl here and no one would stop you; you could do anything to a girl anywhere and no one would stop you if you had a car with tinted windows and a stereo system that drowned out all screams.

'Maryam, please,' Zahra said.

'Could you please take us home,' Maryam said.

'Of course,' Jimmy said. He reversed out of Napier Road, back into the familiarity of Bunder Road. Maryam rolled the window down all the way, gulped in the fresh air.

*

It was only a few minutes before they returned to the part of the city that they traversed in their everyday lives, and another few minutes before they were driving past the homes of people they knew. When they finally neared the identical blocks of flats along the seafront,

Jimmy said, 'Still want to park further up where it's dark?' and Hammad replied, 'Jimmy, come on, even I am going to be in trouble for getting home this late.'

The dim bulb in front of Zahra's block showed only the silhouettes of the two men standing outside, one smoking, one pacing. As soon as Jimmy's headlights swung round to illuminate them they rushed towards the car.

Jimmy cursed, his voice high-pitched, and reversed all the way back on to the street, away from the men waiting for their daughters to come home. 'Out, get out,' he shouted even as he slammed on the brakes. 'Come on, Zahra,' Maryam said, but Zahra needed no prompting to open the door and tumble out. Jimmy peeled away, and Zahra ran straight into her father's arms. She was aware of Maryam's father approaching more slowly, shaking his head at his daughter.

'How could you?' he said.

'Let's go upstairs,' Zahra's father said, quietly.

Upstairs, there was Zahra's mother, and instead of the expected scolding, the tightest of embraces.

'Zeno?' Maryam's father said.

Maryam's mother was bent over on the sofa, elbows on her knees, her palms covering her face. When she moved them away her mascara was smudged, and for the first time Zahra saw that Zenobia Khan wasn't more beautiful than Shehnaz Ali – she was only more elaborately arranged.

Zeno stood up and walked over to her daughter. 'Are you going to say something?'

'Sorry for being so late,' Maryam said to Zahra's parents.

'Late?' Maryam's mother said. 'Don't think we don't know what happened. Saba told us. What she didn't see,

108

the drivers did. Do you know how lucky you are to have a friend like Zahra? Did you think of the position you were putting her in?'

Zahra formed the sentence in her mind that would say that Maryam had been the one who wanted to go back to the party, and that she, Zahra, had got into the car when they could have walked through the gates to safety. But they would ask her why, and how could she say, because Hammad's wrist, because the tinted windows and the unknown man in the driver's seat?

'Are you both all right?' Zahra's father said.

Zahra and Maryam nodded, both smiling reassuringly as if they'd already discussed the matter and agreed there was no point giving their parents any more worries with talk of running red lights and cars sitting in darkness in the middle of the road and transactions that had certainly been criminal. They lived so close to the edge of violence every day, and Zahra knew the directions in which her parents' minds would have gone – directions in which her own mind had raced as Jimmy drove fast through the empty streets, one hand on the wheel, one on his thigh. But in the end, nothing terrible had happened. Really, nothing had happened. They went for a drive, he stopped to pick something up along the way, they came back. She'd been in cars with crazier driving – Saba's brother had once driven back from the beach on the wrong side of the road to avoid a traffic jam, trucks and buses charging at them with blinding headlights for an endless stretch of time. Now it was just a story of daring that Saba told those who hadn't been here.

'They're fine!' Maryam's mother said. 'Look at them. They've had a grand adventure. We're the ones who've been sitting here worried sick. Habib, Shehnaz – I'm so sorry about my daughter.'

'We've all done stupid things at that age,' Zahra's mother said. 'Maryam's a good girl.'

'That's kind of you, but hardly true,' Maryam's mother said. 'Come on, Maryam. We're going home.'

On the way out, Maryam reached for Zahra's hand, clasping it. Zahra pressed down against her friend's fingers.

*

Maryam woke into a feeling she didn't recognise but which became anger as soon as it had someone to alight on – her parents, who greeted her at breakfast as though nothing had happened the night before; her younger sisters, whose persistence in wanting to know what had happened sharpened the contrast with the parents who didn't want to know; Hammad, who was clearly the person who kept calling and hanging up when someone other than Maryam answered the phone; Saba, who must have told her aunt, Mrs Hilal the biology teacher, that two of her classmates had gone off in a car with Hammad and a strange man, which was why the headmistress had called to say she needed to see Maryam and her parents in her office first thing Monday morning.

'What are we going to do if she wants to expel you?' Maryam's mother said, opening the bedroom door forcefully but then standing in the doorway, as if there was only so far she could go in asserting her authority over her firstborn.

Maryam looked up from the art pad she'd been sketching on. 'I'll drop out of school and go to work at Khan Leather.'

Her mother shook her head and retreated down the hallway. Maryam looked down at the sketch – she'd drawn a rear-view mirror, a pair of eyes reflected in it.

Maryam ripped out the sheet, folded and folded it into a tiny square of paper and placed it between her teeth, biting down hard.

What is it what is it what is it, she whispered into the empty room. What was this feeling that made everything seem wrong, with no route back to right?

The fear she'd felt last night had been activated by a knowledge inside her body, a knowledge that was *about* her body. She knew that Zahra's terror was related to hers, though that man – Jimmy – didn't look at Zahra the way he looked at her. Knew also that Hammad felt no trace of it; he might worry that Jimmy would drive them into an oncoming car, or that the police would stop them at a checkpoint, or that he'd be home so late his father would clip him around the ear, but he couldn't know this feeling of – she had it now – inescapability. Ever since her body had become a strange new home in which she had to learn how to live, this was what she had glimpsed from the corner of her eye, this was what was present in the men brushing against her on the Tube, the uncle pulling her close in an embrace, and even Hammad resting his eyes on her breasts as he walked down the school corridor towards her. She was a target now, her body a target. She placed the palms of her hands on her breasts, felt their weight.

She was beginning to understand why men and women walked so differently, stood so differently. Men strode, owning the world. Women walked with smaller steps, watched and watchful. Her anger deepened into rage, and she felt the strength of it, the strength of her own will. Not her. She would stride always, even in the presence of a Jimmy, especially in the presence of a Jimmy. She took the paper out of her mouth; it was sodden, tooth-marked. She flicked it with her thumb and finger across the room, a perfect soaring arc, into the wastepaper basket.

'Nice shot,' said the only voice in the world she really wanted to hear. Zahra came further into the room, Maryam scrambled off the bed, and they embraced, arms tightening around each other, staying like that for a very long time. Maryam felt the world start to tilt back to OK.

'Have you received the summons?' Zahra said when they finally separated and took up their side-by-side positions on the bed.

'Yes. Why is it the school's business anyway?' Maryam said.

'We expect our students to maintain certain standards at all times,' Zahra said, in a perfect imitation of the headmistress's voice. She picked a book off the bedside table – *Lucky*, which Maryam had turned to for comfort last night. With her other hand she cupped her neck as she did when she was feeling insecure about something. 'I'll tell her I was the one to get into the car when you wanted to – tried to – go back inside.'

She was looking at the book, attempting to keep her tone light. Maryam watched her friend. She knew the request that was being made of her, that couldn't be voiced. Zahra's closely guarded reputation would be sullied if she changed her role from concerned friend who'd gone along to protect Maryam to the one who'd insisted on getting into the car. Perhaps she wouldn't make it to Head Girl, perhaps a teacher would be a touch guarded in her praise in a university letter of recommendation.

There was a part of her that wanted to yell, *Why did you do it?* It was the most un-Zahra-like behaviour, the first completely inexplicable thing she had done in all their years of friendship. Or perhaps not so inexplicable. For a while now, Maryam had suspected that for all Zahra's bookish intelligence she could be very foolish about the world. And despite everything else, she felt triumphant in having this confirmed, and then immediately disliked herself for the thought and hoped Zahra would never know she'd had it. She certainly would never say it. Zahra wasn't uttering a word of blame for any of the events of the night, and perhaps – she felt grown-up thinking this – perhaps friendships weren't all about what you said to each other but also about what you didn't say.

'Don't be silly,' Maryam said. 'You'll tell her no such thing. We got into the car at the same time, and I'm the one who organised the whole thing with Hammad. Do you think Saba found my shirt in her flowerpot?'

'I bet she'll keep it and wear it at the next party she knows you're going to be at.'

Zahra's voice was full of relief and gratitude as she took Maryam's hand, squeezing it tight.

*

Monday saw them in the headmistress's office – Zahra and Maryam and all four parents. The room was large, dominated by a vast desk, behind which the headmistress sat in a black gown over a beige shalwar kameez. The walls were covered in photographs of the school's staff over the years, the headmistress herself going from bright-eyed recent graduate to a woman of authority in the course of several decades.

She had looked up without smiling when the Alis and Khans walked in, though Zahra's mother stood beside her in many of the pictures on the wall. Personal relations were secondary to the question of the school's reputation, and the school's reputation was indivisible from the students' reputations.

She asked Zahra and Maryam to step forward, which meant they were standing beside each other, yet nowhere close to being in the same moment. Ever since the headmistress had called to summon Zahra and her parents to this meeting, Zahra had imagined her future disappearing into a dark void, regardless of her parents telling her she was overreacting and Maryam's assurances that she wouldn't let Zahra take the blame for anything. A girl could be expelled from school for going off with a strange man, and if that happened she'd carry that stain with her forever. Girls who were expelled didn't get scholarships to Oxbridge, they didn't graduate summa cum laude from Ivy League colleges, they didn't go on to shine brightly in the world, leaders in their chosen fields. Disgrace and failure: the words brushed against her, feather-light and horrifying, like Jimmy's touch on her cheek. By contrast, whatever happened to Maryam today wouldn't matter very much. She'd still inherit a business and a place in society. The rich lived in a different universe.

The problem, the headmistress said without preamble, was that on the face of it both girls had done the same thing – gone for a joyride late at night in a car driven by a boy they didn't know, the kind of boy who drove around with tinted windows, which led to all kind of speculation about what went on inside the car.

Maryam glanced at Zahra when the headmistress said 'joyride', as if this was a moment to quibble about vocabulary.

The headmistress continued. What punishment awaited one girl must befall the other, she said. Several of the teachers were in favour of suspending them for what little remained of the term; of course the timing meant they would then miss their exams and that would show up on their transcripts and could affect their university admissions. And now Maryam's hand reached out, shielded from the headmistress's sight by the desk, and gripped Zahra's hand, steadying her.

The headmistress's expression softened. No one in the staffroom wanted Zahra to suffer long term repercussions for what everyone understood to be a large-hearted though misguided act of friendship. She was one of the school's brightest stars, a responsible, hard-working, admired student who had the potential to one day be Head Girl, though for that to happen in the light of these new events she would have to stick to the straight and narrow without exception. It was to Maryam's credit – and her tone of voice made clear this was the only thing to Maryam's credit – that she had chosen such a best friend, and it was to be hoped that this escapade would cause her to reflect and to learn from Zahra.

Fortunately, the headmistress said, there was another way to look at the night's events. The girls had agreed to be dropped home by a fellow student. There was nothing wrong with this. The school should be responsible for ensuring that none of its students were boys you wouldn't feel safe going home with. They didn't know – did you, Zahra? – that some other boy, from some other school if he'd ever been to school at all, was driving and had his own plans. The drivers – it was very unfortunate that drivers had to witness all this – had said the girls had started walking back to the house but Hammad's friend had driven up and, in some accounts – she emphasised the *some* – Hammad had all but kidnapped them. Hammad, of course, had been expelled. It was a shame they hadn't found a way to do it earlier. A bad seed from an early age.

The black gown, it was now clear, was meant to call to mind a judge's robes.

And so, the headmistress said, placing the palms of her hands flat on the desk, there would be no punishment for the girls from the school. She would leave it to the parents to decide their own ways of responding.

It was only now that she half stood up so she could reach across the table to take Zahra's mother's hands in hers. 'My dear, we miss you terribly,' she said.

It was understood that Zahra's parents would stay on, and tea and biscuits would soon make an appearance. They and their daughter had been exonerated; all blame fell on Maryam and the parents who hadn't known how to raise her properly. Zahra looked at Maryam, wanting to convey her embarrassment at the unfairness of this judgement, but it appeared Maryam either hadn't noticed or didn't care.

'What a relief,' Maryam's mother said when they were out in the schoolyard again. There was no one around, not even in the playing field, but Zahra looked up to the latticed windows cut into the school building and wondered if anyone was watching and relaying information back into the classroom about the disgraced girls and their parents.

Maryam's mother rubbed Maryam's shoulder and smiled at her in a manner that was almost cloying. She wanted so much for her daughter to like her.

'Hold your heads high,' Maryam's father said, sounding for the first time like the Patriarch. 'Don't let anyone smell weakness.'

There was no point going back to class when Maryam's parents departed. It was break time in a few minutes, and anyway, Zahra's legs didn't feel as though they could carry her up the stairs. They made it to the school bell and collapsed on to the ground, leaning back against the solid brick of the archway.

'Thank god that's over.'

'Is it?' Maryam said.

'Oh god. I forgot about Hammad.'

'Please. I'm glad he's been expelled. But what about Jimmy?'

'What about him?'

'He just gets away with it? How is that right?' Maryam frowned a little, and her voice was unusually thoughtful when she said, 'There's no justice in this world for girls, is there?'

Zahra never wanted to have to think about Jimmy again. Already, he was receding in the way of a nightmare. 'Well, no harm done in the end, right?'

Maryam was silent. Zahra drummed her fingers on her friend's arm. 'That whole ride, I kept wishing I was more like you. You weren't afraid at all. I've never seen you afraid of anything.'

'I was afraid,' Maryam said, her voice low. She looked at the palm of her hand as if it could tell her what future lay beyond this moment. When she looked up again, she was grinning. 'I was afraid of getting you suspended. I didn't know if our friendship would survive it.'

'Idiot,' Zahra said, bumping her shoulder affectionately against Maryam's. But she knew it was possible the friendship wouldn't have survived it, even if the incident had been mostly her own fault.

Soon, the bell would ring and the students would rush out to hear if Maryam Khan and Zahra Ali had been suspended or expelled; Saba would feel more important than ever, as she retold the story from her point of view; students as young as Class 7 would nudge each other as they passed the girls to say, that's them; Babar would want

117

to sit with them to be supportive and perhaps continue what he had tried to start on the dance floor, but he was just troublesome enough in the classroom that Zahra would be ignoring the 'straight and narrow' injunction if she even considered the option; some students would be kind, and that would be shaming; Hammad's friends would be resentful that he had to bear all punishment when Maryam was the one who had turned up in a white tank top and sat in his lap; some would whisper that Zahra wasn't nearly as unwilling as everyone said; and everyone would wonder what really happened in those lost hours of their lives. All that would happen, and soon. But for now Zahra could lean on her best friend's shoulder, the sounds of the city reaching them from the other side of the high boundary wall, and know how lucky they had been for everything turning out all right when there were so many ways in which it could have gone wrong.

*

Her grandfather had been in Malaysia, discussing the new line with Khan Leather's designers, a week-long trip that felt endless to Maryam as she waited for his return. He was due back on Saturday, but on Friday evening she was summoned to see him in the drawing room, which was where he always liked to be received. In the summer silk curtains blocked out the sun, but now the curtains were drawn back from the French doors, framing the garden with its hibiscus bush and frangipani tree in flower. He was in his armchair, palm atop his walking stick, Maryam's parents on the nearby sofa.

Maryam moved with rapid steps towards him, and he flicked his wrist. The walking stick, parallel to the ground, measured the distance she had to keep away from him. She came to a stop, halfway across a Persian rug with a hunting scene woven into it. Her first thought was that he had injured himself and her embrace might aggravate the wound.

'I thought firing Abu Bakr would have taught you a lesson about lying, conniving and implicating other people in your crimes,' he said. 'I'm amazed Zahra's parents haven't banished you from her life.'

She looked at her parents, full of contempt. Of course they'd told him their own version of what had happened, based on exactly zero questions to their daughter about the night's events.

'I told him to take us straight home as soon as we got into that car.'

'You went through all that trouble only to get a ride directly home?'

'I didn't know that other person – Jimmy – would be involved. Hammad never mentioned him.'

'I see. Who would have imagined you could tell a seventeen-year-old boy you'd leave a party with him and everything that followed wouldn't be exactly as you wanted it to be?'

'I know Jimmy's licence-plate number. I memorised it as he was driving away.' She jutted her chin out, waited for him to commend her. Outside, her sisters were crawling along the grass on their elbows, trying to get to the French doors unnoticed so they could put their ears to the glass and listen.

'To what end?' her grandfather said.

'You can find someone with their licence number,' she said, hoping this was true in Karachi and not just in American cop shows.

'You want me to call the police? I should send them after him – for what crime exactly? And what happens

119

when they say, what was a girl from a good family doing in that car? Do I say, she lied to her parents about where she was going, and how, and then she took off her clothes and got into a stranger's car, half-naked? They might give that Jimmy a medal for getting you home safely when most men would have done something very different.'

'Is no one going to ask me what happened?' Her voice was childish, tearful.

She saw her grandfather glare at his son and daughter-in-law. 'I assumed someone had.'

Her father bit his thumbnail and looked into the middle distance, her mother made a face that recognised the process to be inadequate but stopped short of claiming responsibility. Maryam felt power shift back to her as she told her grandfather everything that had happened once they were in the car – no point in dragging Zahra into this, and anyway her grandfather valued loyalty, it would count against her if she tried to shift blame to her best friend. She described Jimmy's cheap cologne and shiny shirt, his reckless driving, how he turned off the lights on a deserted street and taunted her, the stop at the port to pick up something, probably videocassettes.

'How do you know it was videocassettes?' her mother said. Maryam had been looking at her grandfather while speaking and now it was a surprise to become aware of her mother's genuine horror. 'It could have been anything. Drugs or guns, that's what goes on at the port.'

Maryam shrugged. 'Didn't sound like drugs. Maybe guns, I suppose.'

'Maybe guns, you suppose?' Her mother touched her hands to her temples, shaking her head.

'And then?' her grandfather said.

'And then I said we know the DIG Police really well, and that he should take us home if he didn't want the police out looking for him.' She waited a moment to see if this piece of quick thinking would make him look more favourably on her, but he continued to stare at her with the same immobile expression that he wore when his employees stood in front of him and confessed some error or failing. So there was nothing to do but admit that instead of doing as she said, he had driven them to Napier Road.

Her mother made a low choking sound.

'What did he do there?' Her grandfather leaned forward.

'He . . .' How to say it? 'He stopped the car and gave me this look. It wasn't the way boys should look at girls.' She was aware of how feeble, how inadequate, that description was. 'And he made me say please to him. Please could he take us home.'

'And then?'

'And then he drove us back to Zahra's.'

Her mother stood up and put her arms around Maryam, trying to pull her daughter to her, but Maryam stiffened, resisted, and her mother went to sit back down.

Her grandfather tapped his walking stick on the carpet, irritated by the interruption. 'So when we come down to it, his only crime that we know of was traffic violations, which aren't nearly as serious as driving around without a licence, aged fourteen. The duffel bag could have been videocassettes, could have been guns, could have been –' he gestured out of the window to the gardener tilting a steel container towards the little flowerpots affixed along the exterior of the house '– watering cans.'

'He wanted to scare us. He enjoyed us being scared.'

'Were you scared?'

'Not at first, but eventually.' A terrible thing to have to admit, particularly because it prompted her mother to look at her with such concern, but how else to make him take seriously what Jimmy had done?

Her grandfather reached for the glass of water beside him and took a long sip. 'If I had been there when he'd dropped you to Zahra's I would have chased after him and thrashed him with my stick,' he said, a glance in his son's direction to underscore his failure to do the same. 'But it isn't a crime to scare someone.'

'If we call the police and it gets out, everyone will think something really unspeakable happened to you,' Maryam's mother said, her tone apologetic. 'And there'll be enough talk as it is.'

'Can we speak alone?' she said to her grandfather.

'No,' he said shortly. 'Say whatever you have to say.'

'I know you can't call the police. But you can make a phone call.'

He waited for her to tell him who he was supposed to call, and she repeated *make a phone call*.

'You want me to call Billoo?'

'Who's Billoo?' her mother said at the same time as her father said, 'Why does she know about Billoo?'

'Do you know what you're asking?' her grandfather said.

'It's not right that he should just get away with it.'

'So what is it you want me to tell Billoo to do?'

Maryam shrugged. He was the adult; he should make these kinds of decisions. She only knew that Jimmy must be taught a lesson.

'Beat him up? Break his kneecaps? Torture him with a power drill?'

She remembered the man on the pathway, screaming, his groin wet. A terrible memory until now, but she imagined Jimmy in his place and the feeling that came on her was satisfaction. She understood for the first time, at the deepest level, what justice meant.

'He made us afraid. I want him to be afraid, that's all.' There would be no reason to even touch him, as he hadn't touched her or Zahra. But please, let him know fear.

'God help us,' her mother said.

'What kind of person are you?' Her grandfather, with a note of unknowing quite distinct from his usual questioning tone that suggested an examiner who has all the answers and is merely testing the quality of his interlocutor's knowledge.

'The kind of person you've taught me to be.'

The sound of upset from her mother was drowned out by her grandfather stamping his stick against the floor. 'You think you can compare your disgraceful demands to the terrible decisions I have to make for the good of the company and this family?'

'What decisions?' she heard her mother say to her father, who hadn't made a sound or said a word, and still didn't.

Her grandfather was looking at her the way he looked at disappointing product samples. 'I thought I could make you what you need to be. But you're just a girl, aren't you? You'll always be a girl. And there'll always be Jimmys out there who'll see through everything else and know that. Perhaps I should be grateful to him for making that so clear.'

'A girl is running this country,' she said.

'She'll never run anything. Already we're hearing more about her husband than we are about her. And god knows what kind of decision you'll make in that department when the time comes to it. This Hammad – I'm told the headmistress said he's always been rotten.'

She couldn't help rolling her eyes, though she knew he would hate that. 'I wasn't planning to marry him.'

He stood, placing his weight on his stick, and turned to her mother. 'Do what you want. I won't stop it.'

Her parents' startled looks told her something dramatic had happened. Her grandfather lifted his hand off his walking stick, it wobbled, and his hand descended again to catch it before it fell sideways. A familiar tic, but as he raised his arm the phrase 'under his wing' went through her mind. That was her place, and the temporary withdrawals of his favour were merely a sign of it. Was her family really blind enough to think otherwise?

'I'm sorry,' she said to her grandfather. 'I know I still have a lot to learn from you.'

He was shaking his head. 'You're learning all the wrong things. Self-absorbed and wilful. No moral centre. You'll never be who I need you to be.'

On the other side of the French doors her middle sister was pulling a grotesque face at her, full of triumph and spite. Her youngest sister put her arms across her own body. 'You going to try to make one of them your heir?' She flicked her fingers towards them, stung into playing her trump card for the first time.

Her father sat up. 'I'm his heir,' he snapped.

'No one thinks you have any intention of running the company,' she said, rage undamming. 'And you couldn't even if you tried.'

'He wants to sell it when I'm dead,' her grandfather said. 'Oh, you thought I didn't know that?' This was to her father, who pressed himself into the sofa cushions.

Once, walking on the gunwale of a wooden sailing boat, she had slipped on an oil patch. There was the endless moment of losing her balance, clawing at air, and then the cold dark waters that all her years of swimming in the ocean hadn't prepared her for. The absolute immobilising shock of it. Just a few strokes away from the boat, twice junior champion of the swimming gala, she'd had to be rescued by one of the crew.

'He can't sell it. It's our family business.' She addressed herself only to her grandfather; no one else mattered in this conversation.

'That has always been my thought, my dream. But Allah gave me only one useless son, and no grandsons.'

'I can run it.' Clawing at air. 'Dada, please, it's our company, my company. You've always said.'

'My god, what ideas have you been feeding her?' her mother said. 'She's a child. And Toff is your son. He's your son.'

'Yes,' her grandfather said. 'That seems to be my fate.' He raised a finger towards Toff. 'You will stop having conversations with other people about selling so long as there's a single breath left in me, do you understand?'

He was looking over Maryam's head, speaking to his son as if this conversation had nothing to do with her.

'He can't sell it, not ever, you said it's mine. Please, Dada.' She clutched at his sleeve and began to cry, no more than the helpless girl Jimmy had seen and revealed.

He prised off her fingers, embarrassed by it all. And then he was gone, and her father stood up and walked out of the room, saying he didn't want to talk about any of this ever again.

So it was Maryam and Zeno. She pushed off her mother's attempts to comfort her. 'What did he mean, "Do what you want. I won't stop it"?'

A sound from outside. Her sisters had put their hands to their mouths as if they already knew what their mother planned for Maryam, and it was something far worse than they would have wished upon the sister they didn't even like. Didn't they understand? Her future had been torn away from her by the grandfather who had always

125

been her protector. Whatever else happened didn't matter, how could it? Beneath her feet, a stag with a quiverful of arrows through its heart.

*

The weekend morning traffic was light, and most shutters were still down along the stretch of Bunder Road to which Maryam had driven, but the neon-lit hole in the wall for which she and Zahra had come was open. She parked the Mercedes in a no-parking zone and turned to Abu Bakr in the back, who nodded to say he'd stay with the car in case the traffic police turned up. He got out of the car and leaned against its door, letting the men at Cafe VIP who watched the girls' approach know that he had an eye on everything.

All the tables inside the white-tiled cubbyhole were available, but the tables on the pavement were taken by young men whose lab coats marked them as students from the nearby medical university. A radio was perched on the counter that took up part of the entryway, broadcasting the West Indies vs Pakistan one-day game from Hobart. Zahra looked inside the cubbyhole, said again to Maryam that this really wasn't necessary. Maryam walked up to the counter, asked for chai and paratha for herself and her friend and the same for her driver back there, and a table outside. No, she didn't want to sit inside, she said, a little louder. Two of the university students stood up, moved their chairs to the table a few inches away, and told the owner to bring out chairs for Maryam and Zahra. Maryam looked at the four men now huddled around a two-person table, elbows knocking into each other, which required an act of choreography to bring teacups up to mouths without spillage, and said if they joined both tables there'd be space for everyone. This plan duly executed, Maryam and Zahra sat at one end of the conjoined tables, and the men all angled away from them, which simultaneously ensured their knees wouldn't touch the girls' and allowed them to continue their conversation about the cricket match uninterrupted.

A crow hopped on to the handlebar of a motorcycle that had been parked on the pavement to circumvent the no-parking rules and cocked its head at Zahra. She'd told Maryam she'd been afraid when the pavement men at Cafe VIP looked into the car, and Maryam had said that had been the safest moment of the ride, she must stop being frightened of everyday life. She knew Maryam was right; she wanted to be more like her best friend and not to have to live with fear as a constant companion.

It's not just fear, it's girlfear, Maryam had said with Maryam-like certainty. *Boys don't have it the same way.*

'They should play Saeed Anwar,' Maryam was saying now, breaking into the men's conversation about the disastrous start to the cricket series, which was unlikely to take a turn for the better given the way Desmond Haynes was batting, merciless against a bowling attack that included Imran, Wasim and Qadir.

The men turned to look at her. She blew on the surface of the hot tea, her breath wrinkling the skin of cream. 'Your father says he's one of the best young players he's seen in a long time, doesn't he, Za?' To the men she added, 'Her father is Habib Ali.'

The medical students were amazed. They wanted to know what her father said about Saeed Anwar, a Karachi boy, one of their own. One of the students had seen Saeed Anwar play at NED University. He

127

recounted the highlights of the innings, breaking off to applaud Haynes's century. A few balls later, Imran finally took Haynes's wicket and there was more applause – both for the batsman and the bowler who'd finally got him. Viv Richards came on to bat, facing Imran, and one of the men murmured both their names the way people in another age might have said 'Hercules Achilles' or perhaps 'Nargis Raj Kapoor'. Her father had once said that what set these two cricketers – and, he grudgingly added, Botham – apart from all others was the glow of victory that enveloped them even in the midst of carnage. Maryam has that, Zahra thought, watching her friend wipe her fingers very thoroughly on a square of newsprint, as though she wasn't accustomed to the finest linen at home. Any space Maryam entered, she owned.

The men had discovered that Maryam played cricket. They started to talk about the match between an all-women's team and a men's side due to take place in Karachi later in the month that had been called off after the religious parties staged protests.

'They can't stop a woman from running the country so they interfere in cricket matches instead,' said one of the students, his lips shiny with paratha grease.

'He's only saying this to impress you both,' said another student, who wore his hair long like a fast bowler. 'He won't let any of us even look at his sisters.' He caught his friend in a headlock, and the other men shouted out to watch it, watch it, don't knock over the tea.

'Do his sisters look like him?' Zahra said. There was a moment in which she was horrified at herself for assuming they would accord her the right of banter and insult, and then the shiny-lipped student held up his hands to say, I'm defenceless, don't attack me, and the other men roared with laughter.

'A-one!' the fast bowler said, holding his hand, palm up, towards Zahra. She slapped down on it.

In that moment she stopped standing outside the circle of men, conscious that she shouldn't be here, and slipped into the scene. She had walked into the city's arms, and it had embraced her – such a straightforward interaction, why had she never understood it before? She planted her elbows on the plywood tabletop. If a car were to drive up with two girls in it, they'd look at her and Maryam and know that women could claim this space, this outdoor life, this city.

The innings ended a short while later and the students left, thanking the girls for sharing a table and talking to them.

Maryam called for some more tea and another paratha. 'I love this street, don't you?' she said to Zahra.

Zahra didn't know what there was to love. It was mostly electronics stores. The older yellow-stone buildings had upper floors that had once been the homes of affluent merchants, but now they were falling into ruin, which was the kind of thing that only the rich could find charming.

'In England, everything fits in a little box with its own precise purpose. The cafe is for eating and drinking, the pavement is for walking, the street is for driving.' Maryam's hands described little strips of activity, each distinct from the other. 'And then there's this—' The sweep of her hand took in Cafe VIP with its seating spilling on to the pavement, the motorcycle parked beside the plywood tables, the tree branches beneath which a cobbler had set up shop, the vendor with his cart of sugar cane parked on the street, and down an alley the boys playing street-cricket. 'You know if you go into a supermarket in London and they ask you for one pound and you only have ninety-nine pence they won't sell you what you came for. "Sorry, love," they'll say. Overfamiliar enough to call you "love" but not to forgive you one pence. Who would want to live there?'

Zahra was sure the supermarket comment couldn't be true, and surely they played cricket on the streets in London?

'How come Abu Bakr is back?' she said, dipping her finger on to the surface of her second cup of tea and pulling it out with the skin of cream clinging to it. She wiped it off with the square of newsprint, thought about going back to the Mercedes for the box of tissues that was always there. 'And still letting you drive?' It still rankled that Maryam hadn't told her about the driving until Abu Bakr had been fired for it.

'Oh everyone's being very very nice to me,' Maryam said, tearing off a strip of paratha. 'What do I want for dinner, do I want to go to the beach, here are some lemon tarts from the club bakery. The only good thing to come out of it is Abu Bakr's return.'

'Why are they being nice to you?'

'Do you ever feel that something isn't really properly true until we tell each other about it?' Maryam said.

'Yes. All the time.'

'That's why I don't want to tell you. But I can't not. My parents are sending me to boarding school. In England.'

'No,' Zahra said, automatically. 'They can't. Your grandfather won't let them.'

Maryam dug a nail into the back of her hand. 'He's changed. The way he thinks about me, it's changed.' She rubbed the deep crescent mark on her skin, vicious. 'I'm just a girl.'

'What do you mean?'

'I mean, Jimmy. He made my grandfather see me differently. Well, I see him differently too. I thought he believed in fairness and justice and he doesn't, he won't help me get these things.'

She'd never seen Maryam like this, so wounded. 'He won't help you how?'

Maryam was quiet for a long moment, and when she finally spoke, her voice was uncertain. 'If I tell you maybe you'll look at me the way my parents and grandfather did. Like I'm a child who's asking for grown-up things when I'm too young to have them.'

'I would never.'

'I asked my grandfather to send someone he knows to find Jimmy. To scare him. So he'd know how that felt. And he refused.'

The shock of that left Zahra unable to respond. She knew what it meant in Karachi when the powerful sent someone to 'scare' their enemies. It was part of the character of the city, this other world of personal justice – messages delivered via fists and bullets and power drills. Now the way her parents talked about the Patriarch made sense, always a subtext there that she'd never before understood.

I want you to die. Zahra remembered Maryam's voice saying those words to Jimmy. She had known right away that Maryam had said it on her behalf, because Jimmy had terrified Zahra. And it was at least in part for Zahra's sake that she'd asked her grandfather to send a man to 'scare' Jimmy. All at once she was afraid of Maryam. But then, looking at her friend – so cast down, so defeated – she wondered if that was the wrong response and she should be ashamed that she would never be able to match the infinite reach, the unquestioning love of Maryam's friendship.

'You can't go.' That was what mattered, that was the only thing that mattered right now.

Maryam moved her chair closer to Zahra's, and they sat shoulder to shoulder, looking out on to Bunder Road, all at once immense in its beauty.

'When?'

'Soon. It'll be new subjects, new textbooks. I'm going to spend the whole term trying to catch up. And without your brain to help me.'

'You'll make new friends quickly.'

'What's the point of new friends? I want old friends.' Their heads angled, rested against each other, a deep sorrow passing between the two of them.

'When will I see you again? Not until the summer holidays?'

Maryam sat up straight, rubbed her eyes angrily. 'My parents want the whole family to move. They're sending me ahead, but they're all coming by summer.'

'What about Khan Leather?'

Maryam ripped at what remained of the paratha. 'My father doesn't want to run it. My grandfather no longer thinks I can run it. So when he dies, it'll be sold. Unless I can change my grandfather's mind, but how can I do that from England?' She tossed the remains of the paratha on to the pavement and a cat streaked out from under the table, the crow on the handlebar dived down. The cat won. 'They're taking everything away from me.'

Maryam in England. Never coming back. What would Zahra do without this friend by her side?

'I still don't understand. Why are your parents sending you away?'

'They think I'm too wild, too reckless. They think it's only a matter of time before that'll land me in trouble I won't be able to recover from. So I'm off to the English countryside where the worst thing that will happen is I'll get drunk and wander into a field full of cows. Which is a situation I'm far less capable of handling than getting into a car with a Jimmy.'

'I'll tell them you didn't want to get into the car. I should have told them already.'

'No one will believe you. It's not your fault. Jimmy did this. Not even Hammad, not really. It was Jimmy. That may be the worst thing of all. He's out there in his FX, thinking he's such a big man for scaring a pair of girls. I hate him, Zahra, I hate him more than I'll ever hate anyone, ever.' She exhaled, a long heavy breath. 'Right now, that is the only thing I know for certain about the rest of my life.'

There had been three moments – three of them! – when Maryam had tried to go back to the party and Zahra had prevented it. *It's not your fault.* The acknowledgement and the forgiveness all in one. Zahra looked at the unfamiliar expression on this most familiar of faces as Maryam watched the street – the everyday, taken-for-granted ordinariness of it. Abu Bakr buffing the Mercedes with a square of cloth, the sugar-cane seller feeding the long sticks into a press and extracting green juice, the shutters still down almost everywhere because 10 a.m. was too early in the day for the life of a nocturnal city to begin. Surrounded by a world she'd known forever, Maryam was lost. Zahra felt her friend's pain move into her own heart, sharp and surprising. So this is love, she thought.

She tilted her head back, watching sharp-taloned kites glide against the pale winter sky. She had been waiting so long for disaster to come swooping down upon her, and all the while the disaster had been curled up, waiting, inside her tiny, covetous, coward heart.

LONDON
2019

SPRING

Guardian
23 March 2019

Zahra Ali: 'I know firsthand how authoritarian regimes operate. That's why this government has me so worried.'

The head of the Centre for Civil Liberties on battling for the UK's freedoms, her celebrity friends, and her love for London

It's hard not to think of a panther when Zahra Ali enters the Centre for Civil Liberties meeting room dressed in black from blazer to knee-high boots, dark hair sleek, long limbs moving purposefully. Fortunately, I'm not her prey; she sated herself the night before on the Minister of State for Security during a *Newsnight* segment that cried out *meme me* before it was done. She says she's unaware of the attention she received on social media, which she never looks at – 'Too much noise,' she says, in a characteristically understated way of talking about the death threats and trolling that inevitably, and depressingly, attach themselves to a migrant Muslim woman who has become the voice of Britain's conscience since she took on the position of Director at Britain's oldest civil liberties organisation a decade ago.

'I never thought I'd be doing this so long but, honestly, I can't think of any better place to work. So as long as they'll have me, here I am,' she says, sipping a cup of tea that she takes – 'Pakistani style' – extra strong, with lots of milk and a spoon of sugar. Ali left a successful career as a barrister specialising in human rights and immigration to join CCL in 2009. 'There was a change in my personal life that made me think of what other kind of changes I could make, in that cliched way.' The personal change was the end to a six-year marriage. 'My husband was offered a job in New York which he didn't feel he could turn down. When I decided to stay in London, the marriage ended.' If this seems a curiously dispassionate way of talking about matters of the heart, it may be symptomatic of how carefully she guards her private life.

But when I put this to her, she demurs. 'I'm guarding my ex's private life, not mine. One person shouldn't get to comment on a marriage of two people.' A little later she adds, 'The funny part, of course, is so many women my age rely on their friends far more than their partners for everything from emotional support to belly laughs. But when we talk about people's private lives that isn't ever what we mean.'

Ah, the friends! Among the criticism sent Ali's way is the charge that she spends too much time with celebrities. 'More likely to be seen in the pages of *Tatler* than in the courts of justice,' as the *Sun* recently put it. While the comment reveals a lack of understanding about Ali's role at CCL – as Director she oversees a legal team but doesn't take on cases herself – there is no denying the starry company she keeps. She's appeared onstage with

Annie Lennox, had a cameo role playing herself in a Riz Ahmed movie, and watches cricket with Malala at Lord's. 'If people who've worked hard to get to the top of their profession want to use their high profile to increase awareness of the work CCL does, I'm not about to say no to that – and sometimes you build individual relationships from people's support for your organisation.' She laughs as her own words echo back to her and drops the pre-packaged line of defence. 'Oh come on, who's going to say no to getting up on a stage with Annie Lennox?' Her public persona is formidable to the point of being forbidding, but she's likeable in person: wryly funny, happy to send herself up.

Ali has lived in the UK all her adult life, since she was awarded a scholarship to Cambridge, but she grew up in Karachi during a particularly bleak time in that country's history. She was three when General Mohammad Zia ul Haq seized power in a military coup, and though her home life was happy she was always aware of the mood of paranoia and fear that the dictatorship engendered. She worried about making known her family's anti-Zia views in the classroom, and knew never to say anything compromising on the telephone because the intelligence services could be listening in. When she was fourteen her father, a popular cricket writer and broadcaster, received a message from the military instructing him to work some words of praise about General Zia into his cricket show. Her father chose not to. Ali remembers being angry with him. 'I thought he was endangering himself, and not thinking about his family. And that very day – the day he recorded his show and I was throwing an adolescent tantrum about it – General Zia was killed.' A few months later the young, Western-educated Benazir Bhutto was voted into power. 'I learnt then you should never believe a fight is lost, no matter how many years go by without a glimmer of hope.'

It's easy to see why Ali's childhood has made her a champion of human rights and civil liberties; less clear why she recently declared the United Kingdom was on the road to dictatorship. It's impossible to imagine Jonathan Agnew being asked by shadowy figures to praise the PM during *Test Match Special* and even more impossible to imagine his family being terrified by his refusal to do so.

Challenged, she shifts into a slightly chilly tone. 'I never said anything about a road to dictatorship. That's the tabloid headline version of a very long answer to a question I was asked at the Cambridge Union. I made the point that I know firsthand how authoritarian regimes operate. I recognise their tactics for suppressing dissent and holding on to power. That's why this government has me so worried. Not because I think the UK is in danger of becoming a dictatorship but because the British are too complacent that their democracy is so robust it can't be weakened – things that would set off alarm bells in countries with histories of authoritarian rule are allowed to slide by with little noise here.' She talks at length about the government's escalating rhetoric regarding the 'excessive' powers of the courts, the proposed bill that will limit the right of protest, the planned introduction of ID cards, and the instructions to the Home Office for officials to make wider use of their discretionary powers of rejection 'if something doesn't feel right' about an application for citizenship or settlement. All this with the government just a few weeks in power.

She makes a compelling case for concern, but I still wonder if her view of things might be coloured by her very clear loathing of the new government, which brings a bite to her voice that I've never heard in the decade she's been holding the powerful to account.

'I'm expressing an entirely professional concern about an unprecedented assault on our democratic way of life,' she says. I ask how clear the boundaries between Zahra Ali's personal and professional concerns are, and she says 'clear to me' with a tight smile that tells me nothing will be achieved by this line of questioning.

If she does take the government personally, that may be a two-way street. Earlier this week, CCL won a land-mark judgement in the Court of Appeal against the police's use of facial-recognition cameras. The Home Secretary responded by accusing not CCL but Zahra Ali directly of imperilling Britain's security and siding with criminals. Westminster insiders claim the government sees Ali as the real Leader of the Opposition, having seen off the parliamentary opposition with a resounding victory in last month's elections. Does she ever consider a more direct political role? She looks horrified at the idea. 'I've never met a party line I wanted to toe,' she says, and I believe her.

One final question, and this is the one that yields the most surprising answer. Why didn't she want to leave London for New York?

'Love,' she says, simply. 'I love it here. I even love the weather.' And with that, she's off to make a meal of the next MP thrown in her path, or perhaps to rub elbows with Emma Watson and George Clooney.

Tech Capital News
23 March 2019

Top venture capitalist Maryam Khan talks her career, women in tech, and turning failure into success

Maryam Khan is one of the leading figures in the UK tech scene. She is a founding partner at Venture Further, a leading early-stage technology and internet VC firm in London, and was ranked #13 in the Wired UK Tech 100 list in 2017–18. Her wide range of investments includes the photo-and-video-sharing app Imij, the board of which she chairs. Speaking to TCN's Maha Phillips, Khan discussed her career and the role of failure in her life. She also spoke optimistically of the new UK government's investment in tech.

Khan on reimagining success
Khan hails from a leather-goods dynasty in Karachi and grew up assuming she would inherit the family business. But when she was fifteen her grandfather died and her parents chose to sell the company and move the family to the UK. 'Politically, Pakistan didn't feel stable and

they decided we would be better off elsewhere. It was a blow to have to reimagine my future but, fortunately, I was already fascinated by the world of tech thanks to the Apple IIGS that my parents bought for me when I was thirteen.' She studied software engineering at Imperial and graduated just in time to be caught up in the dot-com boom. 'I was a millionaire at twenty-six and living in my parents' flat because I couldn't afford rent at twenty-seven.' After a few weeks of 'feeling sorry for myself and eating too much ice cream' she walked into the offices of Wright Capital, one of the UK's top VC firms at the time, and convinced the legendary tech guru Margaret Wright that her combination of hands-on experience with start-ups and her smart predictions of which internet companies would thrive beyond the present moment made her a perfect match for venture capital as the industry suffered drawdowns from investors after the dot-com bubble burst.

'Our high failure rate is the dirty secret of the VC world,' Khan says. 'The industry pretends that around 25 per cent of new start-ups fail but the real figure is closer to 75 per cent. At Venture Further we've reduced that percentage substantially, but I never pretend to the companies I invest in that there's a guaranteed path to success. Some people say I'm ruthless about calling time on investments that aren't working out; but no one spends more time than I do following up with founder-CEOs who didn't succeed at their first outing. I bring to the table my experience of how what looks like the end of a dream can be a springboard to success.'

Khan on women in tech
Khan believes the tech industry is trending in the right direction when it comes to greater inclusion for

women, though she recognises there's a long way to go. 'Women must be willing to make demands and take up more space. Of course, there are cultural forces that hold women back from doing so and that's why it's important to have role models. I had Margaret Wright, who continues to be a trusted adviser even now that she's retired, and I hope I have played and will continue to play a similar role to young women in tech. When I look at my daughter and her friends I hear the sound of glass ceilings not just shattering but being blown to smithereens.'

She also has a word of advice for the men who walk into her office for pitch meetings. 'Don't try your power stances and your crushing handshakes on me.'

Khan on finding space in crowded markets
Khan was the first to invest in Imij, seeing possibilities in the video-and-photo-sharing app when other investors thought it would be unable to grow successfully in a crowded social media market. 'Everyone else saw where it replicated existing features – but Imij delivers so much more to its users than its competitors. The editing suite gets most of the attention, but for me the real star is the sophistication of its facial tagging.'

Khan on the UK's new government
Khan is optimistic about the new government. 'It's early days, but they're making all the right noises about investment in tech. And I was very pleased to hear the Prime Minister talk about the need to boost skilled migration. I know there's a great deal of concern around migration numbers but there's little gained by placing every kind of migrant in the same boat. For the sake of our economy and our global standing we need to attract entrepreneurs

from around the world, and we need to retain the best of the students who come here to take advantage of the UK's educational system.' Few people epitomise the benefits of attracting and retaining foreign-born talent better than Maryam Khan.

Zahra sat on a bench in Primrose Hill, sipping her coffee and watching two spaniels bound past in the grass, ears lifting like wings. March in London always brought such a sense of renewal with it. *That part of London does spring so well*, someone who she remembered only by the poshness of his vowels had said to her years ago, when she'd moved to her neighbourhood; she'd thought it a ridiculous statement at the time, but earlier today, as happened every year, she found herself thinking, *yes, it does!* as she walked the pathway from the Hampstead Theatre to the Swiss Cottage Library, where branches heavy with the season's first blossoms called to mind feathered fans such as might have swished alongside Cleopatra on a barge moving down the Nile.

Two young women walked past, in animated conversation. 'I don't know. How can I know?' one of them was saying, in that fraught way of one who felt the rest of her life hingeing on the decisions confronting her. Zahra crossed one booted leg over the other, felt the ease of being a woman in her forties.

She resisted the urge to look at her phone, which was buzzing to announce a new message every few seconds; the new intern liked to scour the weekend papers for stories about civil-liberties-related outrages and send them to Zahra in a cascade of links, with furious comments or emojis appended. Zahra hadn't yet had the heart to tell her to stop, or at least wait until Monday. You couldn't say that sort of thing to a 21-year-old on her maiden voyage into the depths of the world's injustices. Or you could, but with the understanding that her adulation of you would be dented by your insistence on being allowed a weekend. #FascismDoesntStopOnFridayEvening

A few moments later a man and his pointer ambled along the path. The man saw Zahra, dipped his head in a manner that acknowledged he knew who she was but didn't want to disturb her by making the acknowledgement so evident that she would feel compelled to respond. They learnt this form of politeness young in North London – she'd received exactly that nod from a schoolgirl the other day. Maryam claimed it wasn't politeness so much as an English need to make you aware that just because they knew who you were didn't mean they were going to get excited about it.

'Beautiful dog,' Zahra said.

'Thank you,' the man said, with a gravity that extended beyond pet ownership.

He moved on, she took another sip of her coffee. It was a triumph, if you were a woman, to move between visibility and invisibility in a way that suited you rather than being scrutinised and ignored in equal, infuriating measure. She held her face up to the sunshine, too filled with well-being to remember to mind that she was being made to wait, as happened every Sunday, though she'd had to walk almost a mile to get here and Maryam was just down the road. The phone buzzed again and this time she took it out of her pocket, just in case it was something she shouldn't ignore. As expected, her notifications were almost all from the new intern, but nestled among them was a message from a Singapore area code.

Hey – saw the Guardian profile. Just wanted to say wow.* Really impressive everything you're doing. You probably don't have the best memories of me but I'd love to buy you a drink (halal or haram, whatever you prefer) next time I'm in London to try and make up for things and so we can get to know the adult versions of each other. Possible? Hammad (Riaz, from school).

*both the article and the picture

Zahra clicked on the thumbnail-sized profile picture and the screen filled with an entirely recognisable version of Hammad, no sign of the slackening jawline or paunch that had started to blur so many of the boys she'd been at school with even while the schoolgirls turned sharper at their edges as they made their way into their mid-forties. She remembered the word 'taut'.

There was a shift in the weight distribution along the bench. Maryam had sat down. 'It is hard not to think of a panther,' she said, with a tone of revelation.

'Oh god,' Zahra said, slipping her phone into her pocket. 'Since when do you read the *Guardian*?'

'Since the alert I've set up for you tells me you're in it.'

'You have an alert set up for me? And here I thought you were indifferent to my professional life.'

'You don't have one for me?'

'Any attempts to find out what you're up to are stymied by a Maryam Khan, model, represented by Venture Modelling Agency, who is best known in her native Canada for a high-profile shoot in leather trousers

151

and nothing else after years of campaigning for animal rights.'

'I like the sound of my namesake. Everyone should be upfront about having exceptions to their principles if the price is right.'

'Are we walking or just sitting here?' Zahra aimed her empty coffee cup at the nearest bin, and watched it bounce off the rim. She stood quickly to retrieve it before someone with a cameraphone caught her littering.

Together, they turned towards the eastward exit. When they wanted a shorter walk, they'd cut through Primrose Hill towards London Zoo, stopping at the giraffe enclosure to marvel at the improbability of the animals, and then down to the rose garden in Regent's Park. Other days, when they were in the mood for something more urban, the canal path would call to them, taking them through Camden Market to King's Cross. But today it was Hampstead Heath, a decision reflected in their choice of footwear – badly scuffed olive-green Hunters for Maryam, who saw no need to part with anything in her wardrobe once she'd reached a relationship of comfort with it, and gleaming black slim-fit Scandinavian wellies for Zahra, who didn't like the snobbery associated with any of the upmarket rain-boots, so found a pair that cost as much but had a logo that was unrecognisable to almost everyone in London. She'd expected teasing from Maryam about it and had been disconcerted to receive an approving 'good thinking – you don't want to damage your brand' instead.

Her stride shortened, Maryam's picked up pace. How many miles had they walked together in the course of their lives – from perambulations in the schoolyard to these Sunday walks in all weather. Talking endlessly about nothing, or about the same things over and over, with the occasional swerve into the most soul-piercing conversations, which relived the intensity of their teenage years. It was the Sunday walks that had prompted Zahra to buy 'gear' she'd never imagined owning – wellies, rain-jackets, waterproof hats and trousers. Maryam drew the line at the waterproof trousers, but was perfectly cheerful about sopping fabric sticking to her skin in that space between the bottom of her rain-jacket and the top of her boots. 'You look like a pair of middle-aged white ladies,' Zola had said one Sunday, as she opened the door to them coming in from the pouring rain, red with cold, dripping so much they had to divest themselves of their outer layers before stepping inside.

'And she thinks it's the "white" that stings,' Maryam had responded, lifting Zola into her arms before calling out to Layla that their daughter was getting too big to carry, could they exchange her for a smaller one?

Today was sunshine. Their boots were ridiculous as they walked along England's Lane and through Belsize Park, but would soon be necessary for the mud in those particular, known areas of the Heath where rain left its mark long after the ground had dried and hardened everywhere else. It was the first time in months they were walking without bulky winter jackets and Maryam's unusual attention to posture told Zahra she was more than usually pleased with the figure she cut. It was true that the health-and-fitness regime that Layla had imposed on her in the last year in response to elevated cholesterol levels meant that the Maryam striding alongside Zahra was as toned and glowing a Maryam as had existed in a long time, but in losing the slight plumpness that had crept on to her face in her mid-thirties she had also lost all its softness. There came a point in life when your face became more noticeable for character than features; they weren't either of them anywhere near that point yet, but it had begun.

'What do you mean, you think I'm indifferent to your professional life?' Maryam said, as they neared South End Green and Zahra stopped at the fruit and veg stall outside Hampstead Heath Station to consider what she might buy on the walk back. 'I've been signed up to CCL's mailing list for years now.'

'Ever signed one of our petitions?'

'Ever achieved anything with one of your petitions?'

The Zahra of a few years ago would have taken the bait and delivered a lecture that was meant to convey to Maryam the significance of CCL's role in the UK. The Zahra of now simply said, 'Ouch.'

'Did I say that out loud? Stop eyeing the rhubarb. It just rots in your fridge.'

'Yes, and you also said, "You can't put all migrants in one boat," out loud.' Zahra turned her attention from the rhubarb to the early-season asparagus.

'I didn't. When?'

'Your interview. Babar sent me the link.'

'Well, that's an unfortunate choice of words.'

'Mmhmmm.'

'I better make sure Layla doesn't see it.'

'Oh, I already forwarded the link to her during the ritual wait on the park bench for you. I suggested she withhold sex as punishment.'

'Won't happen.'

'Smug bastard.'

Maryam tugged at her sleeve, and they resumed walking.

When they reached the Heath it was more crowded than it had been since New Year's Day, and the pathway leading from the mixed bathing pond towards Parliament Hill looked particularly intolerable. Zahra and Maryam turned on to a wilder, less-travelled path. The trees, bright with young leaves, were unreal in their greenness after the bare months of winter. Here came the mud, a welcome sight, keeping away those who hadn't thought, or known, to prepare for it. They squelched along, Maryam pausing to pet any dogs who came by. 'Maybe a Border collie,' she said, as a black-and-white dog, wet from a pond, came along, sniffing at her. Her own dog, an Irish wolfhound called Woolf, with a philosophical air about her, was too old and infirm now for Sunday walks, and Maryam had taken to talking about the next puppy she'd get, as though this might mitigate the grief that would soon be upon her.

They stopped by a pond with lily pads floating on its surface, a red arched bridge as backdrop, white clouds and blue sky above. Maryam crouched down and plunged her hands all the way into the water to wash off wet dog. 'Did you mean what you said in the interview or is it part of the whole public-persona thing?'

Zahra picked up two pebbles, and attempted to skim one along the surface of the pond. It sank on contact with the water. 'I tend to mean what I say.'

'Don't get huffy,' Maryam said, taking the other pebble. 'I was surprised, that's all. All that stuff about the oppressiveness of growing up under military rule, worrying about the intelligence services listening in on every phone call. I mean, come on, the only thing anyone really worried about was crossed lines with someone from your social set.'

Maryam's pebble skipped – once, twice, three times – across the water. 'I notice you didn't mention that the absolute worst-scariest thing that happened in your childhood took place the day after Benazir was inaugurated – that's really how our experience of democracy kicked off. With the feeling that any awful thing could still happen.'

'What worst-scariest thing?'

Maryam turned to her, jamming her hands in her spring jacket. 'Jimmy.'

Zahra took a moment to consider the direction in which Maryam would have walked to the park bench, the possibility that she might have seen Zahra looking at Hammad's profile picture. 'What made you think about him?'

'I often think about him.'

'Still? Was that really the day after Benazir was inaugurated?' Looking back, what came most strongly to her about that evening was the memory of standing alone and awkward in Saba's garden, feeling the cold seep into her skin but unable to roll down the sleeves of her denim shirt because it would look uncool. All that inadequacy arising from the sight of Maryam dancing close to Hammad, his hand on her waist.

'Of course it was. But I suppose mentioning that would have disrupted the neat narrative arc from suffering through oppressive dictatorship to Director of the Centre for Civil Liberties.'

'Well, we all create our neat narrative arcs, don't we?'

'Meaning what?'

'You at twenty-seven, living with your parents because you were unable to pay your rent. And then boldly striding into a top VC office and using chutzpah and smarts to get a job.'

In the wake of the dot-com crash, Layla had thrown Maryam out of the Notting Hill flat they'd recently moved into together because she was sick of her girlfriend moping around eating ice cream rather than getting on with finding another job. Maryam had moved in for a few days with her parents, who had brought with them from Karachi everything that might help London feel like home – from their art collection to their social connections. It was at their urging that Maryam had gone to see Margaret Wright, who was sister to an Oxford friend of Toff's.

'Oh, that,' Maryam said, acknowledging that Zahra could easily have mentioned there was another part of her story that had deviated even further from the truth – her grandfather's death, the sale of Khan Leather. How calmly she'd talked about it in the interview, how accepting she'd sounded about her parents' decision to move their family somewhere more 'stable'. The Patriarch had died of a heart attack during Maryam's first term at boarding school and when she'd flown back for the funeral Toff was already in talks to sell Khan Leather – Maryam was all grief and rage, more animal than human. She'd lived at Zahra's house during her brief return home, refusing to be anywhere near her parents except during the rituals of mourning.

A knot of women approached the pond and called out in enthusiastic greeting to Maryam, who said her hellos in that pleasant but restrained way in which she'd always dealt with the mothers of Zola's friends so they wouldn't feel encouraged to ask her to join their poker games or spa outings. The sociable Maryam of their teenaged years had been replaced by a woman who guarded family time too much to be drawn into new friendships.

'Oh god, why am I so bad with their names?' Maryam muttered, taking out her phone and pretending to read something off it while using the camera to take a picture of the women as they approached. A single click and the women's faces were tagged, their names flashing up on the screen.

'Thanks for picking her up on Friday, Louise,' Maryam said smoothly to one of the women, who smiled and said it was always a delight to have Zola over.

The women had come to take pictures against the backdrop of the red bridge – it's our spot, one of them said – and there was a slight awkwardness as they pretended that they thought 'Zola's mum' should be included, which Maryam sidestepped by offering to take the photograph, claiming that Zahra was useless at holding a cameraphone steady. Zahra nodded her regretful acknowledgement of this fact. The school mums were full of gratitude, and everyone understood that to be about Maryam's deft handling of the situation. As they walked away, Zahra heard one of the women say, 'She is nice,' as though confirming something they all already knew but remained a little mystified by.

'They were practically giddy to be around you, did you notice,' Maryam said.

'Don't be silly.'

'They were! When I said you couldn't take a picture they had these smiles that said, "Why should Zahra Ali have any photography skills? She's Britain's conscience. Let other people take the photographs. Let Zola's mum do it."' Maryam's tone was affectionately teasing, an apology in there for her earlier sharpness.

'Now you've gone and ruined my reputation as a photographer,' Zahra said, rapping on Maryam's boot with a fallen branch. 'What app were you using there? Imij?'

'Yes. We should start marketing it to older users as a memory aid for ageing brains.' Maryam linked an arm through Zahra's. 'Did I say there's some fish thing for lunch? By popular demand, you're making those green beans with mustard seeds.'

Zahra's phone buzzed. She used her free hand to edge it out of her pocket and glanced down at the screen, angled away from Maryam's sight. Singapore again.

*

Another Sunday, and lunch ended with Maryam's roast chicken reduced to splinters of bone. 'Still astonishing after all these years,' Layla said. It was a long-running joke that the moment Layla realised she'd truly been accepted into the Khan family was when Maryam's parents were able to gnaw through bone and cartilage in her presence without worrying about showing her their most unrefined side.

Maryam's mother extended her hand towards Zola's plate, where wing bones had been reduced to nubs. 'This one really is all Khan sometimes,' she said. Zeno never passed on an opportunity to comment on any similarity she could find between Zola and someone perched on Maryam's family tree, even if the connection was as tenuous as Zola's interest in gymnastics and some great-uncle who'd entertained several generations with his ability to do cartwheels all the way into his eighties – her comments always delivered in a tone that suggested the connection proved something that needed proving about this granddaughter of hers who was composed of no Khan DNA.

Zahra looked across the table to Maryam, an unspoken 'let it go' in the slight movement of her head. All these years later, Maryam could still become enraged when one of her parents revealed the little bit of their hearts that still placed Zola in a separate category to their other grandchildren; she saw too clearly in that revelation the continuing wish that their eldest daughter had gone down another route in life, which they were sure she could have if she'd just been a little more concerned with how awkward, sometimes impossible, it would be for them to reveal to their friends that they had a lesbian daughter with a Black partner and a child born from some sperm donor of unknown family background who they'd found in a binder. Layla almost always thought Maryam was being too hard on her parents, still holding against them their early resistance to the coupling ('What will people say?' her mother had predictably said), but thank god for Zahra, who'd had a lifetime of Zeno to learn all her subtexts.

Perhaps that was the key to the longevity of childhood friendships – all those shared subtexts that no one else could discern. And perhaps shared subtexts felt even more necessary when you both lived far away from the city of your childhood that was itself the subtext to your lives. Childhood friendship really was the most mysterious of all relationships, Maryam thought, as she signalled Zola to get up and clear the plates; it was built around rules that didn't extend to any other pairing in life. You weren't tied by blood, or profession, or an enmeshed domesticity or even – as was the case with friendships made in adulthood – much by way of common interests.

Soon Zahra would be the only one left in London who had been an integral part of her childhood. Maryam's parents were moving back to Karachi after three decades in London, taking all their subtexts with them, a development more unsettling than Maryam would have imagined. Their middle daughter had moved back when she married straight out of university, and was living a life that closely replicated the one they'd left thirty years ago. By contrast, everything in Maryam's life was a mark of her separateness to her parents – her work ethic, her partner, her child. Even this house with its elongated lower floor without demarcations between dining room, kitchen and living room, all cement and oak and stainless steel enlivened by colourful furnishings and huge windows – everything about it was a world away from her parents' Karachi-transplant of Persian carpets, calligraphy on the walls, cut-glass ashtrays and silver ornaments, and the firmly closed kitchen door behind which the hired help cooked and scrubbed.

'Do you think you might do the same one day?' her mother was saying to Zahra, as conversation moved to The Return.

'Go back to Karachi?' Maryam said. 'Some people leave in order to leave, not because they're intent on disrupting everyone else's life before flitting back to where they started.'

'Mama,' Zola said. 'Without the disruption you wouldn't have Mum and me.'

'Exactly,' Zeno said, as though her entire purpose in throwing Maryam to the wolves of an English boarding school had been to liberate her from conventions around sexuality.

'Oh, even if I hadn't been packed off to London at fourteen I would still have met your mum through Zahra Khala and fallen madly in love with her. Any road taken would lead me to you and her.' Zola made a face of disgust at the talk of falling madly in love, but there was no hiding her pleasure at the confirmation that there was no better life Maryam dreamt of that didn't involve her. Layla's foot reached out under

161

the table to rub against Maryam's ankle, and she focused on that instead of the sceptical look her father was sending her way.

The Return had been an idea so long discussed it had felt inevitable it would never be anything other than chatter, but now there were one-way plane tickets and invitations to farewell dinners and shipping containers addressed to a flat in Karachi where her parents could live independently but close at hand to an untroublesome daughter and fair-skinned grandchildren. They would slip so easily back into Karachi life, her mother returning to her round of ladies' teas and charity boards, and her father continuing on with the life of crosswords, outdoor activities (originally tennis, now golf) and socialising that had been his entire adult existence – in London, his wife's canny investments in the property market with proceeds from the Khan Leather sale had allowed him to remain as idle as he'd ever been in Karachi. Home had always been a place waiting for them, burnishing its own appeal with its luxury developments and burgeoning restaurant scene and a dramatic reduction in crime due to 'operations' by police and paramilitary forces – all this, when placed alongside the pound-to-rupee conversion rate and the salaries of domestic staff, made it the only possible destination for a comfortable old age.

Zeno returned to her conversation with Zahra as if no interruption had occurred. 'I thought maybe with your parents getting older, Zahra, and so much to be done in human rights there.' And without a family to keep you here, said her subtext. 'Of course, I can see why you might prefer to stay.' It's easier to be a single woman in London, the subtext continued.

Zahra rested a hand on her chin, gave Maryam's mother that slightly teasing look that had crept into their relationship through Zahra's university years when the older Khans made it clear that their London flat was Zahra's home. Unspoken reciprocity for those school holidays when Maryam flew back and lived with Zahra and her parents while the rest of her family summered in Europe, refusing to countenance Karachi heat.

'Admit it, Aunty Zeno. The real reason you're leaving is you've finally given up on setting me up with a nice boy from a good family.'

'There's time before I leave for that final one up my sleeve,' Zeno said. 'Oxford, Wharton, does something with hotels. Not the most good-looking but perfect manners, and none of the usual British Asian hang-ups.'

'What are the usual British Asian hang-ups?' Zola asked.

'When you don't understand what your grandmother means, it's safe to assume she's talking about class,' Maryam said.

'Oh,' said Zola, putting a hand to the side of her face so she could roll her eyes without her grandparents seeing it. 'Anyway, Nani, there's no point. Zahra Khala is asexual.'

'Good god,' Maryam's father said.

'Your Zahra Khala is single by choice, Zola. That's not the same thing,' Layla said in the conversational tone she used whenever Zola let slip a new concept that Maryam didn't see any reason for someone of her age to know. 'People can be responsible about having sexual partners without . . .'

'Could we not have this conversation in front of my parents,' Maryam said at the same time as Zahra made a prolonged sound of agony.

'You think the problem is your parents rather than a ten-year-old?' Zeno said.

'Yes,' said Maryam and Zahra together.

'How many sexual partners do you have right now, Zahra Khala?' And now Zola was being wicked, not about to pass on the rare event of finding both her mother and her godmother so discomfited.

What was it right then in Zahra's face, the strange furtiveness of her expression?

'Isn't it lovely outside,' Layla said, looking towards the glass doors that led into the garden. The afternoon was sun-drenched, showing off the wisteria clambering up Layla's studio at the bottom of the garden, and the flower beds, sumptuous with colour. 'Why don't you all leave me to do some cleaning up. No, really, it's faster this way.' The other adults trooped on to the deck, Zola and Woolf following, and took up positions on the rattan sofa set: Maryam's parents on the two-seater, Maryam and Zahra on the armchairs. Woolf settled at Maryam's feet, Zola perched on the arm of Zahra's chair.

Very soon, everyone well-fed and a little drowsy, talk stalled. It didn't bother any of the adults, happy to look at the garden in bloom, feel the warmth of the afternoon, listen to the sleep-rumblings of Woolf. But Zola, barred from using her tablet when her grandparents were over, needed some form of entertainment and attempted to convince Zahra to play Would You Rather? with her.

'Later, sweetheart,' said Zahra.

'Why are grown-ups so boring?' Zola demanded. There was something new in her voice these days when she was disappointed, an undertone of rebellion that foretold the adolescence for which Maryam wasn't anywhere close to ready. At ten Zola still had a child's body, but her underarms had a new etching of dark hair and she had become self-conscious about sleeveless shirts now that warmer days were here. Of late, she'd worn nothing but her black leggings and an oversized Billie Eilish sweatshirt, both of which Maryam would have to steal out of her room while she slept tonight so she could wash them.

'I was going to invite you backstage with me for a BST concert in Hyde Park, but you won't want to go with someone boring,' Zahra said.

Zola let out a little scream and wrapped herself around Zahra.

'Is Annie playing?' Zeno said, her first-name familiarity with Annie Lennox based on the principle that anyone known to Zahra was a Khan intimate by proxy.

'No,' and Zahra threw out the name of one of the world's biggest music acts as if to say she didn't want to brag about her starry fandom, and was only saying since Zeno had asked. Zola squealed; Zeno pretended to know who Zahra was talking about even while misspelling the name into her phone's search bar. Toff looked disappointed and said he wished it were Barbra Streisand, whose upcoming summer concert was the only one that had crossed his radar.

Maryam bent to pet Woolf and looked up at her father. He winked at her and she couldn't help the conspiratorial smile she returned, pleased by his refusal to be impressed by Zahra's name-dropping, which was never more blatant than in the company of the Khans, as if they might hold some view of her that made it particularly important to stress how vast her footprint in the world was, how coveted her presence at North London dinner parties. The wink and smile ended the silent battle Toff and Maryam had been engaged in for most of the afternoon, which had grown out of Layla's complaints about a local arts organisation that had invited her on to their board in the name of 'change' and then made it clear that her presence there was all the change they intended to bring about. Well, obviously, Maryam had said. No one gives up power, not even if they're incompetents about handling it; they hoard it or they sell it. Her father had launched into a funny story about a king and his sons, the speed with which he moved to charm the table making it clear he knew exactly which incompetent was on Maryam's mind.

'Shouldn't someone be helping Layla?' Toff said, looking pointedly at Zola, who was still squealing. The onset of his seventies suited him remarkably well; the indolence of his earlier years was recast as the earned repose of later life. Maryam hadn't exactly forgiven him either the sale of Khan Leather or her grandfather's death, which she was certain was due to the strain of going through every day knowing his beloved company would pass into the hands of strangers, but, three decades on, those feelings tended to come out as withering asides rather than rage.

Maryam glanced indoors. Layla was walking towards the sliding door with her characteristic upright posture that could sometimes be brought to slumping by the company of Toff and Zeno, but not today. She had emerged from the silent interlude in the kitchen wreathed in graciousness, bearing the silver coffee set that had been a gift from Maryam's parents and which was never used except when they visited – a Layla courtesy; Maryam said it only encouraged the buying of gifts that showed the narcissism of the gift-givers in reflecting their tastes rather than those of the recipients. Maryam stood, opened the door and, with an apologetic kiss on Layla's cheek, used the opportunity to slip into the house and make straight for her phone, which was charging at the breakfast bar. Zola wasn't the only one banned from devices when Zeno and Toff came for lunch. There was a string of messages with 'Imij' in the subject line from investors and members of the Imij board, which Maryam chaired.

Maryam clicked on the link in the first of the emails. IMIJ ALMOST KILLED MY CHILD ran the headline over a picture of a girl in a hospital room, bandages around her wrist. Maryam placed a hand over her stomach. A thirteen-year-old schoolgirl had attempted suicide because of bullying, much of which had taken place on Imij. The schoolgirl in question was Muslim and overweight. Several obviously coordinated accounts used the app's photo-editing tools to bring the girl's eyes closer together and flare her nostrils – a wealth of cruel comments made their way on to those posts from people who didn't seem to know her but had much to say about a piggish girl in a hijab. A column accompanied the news stories. 'Government must intervene to prevent the harm being done to our children by social media,' declared the columnist, who usually saved his vitriol for left-wing politicians and climate activists.

The Imij founder-CEO answered on the first ring. 'I know,' he said, sounding as cheerful as ever. Golden Boy, Maryam and the rest of the board called him behind his back, for the colour of his hair, his youthful success, and the sunniness of his manner. It was meant without any affection at all. 'The government's not going to do anything, are they?' Buyout talks for Imij were under way with a software giant planning to expand into social media, $14 billion and serious multiples on exit at stake. The money didn't matter to Maryam as money – she lived the same lifestyle as she had a decade ago – but it mattered enormously as the biggest tech deal the UK had ever known. It would catapult Venture Further into the top ranks of global VC firms, pave the way for the grand opening of their San Francisco office.

'It says the images were reported within minutes of being posted and no action was taken for over thirty-six hours.'

'Yeah. Cock-up.' Still cheerful. 'The administrator thought the whole pig thing was directed at the girl's weight rather than her religion, which meant it didn't violate the guidelines against discrimination. We've fired him, and we're putting together a statement. Tougher measures blah blah. Shocked and horrified. A few users who misuse our platform etc. Do we mention she's thirteen and the terms of use say you have to be at least fifteen?'

'Not unless you want to open a conversation on ID checks. Keep it brief. The story will go away quickly.'

'True. Fat girls don't stay on front pages.' A snort of laughter at that, which allowed her the satisfaction of thinking, who's the pig now?

She hung up, looked again at the picture of the girl's parents further down the article. Pakistani. Her age, perhaps slightly younger. The father had something in his expression that reminded her of Habib Ali. A certain kindness.

When she returned outside it was to find Zola hopping from foot to foot in the garden saying, 'Please Mum, please, I'm ten!' which wasn't encouraging. Layla had just seen a text, sent over an hour ago, inviting Zola to walk to the park with her best friend, Mark, and his parents and their new puppy. Now the puppy and humans were already at the park, and planning to stay a while, but Layla wasn't about to walk Zola across while there were people over for lunch. Zola proposed walking to the park alone. It was a short walk, the entire route was studded with the homes of her friends, and she would take the spare phone so they could track her. This spare phone, which was used by house guests from abroad, had long been in Zola's sights.

'Absolutely not,' Maryam said at the same moment that Layla said, 'Fine.'

Zola launched herself at Layla, pretending she'd heard nothing else, and hugged her around the waist. 'Thank you thank you thank you thank you.'

Layla's look in Maryam's direction was both apologetic and not about to backtrack. Maryam knew what Layla would say to her in private later on when she objected. It's perfectly ordinary for London kids to start going out in the neighbourhood on their own at this age – her own West London upbringing as opposed to Maryam's chauffeured Karachi childhood a trump card she was always happy to play, even though part of her own childhood had been chauffeured in Lagos. Layla could slip between her Nigerian half and her English half with absolute ease, depending on whether it was to her advantage to play immigrant or native, member of the elite or put-upon minority. She claimed that her slippage between ways of being was far more commonplace than Maryam's unchanging attitude of privilege and belonging, no matter the company or nation in which she found herself.

'You can walk as far as the park,' Maryam said. 'But some adult has to come and meet you at the entrance.'

'I can walk her over,' Zahra said. 'I should get home soon anyway.'

'No!'

Zola would usually give anything to have a walk with her beloved Zahra Khala, without other adults around as distraction. But some other need had got hold of her, and made her come towards Maryam to plead with her. She had Layla's walk, long of stride, to go with Layla's features. Only her eyes, straight out of a Mughal miniature, suggested the Pakistani sperm donor.

169

'I want to go into the world on my own,' she said, a grandiose sentence that was as touching as it was ridiculous. And hadn't Maryam wanted exactly this at Zola's age? She would have been even younger than Zola when Abu Bakr first starting giving in to her demands to detour somewhere on the drive back from school – the one shop which sold Coke in cans rather than bottles, the street vendor who coated sliced apples in a tamarind and chilli sauce from a jar buzzing with flies. She would open the car door, telling Abu Bakr and her sisters to wait for her, and a feeling would settle upon her – so delicious – of stepping out of a cosseted childhood and becoming a participant in the thrum of the city.

Maryam pressed her knuckles against Zola's forehead and Zola leaned into her fist. As if something – some knowledge, some strength – could pass between them. 'Please, Mama.'

She would never be ready for this moment. How to applaud your child for fearlessly claiming her right to the world while also warning her about the awfulness of other people. The racists, the homophobes, the Jimmys – so many routes to girlfear. She knew it was some kind of miracle that she'd made it all the way to fourteen before experiencing it herself. Zahra thought that was because Abu Bakr drove her around everywhere with a gun in his waistband, but she knew it was because of the shadow her grandfather cast in the world, the protective quality of it.

'If Zahra says she can walk her over then what's the point of her running off on her own?' Zeno said. 'Maryam didn't ever go out alone unaccompanied until she went to uni.'

Zola grinned up at Maryam, knowing there wasn't any possibility this was true.

'Only up to the park entrance,' Maryam said, defeated by the allyship of her mother. 'I'll tell Mark's mum to meet you there. And if anything happens along the way that doesn't feel right, call me immediately. I'll put my number on speed dial.'

When Zola had gone, clutching the spare phone in a manner that suggested she wasn't prepared to relinquish it on her return, Zahra stood with Maryam on the pavement outside the house, watching the curve of the road where Zola had disappeared from sight. The phone in Maryam's hand showed a blue dot that moved briskly towards the park.

The street was quiet, reassuringly familiar. It was a long street, but they lived in a bend of it that felt separate. Many of the houses on this stretch of the road had the same Victorian exterior as Maryam and Layla's home, even if no one else had the same shift into twenty-first-century modern architecture when you climbed the portico steps and crossed the threshold. Maryam and Layla and Zola had crossed almost every threshold in the Bend, a friendliness existing between households that hadn't quite tipped into friendship, at least not for Maryam. In recent years she'd learnt, via an app she'd invested in, to identify all the trees and plants in the front gardens – the Japanese maple two doors down, the rowan tree across the street, the Persian ivy sprawling along her own low front wall that she'd never thought to describe as anything other than ivy.

'Why only to the park entrance?' Zahra asked.

'No CCTV in the park.'

'Ten-year-old Maryam wouldn't have believed the worrywort you'd grow into. No one's going to kidnap her.'

'Someone might say something to her. Walk too close. Make her feel uncomfortable.'

'And what will CCTV do for her then?'

'Help find whoever it was and make sure he knows never to try that again.'

Zahra's superior laugh emerged, the one that said she understood the world better than Maryam did. 'I promise you, the police aren't going to go searching through CCTV footage to find someone who makes a Black kid feel uncomfortable on the streets of London.'

'I'd convince them,' Maryam said, but with less certainty than she'd like. In this country she was Maryam Khan, #13 in the Wired UK Tech 100 list, and yet strangely no one. She kept her eyes on the blue dot moving towards the park. The only thing that would be on Zola's mind was a puppy's velvet paws and liquid eyes and the freedom of being able to walk towards that on your own – buoyant, assured. 'What we really need is for every CCTV camera to be a facial-recognition camera, but you're not going to let that happen, are you?'

'You may credit me with too much power.'

'What an admission.'

'You know how the court ruled that facial recognition technology was racially biased and disproportionately used by the police? So, the government's changed the wording on its policies to say the police will make "fair and proportionate" use of the technology – and is expanding its use. It's not funny!'

It was one of the funnier things Maryam had heard in a while, but Zahra was clearly taking it as a personal affront.

'They're racist,' Zahra said.

'The government?'

'Since you bring that up, but I meant the cameras. Can't tell one Black person apart from the other. This is what you want in the world to keep your child safe?'

Does it look more indolent than English ivy, do you think? Zahra had said when Maryam had identified the Persian ivy for her and it was hard to know if this was a joke or Zahra's determination to see racism everywhere in England, even in the naming of plants.

The blue dot stopped. Maryam gripped the phone more tightly. Blue dot moved. It was that moment of April when the magnolias and cherry blossoms were in full bloom and Zola could be brought to a sudden halt by pinks and whites that practically hurled themselves at you as you walked past certain homes.

'Tech, unlike people, can be improved. The Imij facial-tagging feature doesn't discriminate by race.' Or not to the degree that all other facial-recognition software did, at any rate.

'Not to mention the impact of constant surveillance on a society.'

'It's here already, just rebranded.' She waved her phone at Zahra. 'Do you want to know what percentage of Imij users opt in to face-tagging?'

'They opt in to being tagged by their friends. That's a different thing to the police watching you at all times because you're a climate activist or a guy who goes to a mosque.'

'You really haven't been on any form of social media in about a decade, have you? People gave up friends in favour of followers ages ago.'

'Well, friends can be overrated.'

Maryam laughed, glad to see the Director of CCL fading into the background and becoming her Za again. 'So, what was that earlier? That look when Zola asked about sexual partners. Is there someone?'

'No,' Zahra said. Then, 'Just someone in the corner of my eye. Not even worth talking about.'

'Since when do we only talk about things that are worth talking about?'

But Zahra wouldn't be drawn. It was nothing, she insisted. There'd been a moment of flirtation weeks ago, that was all.

'Your usual type?' Maryam said.

Zahra shrugged.

Maryam said, 'Zahra!'

Zahra said, 'Maryam.'

Forty years of friendship compressed an entire conversation into those few syllables.

*

Zahra's flat looked out on to a large weeping willow, allowing her to lie in bed or read on the chaise longue in the living room while imagining a garden or even a stream outside. In truth, the weeping willow stood marooned on a roundabout on which six roads converged, in one of the unlovelier stretches of north-west London. It had been home for over a decade, and she'd chosen it over prettier options precisely for the tree. Growing up by the sea, she'd learnt the pleasures of living in a fast-moving city while looking out of your windows on to a vista that allowed the eyes to rest.

She settled on the gold-and-green chaise longue, and switched on the floor lamp. This was her reading spot, facing the window rather than the TV, a bookcase within arm's reach, though more often than she liked to admit she did her reading off a screen. A new message buzzed on her phone – Mrs Dass on the third floor asking her down for dinner as she invariably did on the rare evenings she heard Zahra moving about overhead as the Dass dinner hour of seven thirty approached.

She knew the Dasses imagined she must be lonely, and while this attitude generally irritated her for its assumptions about the single life, she saw in the couple an echo of her parents' devotion and knew they were only reflecting how adrift each of them would be without the other. She accepted the invitation more often than not, but this was one of those evenings when nothing in the world felt more enticing than putting your feet up in your own home, an R&B playlist streaming through the speakers, while a fiery tomato sauce simmered on the stove. She thanked Mrs Dass and said she'd already eaten – any other excuse, such as tiredness or work, would send Mr Dass up with a plate of food – and now that she was in the message app she scrolled down, without even having to think any more about what she was doing or why, to a conversation dated several weeks ago.

Was that wow* inappropriate?

                                        Yes

My apologies. Let's try this again: Respected Madam, greetings

                    Madam sounds like I run a brothel
Respected Goddess

                              <eye-rolling emoji>
So, now that you live in London do you still wear red saris?

                                        No

That's a crime against humanity. Red dresses? Bikinis?
Inappropriate again?
Hmmm. Maybe you really have become a completely appropriate grown-up
Pity

It was an automatic movement now from the message to the profile picture and then, via the VPN that was always on, to the mobile site for Imij, where she refused the suggestion that she download the app and continued as an anonymous user. He was married; she'd learnt that the first time she'd found his profile page via a trail from Saba to her brother to Hammad. His wife was much younger, all make-up and salon-dried hair, and always posed with the same smile, cheeks sucked in and chin lifted, head angled just so. In pictures of the two of them standing together, his hand rested on her hip bone, proprietary, and she leaned into him. Every picture the same hand on hip bone, the same lean. His feed was largely indistinguishable from that of a number of men she knew from school – the expat life of someone working in the financial sector, socialising almost entirely with Pakistanis, travelling to other countries to watch cricket matches, almost never without a wine or whisky glass in hand, sometimes a cigar. Hammad at a beach resort, Hammad at a rooftop bar, Hammad at Versailles. There were two sons too, grown men, who appeared occasionally and clearly weren't the present Mrs Hammad's children. Since she'd last checked – only yesterday – he'd put up a new post. It was a GIF of Hammad dancing – arms raised, hips swivelling. They seemed to move independently of the rest of his body, those hips. He was wearing the black button-down shirt and blue jeans that were practically the uniform of a certain kind of Karachi man, not unattractive at all. The GIF replayed over and over. She sipped her wine and watched. Marvin Gaye sang.

Tomatoes and chilli and basil scented the room. She stood up, went to the kitchen to add pasta to the boiling water.

She had reached the age when she no longer bothered with the question 'why' in relation to her own character. By contrast, too much of her university years and early twenties had been wasted trying to think or talk her way out of her own desires. Layla, her closest friend at Cambridge, had named the issue early on. There were two Zahras in relation to men – Suitable Zahra and Proclivity Zahra. Suitable Zahra dated the Sri Lankan mathematician who made hoppers for her in the morning; Proclivity Zahra cheated on him with her law tutor. Suitable Zahra met friends of friends at picnics and went out to dinners and movies before deciding whether to move things further; Proclivity Zahra had sex in nightclub bathrooms with men whose names she never asked.

She took the cubed aubergine out of the oven where it had caramelised and folded it into the sauce. She couldn't imagine doing that now, sex in nightclub bathrooms – it wasn't the anonymity but the indignity of the surroundings that would stop her. This is how you know you aren't young any more: you start to care more about thread count than immediate gratification. Was there any life left in this Parmesan rind?

Tom Lennox had come along when she was twenty-four, at first a Proclivity, a forty-year-old man living with his long-time girlfriend. But once he'd left the girlfriend – which he did very quickly – and everyone became accustomed to the age difference, it was clear that he was entirely Suitable. Ticks-all-the-boxes-Tom, as Maryam referred to him. Even her father approved. She'd loved him a great deal for several years, that was nice to remember. Things worked between them for a while, and then they didn't. She still thought of him affectionately, they spoke every year on what would have been their anniversary, and the good feeling between them made her glad she'd twice stopped just short of having affairs to see if that would relieve the captive feeling marriage had given her. Far better that she realised she didn't want to be married – to anyone. And with that understanding, Suitable Zahra disappeared.

Still another eight minutes for the pasta. She wandered back out into the living room, where her phone rested on the side table fashioned out of a tree stump. She touched the screen and Hammad and his hips were there again.

She had long since stopped asking the question 'why' because she no longer allowed the world to tell her what was and wasn't acceptable for a woman to want. The question shifted to safety – physical safety, reputational safety. That kept her off apps – imagine if the tabloids came across her profile? Or one of the men sending rape and death threats her way? She could think about the threats in a reasonably dispassionate manner, having trained herself to stay away from the places where they announced themselves. The need to enter her name in a search bar had long since been vanquished. Unseen, the threats didn't sit heavy inside her; instead, they formed only one seam of the skin of fear stitched on to her, which marked her as a woman and to which she was now so accustomed that most days she didn't even think about it. Girlfear, Maryam had once called it.

She clicked out of the GIF and returned to the thumbnails. Switched playlists so she could hear Chris Isaak singing 'Wicked Game', a song that always placed her on Karachi's beach at night, the moon low and full, the sand cool beneath her feet and Babar's lips warm as he kissed her out of sight of the rest of the party; she had kept her eyes closed, imagined someone less safe than a boy her parents trusted her with. Now, eyes wide open, she scrolled and clicked and zoomed in. She knew men like Hammad, had grown up with so many of them, continued to meet them through Maryam, who had held firmly on to her childhood connections. He was shallow and vain, that was written all over him. Perhaps cruel, perhaps corrupt; why pretend vanity was likely to be his worst characteristic? But that hand on his wife's hip, the way she leaned into him, the posed perfection of it all – he kept his affairs discreet, starting things up with women in faraway countries he might visit on work for a few days a year, and she turned a blind eye when he slipped up. Zahra remembered his hand on her torso, the first sexual touch of her life, and shivered – memory becoming anticipation.

The word 'Maryam' had dropped into her consciousness, and she pushed it out. Thirty years ago, and she didn't have to know anyway.

Just for the record, I've always been completely appropriate, she wrote in the messaging app.

It was the middle of the night in Singapore. She ate her dinner, watched two episodes of *Line of Duty*, spent a good while texting with a group called Keeping It Real made up of four women friends who hadn't known each other a decade ago but were now in daily conversation about their triumphs and irritations, the TV shows they were watching, the people on social media they despised for their attention-seeking behaviour wrapped up in the guise of good politics (they were her social media filters, these friends, sending her screenshots of anything that seemed amusing or enraging or necessary to be aware of). She told them about her exchange of messages with a man from long ago and they cheered the return of frisson to her life. One of them said she admired Zahra's ability to keep sexual relations in a little corner and get on with everything else; another said thank god for Zahra's clandestine entanglements otherwise she'd be too impeccable to bear. The third, Rose, who worked with Zahra, said, *These messages are on an encrypted app, right?*

She was reading in bed when her screen lit up.

I've been watching you online

Creepy

Self-improving
I've learnt so much about the evils of ID cards

She smiled at that. She'd recently been the keynote speaker at a human rights conference in Belfast, where she'd spoken of the civil liberty implications of the government's plans to introduce the cards. She'd been in a trouser suit, largely hidden behind a podium. While he was watching that, she had been looking at him on a beach with his shirt unbuttoned.

Glad to provide civic instruction
What can I provide you with?
I can't think of a thing
You've been thinking about it

Tell me what you've been thinking
Goodnight, Hammad
Goodnight, Goddess

*

A tall steel gate in an unpromising street in King's Cross led into a cobblestoned yard dominated by a structure that looked like two shipping containers made primarily of glass piled on top of each other. These were the premises of Venture Further – a conference room and smaller meeting rooms in the downstairs container, the offices of the three partners and seven other employees upstairs. Bike racks, a ping-pong table and rough-hewn wooden tables for coffee sipping and chit-chat in the yard fostered the impression of a company that was youthful, convivial and open to ideas.

Sometimes it was exactly that, even if there was never time for mere chit-chat in the yard. The company funded start-ups, and Maryam loved nothing more than the optimism and energy that came at the beginning of the process, ideas shimmering, waiting to be guided towards their potential. Other days, and today was one of them, you could start the day failing to convince your co-investors to enter another round of funding for something flawed but fixable, and then move on to ejecting a young founder-CEO from his own company; except it wasn't his own, as she'd had to point out in an ugly tear-filled meeting, it belonged to the investors, and if the founder-CEO consistently failed to listen to any of the advice that would have allowed him to make a success of it, then Maryam and the rest of the board could remove him from the equation and see what profit could yet be salvaged from the wreck of his dreams. He'd called her a cunt on his way out.

At least the sun had finally emerged, and she could hold her next meeting at a table in the yard, drinking coffee from the PhD-level coffee machine that no one but the office manager knew how to operate.

Fat girls don't stay on front pages, Golden Boy had said, but he hadn't counted on the girl's father with his 'caramel skin and long lashes', as one columnist gushed, and that Habib Ali air of decency. The occasional mutterings from all sectors of the media about the corrupting influence of social media on children had found a face and a voice in the guise of a British Pakistani psychiatrist, so eloquent about the harm done to his daughter, his anger that it had been allowed to happen, his fear for all the young girls and boys to whom it was happening right now. He seemed to be everywhere – the *Guardian*, *Good Morning Britain*, the *Daily Mail*, Mumsnet, *gal-dem*. Tomorrow morning he was due to be interviewed on *Today* and rumour had it that he would shift his focus from a generalised demand for social media companies to 'do better' to a call for government to include language in its forthcoming Internet Safety Bill that held tech bosses responsible for the hate and bullying allowed to proliferate on their apps. The phrase 'criminal charges' was being thrown about. A petition had already been drafted in the name of his daughter, calling for government action, but petitions didn't bother Maryam. Soft-spoken men with an air of decency who were championed by both the left- and right-wing media did. *Metro* had called him the Nation's Favourite Dad.

'Shut him down,' the prospective buyer of Imij had said, and venture capitalists with stakes in other social media companies, including her co-partners, said the same.

Eleven minutes after he was due, the man she was waiting for strolled into the yard, looking particularly Golden Boy with a recently acquired tan.

'All this irritation is making my gut act up,' he said, raising a glass bottle in salutation. 'Kefir,' he added and offered the bottle to her after sipping directly from its mouth.

'I don't have long,' Maryam said, keeping her tone mild so that he'd think she was indifferent to his power-plays.

'Sorry, sorry,' he said, with public-schoolboy contrition. Maryam had been his first investor, the first to believe his vision of what was possible for Imij, and he treated her with a courtesy, sometimes even a deference, that he extended to no one else.

'You've tried again to set up a meeting with him?' she said.

'He's still adamant that he'll only have a conversation when we send him proposals to change not only our policies on bullying but also our algorithms.'

The algorithms were the shark under the water in all this. The man's daughter – Tahera was her name – had started to look at self-harming posts after the pig-girl image went viral, and very quickly, her father claimed, her feed was flooded with related content, pushing her over the edge. Thankfully, very little could be proved about Imij's algorithms, and most media outrage continued to centre on the bullying. For the moment, at least.

'What does he want us to do, subvert the entire *give people more of what they want* ethos of the internet? It's undemocratic, that's what it is.' He wasn't looking at her while he spoke, swiping his fingers along his phone screen.

'I hope that's not the proposed strategy you've come to talk to me about.' She waved her coffee cup at the office manager, who was knocking on a window upstairs to tell her that she had a conference call starting in a few minutes, hoping this would indicate both that she was coming up soon and that she needed a refill.

He smiled as he passed her his phone, and she saw something of Saba in his expression – the joy of knowing an unpleasant secret – before she looked down at the screen.

There he was, the Nation's Favourite Dad, sitting at a wooden table much like the ones in the yard, leaning close to a copper-haired woman who wasn't the wife from the front page of the newspapers. Her hand cupped his face, his mouth pressed against her palm.

'This was the day after his daughter was released from hospital,' Golden Boy said, very pleased with himself. 'Imagine, she's at home with her bandaged wrists and he's out there doing this.'

'Is it genuine?'

'God, yes, of course. I'm not an idiot.'

'Is it from Imij?'

Golden Boy made a vague movement of his head that ended as a nod.

'And how did you find it? I assume he didn't put it up on his profile page.' The Nation's Favourite Dad had an Imij account but he'd taken down all the pictures he'd previously posted – mostly of flowers – and replaced them with a screen that said #JusticeforTahera #ChangeNow against a black backdrop.

'Gift horses, mouth.'

'Sometimes a gift horse is a Trojan horse and if you look in its mouth you'll see the soldiers hiding inside ready to slit your throat while you sleep at night.'

'No one will ever know.'

Almost certainly true. Anyone with an Imij account – or even an anonymous user – could find a photograph on a public account and choose to draw attention to it. There would be nothing to link it back to Imij's facial-tagging feature that allegedly gave users control over who could tag them, was only activated for those who had opted in to the tag function, and absolutely didn't give any face-tagging powers to the Imij CEO beyond his own account.

'You clever boy,' she said to Golden Boy, who sat taller at the compliment. It was possible he had a crush on her. The offer of the kefir bottle from his mouth to hers took on a different shade of meaning. 'Show me? It'll be our secret.'

He smiled, delighted. Men like him always wanted to show off the toys they'd built.

He opened the Imij app, entered the account name @KoffeeKraave into the search bar, and scrolled down to a picture of a man – older, Japanese – smiling formally at a camera. He was in a café, chalk-written menu on the wall above his head. The tags identified him as @KoffeeKraave's grandfather. Golden Boy sat back, watching her as she looked at the photograph. She zoomed into a corner of the image. Behind the man's shoulder, a couple sat at a table at the far end of the café, caught in a moment of intimacy.

'Such exceptional face-tagging features,' she said, waving away the office manager, who was approaching with a cup of coffee.

Golden Boy smiled and made a gesture, like curtains closing, to say that was as much as he was going to say.

'So, next steps?' he said.

She airdropped the picture from his phone to her own. 'I'll take care of it,' she said, standing up. She tapped her watch and he said of course, apologies again for being late. When she looked back from the entrance to the Venture Further offices, he was sitting on a ping-pong table, swigging from his kefir bottle, legs splayed, the April blue sky his backdrop. Master of the Universe.

His face had never known, would never know, anything like the expression of the couple in the picture at the café. Open, unguarded, given the illusion of safety by a strength of feeling for each other that made everything else disappear.

The world was exactly as her grandfather had always taught her it was. Terrible and brutal, unforgiving. But she also knew the truth that followed on from that which he had failed to understand: hold close the ones you love, protect them. There is no other source of light.

*

Unexpectedly last year, middle age had announced its onset in the form of blurred words on the page and a backache that burrowed deep and didn't want to leave until an osteopath performed an exorcism. So now Zahra's office had been augmented with reading glasses, an exercise ball and a ridiculously expensive orthopaedic chair. She took off her glasses, stood up from the chair, rolled the ball out from under her desk and bounced up and down on it, lengthening her spine, working her core. Layla's ceramic sculpture looked at her from a bookcase near the door – an old, heavyset woman whose naked body had lost its battle with gravity, sitting with her hands on her knees, head thrown back in laughter. 'You're right, it is absurd,' Zahra said, getting off the ball mid-bounce. She pulled the privacy screen over the whiteboard that took up one long wall of her office and rolled up the blinds covering the floor-to-ceiling windows that looked out on to a street market, noisy with lunch clientele from around Victoria.

Office workers queued beside the blue-tented kiosks, their presence altering the character of the street for a couple of hours every afternoon. The paella and curries were doing brisk business, though once summer set in the wraps – Greek, Mexican, Lebanese – would dominate. If summer set in. Some years it seemed to pass London by entirely. And yet, it was true, she did love London's weather, its changeability. Astonishing the extent to which this city had stolen into her heart. Some days a particular quality of light would make her catch her breath and think 'April' or 'July' or 'October' or whatever month it was in which the light looked as it did in no other month, no other place in the world. Right now, the afternoon light was falling softly. She'd often read about such light in books while growing up but hadn't really understood what it meant until she came to England. 'Softly' wasn't a word you'd ever think to use about the afternoon light in Karachi, which ran the gamut from bright to harsh.

'Have you heard of the High Table?' Rose said, entering the office with her usual brisk manner. Rose was Head of Legal and the person Zahra called when something awful happened in the world and it was essential to speak to someone who responded to it emotionally exactly in synch with you. Rose's Bognor Regis upbringing was about as far from Zahra's Karachi childhood as possible, and yet it was one of those friendships that was wholly explicable to the outside world.

'Is this another dig at my Oxbridgeness?'

'No. I just had lunch with Clare.' Clare was a mutual friend, an investigative journalist for openDemocracy. 'It's a new elite donor club for the Increasingly Shameless Party. Pay £200,000 into their coffers and win yourself unprecedented levels of government access.'

'They really are shameless,' Zahra said, kicking the exercise ball towards Rose, who booted it under the desk with a deftness that came from weekends spent playing football with women half her age. 'Which arseholes are giving them two hundred thousand pounds?'

Rose raised her hands towards the ceiling. 'Shockingly, they seem to be dragging their feet about declaring their donations.'

'God, it's dispiriting.' She had seen four Prime Ministers come and go in her time at CCL, and with each change of administration she and her team had effectively lobbied for changes in legislation – even when the governing party had a parliamentary majority there were always rebels or restive backbenchers or the ones who put civil liberties above party loyalty. The rolling back of anti-terror laws, amendments to the Hate Crimes Bill, an end to the Snoopers' Charter – all these were, in part, CCL victories. Britain was a different place, a better place, because of this office. She'd made her father so proud.

But there was a new character to Westminster now – all rebels had been expelled from the party, and those who remained were in lockstep with the new government and its sky-high popularity in the polls. It was hard to see when or how any parliamentary victory would come again. As for legal victories, it was clear the government was planning to sidestep court rulings wherever it could, while working on legislation to curtail the power of judges.

'Stop being self-indulgent,' Rose said with the brisk impatience of someone who had been in enough wars, personal and professional, to know how luxurious a position despair was. She walked across to Zahra's desk, extracted a chocolate-covered McVitie's from a drawer and retreated to her office down the hall.

Zahra thought she should be allowed a few minutes of self-indulgence. At a conference last night, the Home

Secretary had amped up her line about Zahra 'siding with criminals' to 'siding with criminals and terrorists'. This in reference to CCL's campaign against the Anti-Protest Bill, as it had come to be known. Though the government had a far more euphemistic name for it: Security and Sentencing Bill. Zahra knew from over-heard comments in the office that the online abuse had peaked again.

She returned to looking out of the window. There was a narrow corridor between one blue kiosk and the next through which she could see Azam, the baker's assistant, in the doorway of Scrummy across the road. She waved at him and he walked out to the pavement, pointed at himself and then at her, and tapped his watch, raising his index finger. She nodded, yes, of course he could come and see her for a minute. Azam often came into the CCL offices mid-afternoon with lemon bars and brownies from the morning bake, insisting they would go to waste if his favourite English people didn't eat them – everyone with a British passport was 'English people' to Azam, including his wife, who had been born in Kabul like him but had come to London as a child. He couldn't wait to become English people himself.

She heard him chatting to the receptionist, Ray, before entering her office in his usual jeans, T-shirt and baker's apron. He was one of those 28-year-olds, full of vigour and optimism, who reminded you of the best moments of being twenty-eight.

'Thank you,' he said, extending his arm across Zahra's desk and unfurling his fingers to reveal a small offering, beautifully wrapped.

'For what?' she said.

'Your help with my application.' Azam had recently applied to the Home Office for Indefinite Leave to

189

Remain, the penultimate step on his road to English personhood. All the complicated checks had taken place when his wife sponsored him for a marriage visa, so it was a fairly straightforward application – but she knew from Ray how nervous Azam was about the process, given all the news articles about applicants rejected by a Home Office increasingly hostile to migrants, so she'd offered to look over his paperwork.

'There's no need,' she said. His application had been so perfectly assembled she'd joked that his baker's skills were showing – the precision, the attention to detail. He'd said it wasn't down to his baker's skills but to his pharmacist wife's clinical thoroughness. Now he made a sound to say her statement was so absurd he couldn't think of the words to rebuff it. The present was a bracelet with an angel charm dangling from it; silver, not just silver-plated. She'd seen his financial disclosure statements and knew he couldn't afford gifts like this, but she couldn't embarrass him by doing anything other than accept.

He didn't stay beyond the one minute he'd asked for, and Zahra returned to work, reading a briefing paper about the Anti-Protest Bill that her team had put together for members of the House of Lords – the unelected chamber was the only place where there was any hope of the government's will being tempered, if not overturned, an irony that was almost unbearable to think about.

This reminded me of you

She swiped the notification off her screen without even looking at the attached image Hammad had sent. He knew better than to expect a response from her during working hours. He was her last thing at night, she was his first thing in the morning. His unmentioned wife probably asleep in bed the whole while.

Campaign focus? she wrote next to a paragraph about the bill's targeting of climate activists. The angel dangling from her wrist cast a shadow on the page. She held it between thumb and finger; it felt unexpectedly heavy.

There was a shout from the reception area, Ray and Azam's voices combined. Zahra stood up and strode to the door of her office, but now the shouting was coming from outside. She turned towards her window just in time to see a man lying supine on the pavement, Azam with his knee on the man's chest, fist driving into his face.

And then Ray pulling Azam back, arms tight around him, pinning his arms in place.

Zahra ran out into reception, the smell of what had happened hitting her before she saw the bag of excrement where it had landed and split open, on the floor between Ray's desk and the front door. An unpleasant squelch and stink as her heel landed in the splatter. She continued on out through the door to the street, Rose and Alex the intern a few paces ahead of her.

Outside, Ray had let go of Azam, who was standing up, one palm covering the knuckles of his hand, Rose's hand on his shoulder. The other man was standing too, nose bloodied, arms behind his back, one wrist gripped by Ray, the other held by the Bangladeshi cook from the Thai kiosk. A line of men – the baker who employed Azam, the trans man from the charity shop, several of the kiosk chefs and cashiers – stood watching with arms crossed, shoulder to shoulder, letting the man with the bloodied nose know they wanted him to break free and run so that they could have the pleasure of knocking him down again.

'You smell like shit,' the man with the still-bleeding nose said as Zahra came closer to him. He was dipping his head forward so the blood fell to the pavement rather than dripping on to his mouth and down his shirt. Ray did something to his grip to make the man cry out in pain.

The sound of police sirens nearby. 'That's for you,' Alex said.

'Me?' the man said. 'I accidentally dropped a bag. Your friend there, he's the one who's going to be charged with assault. Hey, Taliban, you legal?'

Azam pivoted to look at her. He couldn't afford to have a court conviction with an application pending at the Home Office.

'It'll be OK,' she said. 'I promise.'

She saw the look Rose gave her – don't promise, never promise. But the fear slid right off Azam's face, replaced by trust. She moved towards him, and Rose and Alex both took a step away from her; the stench from her shoe was revolting.

*

Zahra said she was fine, there was no need for Maryam to cancel any meetings to come and hold her hand.

'How could you let him get away with it?' Maryam said, while texting Layla to instruct her to go get Zahra out of the shit-filled office that she seemed insistent on hanging around.

'Have to go,' Zahra said. 'Layla's calling.'

Two pitch meetings later, the Karachi Classmates chat group had 168 new messages, all about the events at Zahra's office. Everyone who had settled in America and England was outraged; the Americans particularly likely to use the word 'trauma'. The ones who had stayed in Karachi, racism only relevant to their lives when they applied for visas to travel to Europe or North America, treated it primarily as a cleaning-up issue. *Did it land on carpet or bare floor?* said one. *Is there good ventilation?* asked another.

Lucky to live in a country where it's manure they deliver rather than severed hands or bombs wrote a journalist in Karachi who'd survived an assassination attempt. Zahra was typing a response which came through a few moments later: *Yes, a bagful of shit is the heightened level of civilisation we're at here. A severed hand would have been easier to clean up (not carpet, thank god).* Maryam laughed, even as she started writing a private message for Zahra. *Someone could screenshot that and get you in trouble, idiot.* Before she had a chance to send it, Zahra had deleted the message, resulting in an *OK who here did you think would leak that?* message from Babar. Maryam wrote *Saba!* in the group chat she had with Zahra and Babar at the very instant that Zahra wrote *100% Saba.*

Officially, of course, Zahra had taken a different tone with the BBC reporter – a friend of Zahra's – who had been on the scene in minutes. 'An attack on civil liberties', 'a symptom of a much wider malaise', 'the finger of blame must point at those in power who use dogwhistle politics and then claim to be appalled when things like this happen'.

Zahra so clearly loved it all. Not the attack on the office, certainly, but the persona she inhabited as Director of CCL – poised and brave and replete with moral certainty. Funny to recall how timid she'd been as a young girl, always afraid that something awful was going to happen. Maryam softened, remembered how proud she was of her best friend even when she didn't agree with her. Zahra had made herself exactly what she'd always wanted to be – Someone.

Maryam placed the phone on her desk, which was maple and stainless steel and had its own model name – the Zieg 2000, an apparently long-awaited successor to the Zieg 1500. The Zieg 2000 ran the cables from her monitors invisibly through its structure, which was the closest she'd get to buying furniture with 'features'. She didn't approve of show-off tech and could barely glance without shuddering at her partner Connor's desk, with its integrated touchscreen.

'And they call you tech guru,' he'd teased her one day, and she was startled to remember that even someone like Connor, who had worked alongside her since her earliest days in VC, didn't know that there were generations of classical design in her blood, which brought with it a disdain for 'faddishness'. Her office furniture was all clean lines, the sage-green walls hung with watercolour reproductions of vintage ads from Pakistan that she'd commissioned from a Karachi artist just graduated from the National College of Arts who was now showing at Tate and MoMA. The watercolours included a Khan Leather ad from the 1950s, when the company had first branched out from suitcases. LIVE A KHAN LEATHER LIFESTYLE WITHOUT LEAVING HOME!

She put on her headset and dialled in to an update call with a Venture Further founder whose biotech company used AI for early breast-cancer detection. While he talked, she clicked on the link Babar had posted on the class group. CCTV footage had made its way online from a camera on the street where Zahra had her office. It caught the man opening the door to CCL and throwing a bag inside, his arm slinging back and hurling. Before the door had swung closed a second man in a baker's apron ran out and tackled the first man, dropping him to the pavement. There the footage ended.

She said, *How much cash are you burning on that?* to the founder and scrolled down to the comments. Someone had identified the man, he worked at a hardware store not far from the CCL offices. There was a pile-on of comments directed to his employers asking how they could have someone like this on staff. Other people called him a hero, someone offered to put together a GoFundMe page if the woke brigade succeeded in getting him fired. This was what happened when you tried to control a narrative on social media.

She stood, stretched her arms over her head. *If it doesn't work, you're going to have to sell your user data.* And then, *So make sure no one finds out.*

She ended the call, did a few more stretches. Golden Boy had wanted the pictures of the Nation's Favourite Dad to go public, but she knew that was dangerous. People would want to know where the picture came from, and even if nothing could be proved, enough could be guessed. So instead she made a phone call. Not to a Billoo – she didn't need anyone like that – but to an investigation company that had often brought her information on people it was necessary to know more about before she could make responsible decisions about how to use her investors' money. They valued her as a client well enough to take on what was an almost amateur job: stand outside the BBC's Broadcasting House, waiting for the Nation's Favourite Dad to show up for his *Today* interview and hand him an envelope with a photograph inside.

The interview never took place. A social media account linked to the #JusticeForTahera campaign said the family was asking for privacy and that Tahera's father would be making no more media appearances; his first duty was to be at home and look after his daughter. Without his caramel-skinned, long-lashed face of decency the campaign foundered and fell off the front pages. Maryam was glad for how quietly she'd allowed him to retreat. There'd never been any question of letting him win, but she hadn't wanted him destroyed, only defeated. Her grandfather would have been proud of her.

*

'How do you feel?'

There it was. Zahra had wondered how long Layla would be able to keep from saying it. It wasn't the tone she'd struck to begin with. 'You can't stay in that stinky office. Send everyone home and let's go buy you some new shoes,' she'd said. That had been a while ago. Now they were sitting at a pavement table outside a fish-and-chip restaurant on Marylebone Lane, making their way through a large plate of chips doused in vinegar. Zahra's new grey ankle boots were on her feet; her old grey ankle boots were in a bin outside the CCL premises.

'I'm fine,' Zahra said.

She really was. It had been a shock, yes, but the shock had quickly been overtaken by concern for Azam, and she was still lifted by the glow of making sure he was OK. Victories were hard to come by these days.

Both matters had been dealt with via community resolution, no criminal record arising from either offence. 'Are you sure that's what you want?' the police officer – Asian – had said to Zahra, when she suggested it. The man with the bloodied nose accepted his guilt, Azam did the same. They were both required to say they were sorry, which they each did without clarifying what they were apologising for. The police officer didn't object or linger; she'd heard Azam's accent, saw his terror, knew the country she was living in.

'You're not fine. You don't need to say you're fine.'

Well, what were you supposed to say to a thing like that?

She didn't say anything, just concentrated on following a trail of salt around the plate with a half-eaten chip. Layla sat back in the bistro chair, arms crossed, waiting for Zahra to admit to some feeling of – what? – violation, terror, hatred? Hard to feel any of that about a spindly man with all that rage and no way to express it except via a bag of his own excrement. He had the look of someone to whom the world had never done a single favour, and she suspected seeing him handcuffed and put in the back of a police car might have made her feel she was part of a cruel system.

'Who did the clean-up?' Layla said, relenting.

'Oh god,' Zahra said. 'That was awkward. A good proportion of the office were united in the opinion that Ray and I and Goldie in Legal couldn't possibly be allowed anywhere near it because, you know . . .'

'Only three non-whites in the office?'

'I'm not sure if they thought the optics would look bad or that our assumed childhood traumas were being triggered.' She stepped down on the heel of a boot that made barely a sound against the pavement – with the old pair you could hear her striding through the office. 'You never had anything like that happen, did you?'

'When you're achingly middle class, the racist shit of your childhood is largely metaphorical.'

Layla ripped open a paper packet with her teeth, shook more salt on to the chips. When they'd first met as nineteen-year-olds – each reaching at the same moment for a bell hooks paperback at a used book stall in Cambridge Market Square – Zahra had known immediately that this striking woman in an electric-blue jumpsuit was someone she wanted as a friend, and it was for this reason only that she'd said perhaps they could split the cost of the book (it was 50p) and each read it in turn. And perhaps meet sometime to discuss it? Layla had relinquished her hold on the book. 'I was buying that for a friend. I get my wisdom from Nina Simone, the Clash and Linton Kwesi Johnson. How do you feel about chips?' Zahra had already found her tribe in Cambridge but was beginning to tire of staying up until dawn arguing about whether the Truth and Reconciliation Commission was a cop-out or an elevated form of justice with people to whom questions of democratic transitions or even basic injustice were purely abstract. In Layla she found a friend with whom she could eat oversalted chips and who would take her to galleries to introduce her to contemporary art and tell her off for the limitations of her musical preferences. ('Bryan Adams? Can we blame dictatorship for this too?') Zahra hadn't known someone could be so unimpressed by your tastes and reference points in such an uplifting way.

Layla looked at her phone and whooped. 'They think it's all over; it is now.'

The shop where the attacker worked had posted a statement to say they operated a zero-tolerance policy on racism and had fired the man with immediate effect.

'How do we feel about trial by social media?' Zahra said. Cameras watching, people judging, forms of punishment being demanded that improved nothing at all. The Home Secretary was as secure in her position as ever, standing up in Parliament to say how appalled she was by the attack on CCL while the Opposition listened in collegial silence instead of shouting 'hypocrite'.

Layla threw a chip at her. It bounced off her nose, and she caught it as it fell. 'It's a terrible thing except when it's a wonderful thing. Admit you're pleased.'

'You sound like Maryam.' It was an entirely Maryam move to sweep aside anything that sounded like a value and ask what, deep down, in the most animal places of your heart, you felt. As if your basest emotions trumped everything else; as if only they were truth and all else was just posturing. Sometimes Zahra wanted to say that was the kind of thinking that had led the teenaged Maryam to want to send a thug to beat up Jimmy, but that would get them into a conversation about that night in the FX, which she wasn't keen to pursue. She wondered how Maryam thought about her demands to her grandfather now. Was she horrified by herself? Or still felt justified? The problem with childhood friendship was that you could sometimes fail to see the adult in front of you because you had such a fixed idea of the teenager she once was, and other times you were unable to see the teenager still alive and kicking within the adult.

'People do rub off on each other after twenty years,' Layla said genially, wiping her fingers on a napkin and immediately reaching for another chip. 'But you are pleased.'

Yes, she was pleased. So what? She hated the undue attention given to every individual's feelings that was so much a marker of the present moment. *Be bigger than yourself* – that was one of her father's lines.

'Speaking of rubbing off on each other, did you know she has some refugee food-delivery company in her investment portfolio? She told me this last week, as if she'd done it as a gift to me.'

'Delivering food to refugees?'

'Of course not. Getting refugees to cook and deliver food around London. She's already had to talk the founders into focusing on the cooks and not advertising the fact that the delivery drivers are refugees too. She said, once the British welcomed refugees but didn't much care for world cuisine, and now they'll eat their way around the globe, but spare them the asylum-seeker at their doorstep.'

They both laughed at that, their laughter taking in Maryam's ability to deliver a critique that might be considered left-wing if she weren't so interested in how to profit from it.

Both the chips and the evening had turned too cold to countenance, so they set off together towards Regent's Park. It was just dark enough when they emerged from the park to make a walk through Primrose Hill feel unappealing – Zahra registered a background thrum of envy for the man in running clothes who charged in without thinking twice about the rapidly failing light. She and Layla said their goodbyes and continued along well-lit streets in their separate directions – Zahra heading for the bus to Swiss Cottage, Layla on her way to pick up Zola from Mark's house.

Zahra had only gone a few paces when she heard Layla calling her back, holding up her phone. While they'd been walking, a tabloid had posted new footage on its home page. Azam smashing the spindly man's face, his expression ugly. Alongside the looping footage, a still image: the spindly man, leaning forward, his face smeared with blood, each wrist held by a dark-skinned man. Something had been done to the image to make his blond hair shine so brightly, Ray and the Bangladeshi cook's skin darkened to the colour of coal. The blond man's arms were spread slightly apart as he tilted forward, just enough to make explicable the replication of the image all across social media with the hashtag 'crucifixion'.

*

You OK?

> *Fine, other than having to throw away*
> *my favourite shoes*

Because?

> *It'll kill all erotic charge if I tell you*

I'll never ask again. Hope that Afghan
is getting a medal

> *He was stupid to do that. What is it*
> *with men and violence?*

Can be satisfying. You never wanted to
punch me in the face?

That was a surprise. They'd both avoided – carefully, she thought – any mention of that night that led to his expulsion from school.

> *Oh, you're going there*

Should I backtrack?

> *Did you ever punch Jimmy in the face?*

For what?

> *You were terrorised on that car ride too*

She hoped he would know she meant it as taunt not forgiveness. With Hammad she could be unkind.

No one was 'terrorised'

> *What word would you use?*

Bonjour

> *?*

I have to be in Paris for work this summer
                              Changing the topic?
Don't pretend you don't know what I'm asking

She went to stand at her bedroom window, watching the life on the street. Two men conversed under the awning of a café across the road, cigarettes in their gesturing hands. For the first time in years she wished she still smoked, as she had from university through her twenties. She imagined herself from a distance, a woman who had stepped away from her rumpled bed wearing only a dressing gown, smoking a cigarette, contemplating whether to allow herself what she wanted. Unchaining the animal places of her heart. She exhaled, and instead of smoke rings there was a little misting of the window. She traced a YES in it.

*

Maryam thought the word 'home' with pleasure, as she so often did, returning from the night walk with Woolf, the chill of outdoors closed out as she shut the door behind her. The dog edged past her as they entered the house and made her way on her stiff legs down the stairs. Upstairs, Zola's bedroom light was off.

Down in the kitchen, the dinner plates still hadn't been cleared away as she'd promised Layla. Instead, she'd fallen down the rabbit hole of work emails – no time of day when investors or CEOs weren't awake somewhere in the world. She put the kettle on to boil, cracked open four cardamon pods between her teeth and dropped them into two mugs. *Back*, she texted, looking out towards the studio in the garden into which Layla had disappeared right after dinner.

While waiting for the water to boil, she glanced at her email again, fired off a couple of responses, and then walked around to the floating display cabinet with its trio of sculptures – the goddess Hariti from Gandhara in grey schist and Oshun the Yoruba deity in bronze flanked a clay woman whom Maryam lifted off the cabinet, looking closely at her for the first time in years. She was a small-scale model of a much larger sculpture in white marble that had been Layla's contribution to a group show at Whitechapel Gallery, in the early days of their life together. Layla had called the piece *After Phidias* – it was a response to the absence of women's genitals in Greek art, and had attracted considerable attention at the time. The clay figure reclined, nude, thighs indolently parted, revealing everything. A huge fight had ensued when Maryam had recognised – belatedly, because it wasn't something she'd ever looked at for very long – the sculpture's replication of parts of her own anatomy. *It's an homage*, Layla had said. *And no one but the two of us knows it's you. I mean, none of your ex-boyfriends are the sort to wander into art exhibitions in the East End, are they?*

She'd been in the early days of a relationship with one of the ex-boyfriends when she'd first met Layla. An autumn day in 1993 that placed the word 'russet' at the forefront of your thoughts. Maryam had walked into the Cambridge home that Zahra was house-sitting to find a woman balancing a mug of tea on a denimed knee that was drawn up against her chest, demonstrating a striking foldability of limbs. She'd been prepared to dislike this Layla-pronounced-the-English-way of whom Zahra spoke so adoringly, but Layla made that quickly impossible. Layla hadn't stayed long but, before leaving, she embraced Maryam. The muscles of her arms, the thinness

203

of the fabric of her T-shirt. On the train back to London that evening, Maryam became aware of a shift within her. A truth, already known, fully acknowledged. But it seemed only to be a partial truth at the time – she liked her boyfriend well enough – so she decided to ignore the inconvenience of it. It was several years before she encountered Layla again, in a pub garden on Zahra's twenty-fifth birthday, and everything that followed was inevitable.

Maryam noticed, with some amusement, the dust gathering between the clay figure's legs. Nadya, their cleaner, was usually zealous about keeping everything spotless but there were clearly places she didn't want to go. Maryam carried the sculpture over to the kitchen counter and rubbed her down with a damp cloth. How much time they used to spend on art and war. Endless hours in galleries, from warehouses in Bethnal Green to the Tate Modern, which they first visited the day it opened its vast doors to the public – when the century was new and still filled with optimism. They'd largely agree about the art, furiously disagree about capitalism's relationship to art, and often end up stalking away from each other or kissing in a corner, overlooked by a giant spider or a glittering woman made of elephant dung. A far more perilous activity then than now, but not kissing hadn't really seemed an option.

Maryam followed the damp cloth with a dry one, then placed a fond kiss on the wide-openness of her desire when she was done.

When was the last time Layla had talked to her in more than the most cursory fashion about any exhibition she'd been to see? When, for that matter, had Maryam last been to see an exhibit with her? Their conversations were almost all domestic now – about Zola, mostly; but also grocery shopping, home improvements, summer holiday plans, whether it was time to invite some or other combination of their families over for lunch. They didn't fight much any more – Layla's attitude towards their differences had moved to 'acceptance', aided by a great deal of yoga and meditation. Occasionally, it felt like diminishment. Occasionally, also, Layla herself seemed diminished from the woman Maryam had fallen in love with. Not in any startling way, just the ordinary way in which young people filled with energy and promise settled into middle-aged contentment, at peace with a position as an art and English teacher in a state school when once she was one of the most promising sparks in a cohort whose other members now had solo exhibitions at the Royal Academy and commissions from Artangel. 'You turned her into a wife,' Layla's ex had once said to Maryam. Maryam had been unusually wounded by that, though Layla had laughed when she repeated the line and said, 'Growing up, solo exhibitions seemed within reach but I never dreamed this life was possible.' And she'd gestured around to the bedroom she shared with Maryam, the toddler clambering about her legs. Later, Maryam had heard her yelling down the phone to her ex about 'heterosexual paradigms'.

The studio light went off, and a few moments later Layla walked through the sliding door and laughed to see Maryam with the clay woman.

'Darling, you haven't changed a bit,' she said, dropping a kiss on to Maryam's neck before taking her hand and pulling her on to the sofa. 'Did you make us some tea?'

Maryam gestured towards the kitchen counter where the mugs sat next to the kettle. 'I could bring it over, but that would mean getting up.'

Layla shifted, wrapped her legs around Maryam's waist and held her in place. Maryam rested her head on

Layla's chest, felt the comforting rhythm of her heart, fifty-eight beats per minute at rest. Some of Maryam's favourite moments in life occurred at the end of a busy day, when everything that had come before fell away and there was only Woolf's rumbling breath, the particular quality in the air that arose from knowing Zola was safely at home but not likely to need anything further until tomorrow, Layla silent with her in the way they'd always been able to be with one another.

'I spoke to my aunt today,' Layla said after a few minutes. 'She seems to have started redecorating the whole house in anticipation of our arrival.'

Maryam took Layla's hand and pressed it to her lips. Soon after Zola was born, Layla had sat Maryam down and talked to her about the two years she and her brother had spent with their parents in Lagos when they were nine and eleven. It had been transformative to not see your Blackness as contrast, Layla had said. She'd like Zola to have that experience one day, and also the experience of living within a large family. Maryam had agreed, as was the civilised response to any demand from the lactating and sleep-deprived love of your life. In the years since, she'd shaved the two years down to six months, Nigeria's homophobic laws coming to her aid. Layla could take a term's leave from work, Zola could go to the same school as her cousins in Lagos, Maryam would fly in to visit as often as she could. They were to leave after Christmas.

'Life will be very rubbish without the two of you here.' She tried to say it lightly, but Layla squeezed her hand in apology.

'I've told Zahra to clear her social calendar for next spring. She promises she'll be here at least once during the week as well as your usual Sundays.'

'I don't need a babysitter,' Maryam said, but she was pleased.

A little later, Layla slid a tablet off the coffee table. Maryam took it from her hands and propped it against her knees so they could both watch Zahra on *Question Time*.

'Oh, hello,' Layla said, as the camera focused on Zahra, sitting on one side of the moderator around the crescent-shaped desk. She always wore a jacket in muted tones with a black shirt beneath for her TV appearances, but today the shirt was red and the neckline a V rather than a scoop. The four men and one other woman around the desk were all in different shades of black and white, their hair white or blond. You would look at Zahra and think, *One of these things is not like the other things*, even without the red shirt. But the bright colour added an air of flaunting, a deliberate setting apart, which she should by now know better than to attempt if she was also going to say the kinds of things she always said.

'Do you think she's doing that for her mystery man?' Layla said.

'Has she said anything more to you about him?'

'He's in a different time zone, she knew him slightly years ago, he might come to London some time this summer. Also, she hasn't had an orgasm that hasn't been self-induced for much too long.'

'That is the kind of sentence I can't imagine Zahra saying.'

'It's because you grew up with Upright Zahra. I first met Horizontal with the Tutor Zahra.'

'I suppose he's where it started.'

'It' was Zahra's taste in men, which ran to the clandestine. Zahra liked to call it a proclivity, but really it was a guardrail. You don't expect to go very far when you walk down a dead-end street, and one failed marriage was all the emotional upheaval Zahra was willing to risk in a lifetime. Layla said she was starting with the patriarchal assumption that coupledom had to be the emotional centre of every woman's life, and there was no evidence that Zahra wanted anything more than she received from her entanglements. But inside Maryam there still remained an adolescent, fierce about her best friend, who wanted to yell 'You aren't good enough for her' at all the unworthy men who stopped short of loving Zahra Ali, even if love wasn't what Zahra wanted from them.

'Is this her first time facing the Valkyrie since she said that thing about criminals and terrorists?' Layla said.

The only other woman at the desk was the Home Secretary, who had blonde hair like a helmet and the languid air of centuries-old privilege. Zahra blamed her for the attack on her office, though it was perfectly clear that it was Zahra's own words, not anyone else's, that made certain kinds of people hate her.

The questions from the audience started. Zahra did what she always did, with her perfectly formed sentences and witty asides and very human anecdotes that made it clear she understood the human cost of policy and polling decisions: she made everyone else look insincere, ill-informed and second-rate. Maryam's interest wandered to Layla's hands moving under her shirt and then lower, so she missed the next few questions and only focused again when a woman in a hijab with a Birmingham accent stood up to say she had been distressed for weeks about that schoolgirl, Tahera, whose attempted suicide had been a result of school bullying, much of which took place on Imij.

Layla's hand stilled, aware of the shift in Maryam's attention. Why had everyone stopped talking about it so quickly? the woman was saying. Shouldn't the government have stepped in and taken action against the rampant Islamophobia and racism that was allowed to go unchecked?

The moderator turned to Zahra first. Did she support government action? he asked.

'Absolutely,' Zahra said. 'I absolutely think the government should take action against rampant Islamophobia and racism. A good starting point would be an internal inquiry into their own party, looking first at the leadership's use of language and extending out to government policies.'

Layla hooted in appreciation, the audience applauded. Maryam watched the Valkyrie, saw the bright red marks on her cheeks.

'This government is unequivocally opposed to all forms of discrimination,' she said. 'So yes, we will be taking measures against Imij. The Prime Minister has made it very clear there is no place in Britain for companies turning a blind eye to racism for the sake of profits.'

That brought on the loudest round of applause of the evening.

Maryam kissed Layla's hand in apology while moving it off her and stood up even as her phone started to buzz and ring at the same time.

'Load the dishwasher and bring me some tea,' Layla called out as Maryam crossed to the phone on the kitchen counter, reaching it before the second ring, winged sandals on her feet now that the battle she'd thought she'd averted was here.

*

*Sorry, was on a conference call when you were doing
your TV thing*

Where in the world was he? *Question Time* had aired
before 6 a.m. Singapore time.

> *That's OK. It was nothing to write home about*
> *I disagree*
>   *Based on?*
> *Couldn't listen but was watching on my*
> *phone. You in red. Stuff of fantasies*

Perhaps he was in some other city where he had an
affair on the go. She never imagined she was the only
one – there was something so recycled about many of
his lines.

> *Is having me on mute also the stuff of fantasies?*
> *No I want to hear every sound you make.*
> *What colour was your bra?*

Recycled, and yet it sent a charge through her, made
her feel the right kind of dirty.

>   *What bra?*
> *You're killing me*

*

Maryam walked along the quiet Kensington street,
hands in the pockets of her belted suede coat. A
retro-stylish 1980s Khan Leather saddlebag was slung
cross-body and bumped against her hip with every step.
She glanced, by habit, towards every passing window
to see what piece of life she might find on display in

street-facing rooms on ground floors and in basements. Here was a room that was all television, here another that was museum-like with its red walls and expensively framed paintings, but that drew attention far less than the one that was in total shambles – dust thick on piles of books that were a nudge away from toppling, brown rings from teacups on carpet and furniture; it conjured up an image of occupants who shuffled about in stained clothes that were both moth-eaten and smelt of mothballs. As a child she'd once been taken to such a home by her parents and assumed the couple who lived there – her father's guardians from his boarding-school days – must be too poverty-stricken to afford new clothes or even a spray can of Mr Sheen; she had greeted with first disbelief and then scorn the information that quite the contrary was true, but if you're English and posh you don't ever want to be seen as trying. Years later, when she'd entered the heady world of dot com with its promise of new ways of doing things, she had understood that Britain was a place that had invented nonsensical rules to wrong-foot outsiders at a time when being an insider placed you at the very heart of global power; by the close of the twentieth century the rules were tired and silly, the arcane rituals of a club no one took seriously when the clubhouse itself was up for sale.

But she'd underestimated the club members, as evidenced by her need for assistance today from Baroness Margaret Wright, CBE, descendant of one of the lesser-known Viceroys of India, power-broker, philanthropist, and not only Maryam's former boss but now, in retirement, valued investor in funds raised by Venture Further. The clubhouse might be almost entirely sold off, but club membership remained restricted to those who had grown up playing on its grounds. *You don't mind the exclusivity, you just mind that you aren't part of it,* Layla had said once, as if this was a Maryam-specific attitude rather than absolutely everyone's objection to exclusivity.

Climbing the steps to Margaret's front door, she grasped the lizard-shaped knocker with her usual distaste – one of the few things she'd never missed about Karachi was its geckos. A few moments later she was being ushered by the housekeeper through the chandeliered house, Margaret's brocaded ancestors watching from the walls, and down the stairs to the patio.

She smiled to see Margaret sitting on a patio chair bare-armed, little evidence in her toned biceps of the seventieth birthday that she'd celebrated last year at the British Museum, where she was a trustee. She had a cigarette in hand, and plumes of smoke drifted from her mouth.

'Still a cold-blooded dragon lady,' Maryam said in greeting. Earlier in the afternoon it had been summer, but now clouds had moved in and brought back the sharp chill of spring.

Margaret received this as the compliment it was intended to be, raising her cheek for a kiss, her smile showing teeth discoloured with wine and nicotine. Her careful attention to appearance had never made its way inside her mouth.

'I see the Minister for Children and Families has backed the Home Secretary's comments about Imij this evening,' Margaret said, as Maryam sat down. 'Who even knew there was a minister for such a thing?'

'I imagine he said it just so we do know there's a minister for such a thing,' Maryam said.

'Terrible moment for all this noise, given acquisition talks, isn't it?' Margaret took another drag on her cigarette, her mouth curved into a smile of secret knowledge.

'You already know about that?' She'd come here prepared to reveal this highly privileged information to Margaret only if doing so proved necessary in order to enlist her aid. Even now, she continued to underestimate the club members.

'I might have had a hand in getting that ball rolling.'

Margaret's housekeeper reappeared with a bottle and two crystal glasses. The bottle had gold lettering and a gold icon of a winged horse on it. Since turning teetotaller, Margaret had become a connoisseur of fine water.

'Eight thousand years old,' Margaret said, holding up a glass. 'Puts all those vintage wines to shame. According to legend, Pegasus struck his hoof on the ground and this spring issued forth. It's wonderful with oysters.'

'Now you're just pulling my leg,' Maryam said. She took a sip and wished you could come to visit Margaret and ask for a cup of tea. 'About all the noise around Imij. Could you do something to quieten it down?'

'I'm pulling my weight in other directions at the moment. But I've been meaning to talk to you about the High Table.'

'The what?'

Margaret explained. She had always said political donors' clubs didn't provide a significant enough return on the investment, but the High Table was different, offering monthly meetings with the Chancellor to discuss the country's economic affairs in addition to the usual dinners and receptions with the Prime Minister and other members of the Cabinet. Join the High

Table and your phone calls to Number 10 will never go unanswered, Margaret said.

'You know I don't even vote for them.' Maryam wasn't impressed with any political party, but had voted Green in the last couple of elections because Zola asked it of her. Her constituency was one of the safest of safe seats; her vote couldn't change outcomes in the world, so it might as well influence relations at home.

'No one's asking you to vote for them. That is a matter for your conscience; this is a matter for the firm.'

When she'd first met Margaret and heard things like this it had been hard to believe that someone who sounded so like her own grandfather could appear in the guise of an Englishwoman.

There was no need to ask if Margaret was a member of the High Table. She didn't have to buy influence. Maryam felt the lightest touch of the term 'nouveau riche' attach itself to her, but she shrugged it off the same way she shrugged off words such as 'migrant', with its whiff of misfortune. England taught you the subtleties of language – 'When did you arrive here?' was something you never wanted to hear; 'When did you move here?' was fine. The movers had options, the arrivers simply followed a trajectory out of a hellhole and washed up on some better shore. She was a mover and therefore not a migrant but an expat or even an émigré. Sometimes she liked to think: conqueror.

'Play this right, and there's no limit to what you can get out of it,' Margaret said. 'Between Brexit and the last round of bloodletting in the party, they've lost a great many donors – there's an enticing desperation to their fundraising efforts.'

There was a new feeling of warmth. The sun had lowered, breaking free of the clouds. Maryam tilted her face towards it and closed her eyes. The patio's scent of dwarf lilac entwined around the cigarette smell to evoke long-ago parties in her grandfather's garden – night-blooming jasmine and women's floral perfumes, everyone smoking, and always the air of intrigue: marriage alliances brokered, favours called in, introductions made, information traded. She touched her fingertip to her tongue, tasting the familiarity of it all.

*

The first two sentences were in bold, a larger font than the rest of the letter. **Your application for leave to remain has been refused. You must now leave the United Kingdom.**

Zahra read with her eyes but the sentences registered, as ever, deep in her gut. She'd been rejected for a student visa when she'd first applied for one in Karachi as an eighteen-year-old. An administrative error, quickly corrected, but when she'd read the rejection letter there was a feeling of being upended, the phrase 'rug pulled out from under your feet' revealed for the first time not as a cliché but as a true description of the feeling of flailing, falling. And the life she'd felt herself severed from when she'd read that letter hadn't even been her life – it was just an expectation of a life to come. Thereafter, she'd felt an echo of the upended feeling each time she'd had to apply for a visa extension, a new visa category, Indefinite Leave to Remain and finally citizenship itself.

Her own experience didn't begin to compare, of course, to what someone like Azam must feel, but that was precisely the point. It had felt like an extinguishing, and yet it didn't even begin to compare.

215

She glanced up at Azam. There was that hunted look already in his eyes, she'd seen it in so many of her clients when she was a barrister. Ray had texted her in the morning and said he knew it was the weekend but Azam was falling apart, could she speak to him? And so they'd met near the Finchley Road tube station at a new café that in its stylish wood interior and attractive young baristas tried to defeat the grim thoroughfare quality of the street outside but could realistically aspire only to being the least awful place to have coffee on Finchley Road.

She returned to the letter. Azam's application had been refused because his 'assault' on the man outside CCL's office made it undesirable for him to remain in the UK based on his character and conduct.

'You said –' Azam said, and stopped himself.

But she had said. She'd said it would be OK. She hadn't counted on the CCTV footage going viral or on the Home Office using that footage as grounds for refusing a man settlement based on phrasing in their guidelines that was so vague it allowed them to reject any applications they wanted to reject.

Azam tapped his finger alongside a paragraph halfway down the page. *Little weight should be given to a private life established by a person who is in the UK with precarious immigration status. Any private life in or ties to the UK have been developed with your full knowledge that you did not have permission to remain here permanently.*

'How can they write this? I've come here on a spouse visa.'

It was the standard phrasing to deny a claim to residency based on family ties, but it felt grotesque to use the words 'standard phrasing'.

'And this,' he said, jabbing at another sentence. *There is no reason your wife can't join you in Afghanistan, particularly given her ties to that country.*

'My wife's family came here as refugees. They recognised her rights as a refugee. Now they're saying there's no reason she can't live in Afghanistan?'

A barista had approached with their coffees and stood hovering awkwardly. Azam looked up and apologised, standing to take the cups from her, then sitting back down.

'But I can appeal. It says I can appeal,' he said a little while later. 'Will I win?'

'There's a good chance,' she said, choosing her words carefully. She touched her finger to the miniature potted cactus on the table, felt its tiny thorns as pinpricks. 'There are so many people who will write letters of support about your good character. Your excellent character.'

'How long will this take?' He pressed his temples to indicate the chaos the letter had already caused in his brain.

She had to tell him the truth, or at least some of it. It could take between six and twelve months to get a court date. She didn't say, even when you get a court date you might be put on the waiting list, which means your case might not get heard and you'll have to wait another six to twelve months. She didn't say, if the decision goes in your favour the Home Office could contest it and that could be another six to twelve months. Years might go by in a limbo, everything in your life contingent. Your mood will suffer, your marriage will be placed under immense strain, your ability to plan for or even imagine tomorrow will disappear. You might decide to get on a plane and return to Afghanistan, which is probably the whole point of – or at least a welcome corollary to – this drawn-out torture, but if you do that you'll be barred from returning to the UK, even for a visit, for at least ten years.

'Six to twelve months?' He looked at her as though unsure she really knew how the law worked in England. 'And in the meantime, what? I'm supposed to go to work, come home to my wife, meet my mates and live my life as if everything's normal?'

'You can't work, Azam. You're not allowed to work any more.'

He leaned back in his chair, his hands over his face. His wife couldn't afford the mortgage repayments without his contribution; his brother would have to drop out of medical school in Kabul.

She looked away. Two near-empty 13 buses trundled past outside. The day was warm already, and much warmer on this shadeless street than it would be on the adjacent Fitzjohns Avenue, tree-lined and red-bricked. London and all its diverging lines.

He had applied only a few weeks ago. The average waiting time for an ILR application was six months. The number of times she'd heard of someone with a faultless record being refused residency because of a single punch following on from a racist attack was zero. Someone in the Home Office had been very keen to deliver this blow. She wondered if Azam or she were the intended recipient.

Zahra took off her reading glasses, set them to one side. She'd get him the best lawyer for his appeal, of course. Beyond that, she'd speak to Azam's MP, one of the good ones, who would raise the matter with the Home Office. Perhaps a rally outside Parliament on his behalf. Everyone knew him as the man who tackled the racist. Tens of thousands, maybe more, would turn up at the rally. They'd hold up placards, they'd chant their chants. They'd cheer her when she stepped up to speak on a makeshift stage at Parliament Square, watched over by the statues of Disraeli and Churchill and, since the previous year, Millicent Fawcett, her presence there usually an uplifting reminder of all that could be fought for and achieved. But – Zahra considered her cup of coffee, didn't have the will to lift it to her lips – she wasn't sure she knew how to win any more. The tens of thousands, maybe more, who showed up at rallies had less and less the air of people determined to bend the arc of history towards justice these days, and more and more that of those in need of a support group. History's losers, for the foreseeable future.

She looked at the letter again. The words blurred on the page, all except the first two sentences. **Your application for leave to remain has been refused. You must now leave the United Kingdom.**

*

Maryam walked up the gravelled path of a Chelsea mansion in a floor-length, scoop-necked black dress and black fitted bolero jacket with beaded collar. A door opened on her approach, and a maid in a pinafore offered a tray of champagne flutes. She took one and followed the sweep of the butler's hand into the next room, where another butler was waiting to show her the doorway leading into the garden. On her way out she glimpsed a Matisse, a Miró, and a sketch that might be a Van Gogh.

She stepped into the garden, into the noise of men taking pleasure in being alpha dogs among alpha dogs. White men in black tie on a London evening, their shadows long. It could be a movie scene from any era – except this one, you'd think, but you'd be wrong.

There were two other women present. One was the lady of the house, whose husband was chief executive of an oil and gas company; she was the only plus one allowed into this gathering. The other woman was married to a Russian oligarch with close enough ties to the Kremlin that his name wouldn't look good on a list of the party's top donors, though his last name was so distinctive that the wife who shared it was hardly much of a camouflage. People bothered less and less with veneers these days.

Oh, and there was a third woman. The Valkyrie. She smiled at Maryam with one of those 'hello the sister-hood' smiles. Maryam responded with a vague look that said she believed the smile was for someone else. There were schoolyard rules about the enemies of your friends. She walked towards the newly minted Chancellor, whom she knew a little from a lunch with Margaret at the Athenaeum two governments ago, when he was Business Secretary and there were rumblings about an anti-monopoly bill aimed at Venture. He'd assured them he was on their side, but both she and Margaret noticed that he insisted on ordering wine by the glass and then drank enough to fill a bottle and a half – that said everything they needed to know about his reliabil-ity. Layla had later said *I could have told you all you needed to know about him* in that way she had of claim-ing authority about everyone of Nigerian heritage. On spotting Maryam now, he cried out 'Olé' and it took her a moment to make the connection to her bolero jacket.

'We were all delighted to see you on the guest list,' he said. 'We're trying to beef up our community outreach. Thought you might want to get involved.'

'Only so far as to tell you that it might be best to avoid the phrase "beef up" if dealing with Hindus and Buddhists.'

'That's very funny,' he said. She remembered previously noticing that he told you something was funny rather than laughing. He looked past her at someone else, his face making exaggerated expressions of delight. A moment later, he started to speak to whoever the person was, quite literally over her head. She moved away with as much grace as was possible in the direction of a man she didn't recognise who was waving hello to her.

He'd been at Wharton with Babar. She'd met him with Babar in New York at the 21 Club – he'd recommended she order the burger. She remembered the burger, not the man, but was quickly stuck in a conversation about girls' schools in London. He was moving to London with his family over the summer – taking over the European division of his family's construction empire – and had flown out from New York for this party; he'd joined the High Table before finding himself either a place to live or a school for his children.

She finished her champagne quickly so she could look around for a top-up and complain about the poor service, leaving him no option but to offer to find her another glass. Once he was gone, she was able to survey the garden. There was a particularly large cluster of men near the tulips; that would be the Prime Minister. She didn't know him at all, but her impression of him was confirmed when she moved closer and saw that he was appearing to listen intently to what was being said to him, arms crossed over his body, head bent down – but the bent head was only so that the men around him couldn't see his eyes scanning the garden for new entrants. The eyes arrived at her breasts, stopped, looked up.

'Fuck off,' she muttered to herself, then raised her empty champagne flute in his direction.

He was by her side in a matter of seconds. 'Maryam Khan,' he said, unexpectedly. 'I've been waiting for you.' There was the flirtatious smile, the hand on her arm. *Don't tell me dressing so straight isn't a deliberate choice*, Layla had said when she'd complained about this sort of thing one time too often.

'Are we about to have a conversation about community outreach?' she said, leaning sideways to place her empty champagne flute on a table, which allowed her to move away without seeming to want to move away.

No, they were not. The Prime Minister had grander ideas for how a woman with the last name Khan could be used to repair the party's image internationally, frayed around the edges as it was. He was launching a 'Britain's Open for Business' campaign to send a message to the world that the UK was a wonderful place to bring investments and ideas, the doors were wide open no matter where you came from. There'd been too much scaremongering about a future unshackled from Europe, he said; it was time to showcase the diverse potential of the nation. Someone like Maryam would be perfect as one of the faces of the campaign.

'Brown outside, made of banknotes inside?'

'I didn't think we said that sort of thing.'

'We prefer saying that sort of thing to hearing the code-word "diverse".'

He laughed, a real laugh. She often ended up warming to the awful ones at work gatherings dressed up as social affairs. And they liked her. *If they were all like you* was a phrase she was as familiar with as *And which lucky man brought you along tonight?* You could hold that against them, or you could find the jester, the charmer, the family man, the lost boy inside. It helped. You had to do whatever helped to get through these evenings.

'So you'll do it?' he said.

'I can't possibly,' she said. 'I'm the chair of Imij, and apparently your government is intent on taking measures against it. How would it look if I'm representing your government and being slapped down by it at the same time?'

'Ah, a conundrum.'

'Here's a further conundrum. We're having conversations at my firm. My partners both want to move out of Britain, given the economic uncertainty here. I'm the only one making a case for staying, but this sabre-rattling against Imij isn't helping me win the argument. Incidentally, we've just had a final close on our latest fund; we've raised £600 million for British start-ups. But I can't be a face of a "Britain's Open for Business" campaign if I'm also moving my company out of the country, can I?'

He dug his hands in his pockets and hunched down slightly so his face was closer to hers. 'You are magnificent, aren't you? All right, I'm not calling your bluff. We'll bury the Imij thing.'

'Or you might say something complimentary about how the company has quickly moved to improve our anti-abuse terms and penalties, making any government intervention unnecessary. Have you thought of signing up yourself? You're on other social media platforms, but we have a wider demographic, and you really want to work on younger voters, don't you?'

'I think this is the beginning of a beautiful friendship,' the Prime Minister said, his hand on her again. His thumb stroked the underside of her arm. 'Perhaps we should set up a private meeting to discuss areas of mutual interest.'

'Margaret Wright said we'd get on,' she said.

'Margaret is always right about everything.' He smiled and withdrew his hand. Margaret was friends with his mother-in-law. 'Now if you'll excuse me, I can't possibly spend too much time standing and talking to someone I actually want to talk to. That isn't in the job description.' A wink, and he was gone.

'Impressive.' Babar's friend was standing nearby, holding two flutes of champagne. He handed one to her, and clinked rims. She felt drunk already. How easy it all was once you were in this circle, how lightly everything could be done. Billion-dollar deals saved in a tone of banter. The classic elegance of a game unchanged across nations and centuries. She took a long sip. New possibilities slipped through her veins, drop by golden drop.

*

Late-afternoon light fell on the olive tree on the balcony and slanted into the living room, dappling the wooden floor with leaf shapes. She could still see the Khan family as they had been, spread out across the room – Maryam's father in the armchair, working his way through *The Times* crossword; her mother on her knees by the teak coffee table examining fabric swatches for the redecoration of one of the run-down properties that she would sell at an enormous profit; her sisters lounging at opposite ends of the sofa, looking at magazines, then laptop screens, then smartphones as the years went by. Maryam stood in the doorway, observing how they could share a space and be separate in it. In a moment she would walk in, and a ripple of disruption would accompany her.

'Feeling nostalgic?' Zahra said, and Maryam shook her head and stepped into the room, empty now, the armchair and sofa long ago donated to charity during one of her mother's bouts of remodelling, the coffee table claimed by her youngest sister for her home in Dubai. Only the olive tree remained – the new owners had said they'd like to keep it, along with the cabinet that had once displayed the Gardner collection, now packed up and on its way in a container to Karachi.

'I never liked this flat,' Maryam said. 'Did I ever tell you that?'

'Because it wasn't the house in Old Clifton,' Zahra said, meaning there had never been a need to tell her.

This had never been home. Only Zahra came close to understanding that moving to London all those years ago had felt like leaving herself behind. Maryam had swiftly won over the popular girls at her new school, did well academically, wasn't exactly unhappy. But there was always this knowledge that she couldn't be known, not really. All her subtexts and shadows left behind; each summer she'd fly back to Karachi to return to them, return to herself.

All that was long ago, before Layla had come along and shown her how one person could step into your life and see you more deeply than you'd ever believed possible. But still there had persisted this knowledge of the thinness of her relationship to this country. 'Home' had once been a city of millions, then it had shrunk to the size of a house in Primrose Hill. But in the last few weeks she'd felt herself expanding out into England, occupying new kinds of spaces in it. She'd thought the word 'home-coming' as she stood in that garden in Chelsea.

'It's so strange without them. Layla thinks I feel abandoned.'

'You were never theirs to abandon.'

'That's what I said. Layla's just worried I'm going to feel abandoned when she leaves.'

'Convince her you will, and she'll stay.'

'Get behind me, Lucifer.' Layla would stay for love of her, and so for love of Layla she had to make it feel all right to go. And Zola was so excited about going to school with her big cousins.

'So, not abandoned but . . . ?' Zahra rubbed her thumb in an indentation in the balcony doorframe, and Maryam remembered the edge of a drinks cabinet that had caused it.

'Turns out, even if your parents are useless you still miss them when they go away.'

Maryam opened the door to the balcony and stepped out. This was a busier Kensington street than the one Margaret lived on, identical red-brick mansion blocks on either side of the road. She leaned on the balcony rail, looking down. Two elderly women were walking on the pavement below – one with steel-grey hair and a yellow jacket, the other taller, white-haired, one hand in the pocket of her red corduroy trousers. When she stumbled a little and righted herself, the hand in the pocket slipped out and there was no hand, only an empty sleeve. The yellow-jacketed woman took hold of the empty sleeve, placed it back in the pocket of the red trousers, adjusted it for jauntiness. The two women carried on walking.

Zahra and Maryam moved closer to each other.

'How different life would have been if I'd listened to you about Hammad,' Maryam said.

'What a strange thing to say.'

'Well, that's what started everything that led to London.'

'London led to Layla and Zola, so are you really still complaining about that?'

226

'Now who's saying strange things? Since when have you decided that an injustice stops being an injustice at the moment you manage to right your life again?'

'Sorry.'

'Remember the gold chains, all that macho posturing? The endless boring phone calls. God, so embarrassing. The things he used to say to me on those calls that I never told you about. He was almost eighteen, I was fourteen. And you know what we've never talked about?'

'I'm going to the loo,' Zahra said, and disappeared inside.

The two old women were almost out of sight at the end of the road, and they seemed to be deep in conversation – perhaps the older one's slight stoop came from a lifetime of bending to hear her friend's whispered secrets.

'What have we never talked about?' Zahra said, stepping back on to the balcony just as Maryam was beginning to wonder why she was taking so long.

'Why was he so keen for you to come along on the ride? Were you a treat for Jimmy?'

Zahra bunched up her fingers and caught hold of a leathery-skinned olive that had clung on to its branch through the winter months and showed no sign of letting go. The leaves flashed silver as they moved in the slight breeze. 'What would you do if you saw Hammad again?' she asked.

'I've never thought about it. I used to think a lot about what I would do if I saw Jimmy – and I did see him. Out of the corner of my eye, all the time in those years right after. But Hammad? Too pathetic to think about. All hat and no cattle, as they say in Texas.'

'How do you know what they say in Texas?'

'Episode of *Dallas*, I expect. Where else does all our deep knowledge of Texas come from?' She pointed to the railing across the road, where there was a sign she couldn't make out from this distance but knew well. POLITE NOTICE it said before going on to deliver a stern warning about bicycles being removed if they were chained there. 'I mark my deep knowledge of London as starting the day I realised how aggressive the words "polite notice" are.'

Zahra ran her palm along the wrought-iron balcony rail. 'England felt like home to me almost right away. Not because of England, but because you were here. And not just you, but this flat, with its paintings and furnishings from the Old Clifton house. I walked in here for the first time and it was Wednesday afternoons after school when my father was in the TV studio.'

'Remember, my parents wanted to take you to some fancy restaurant for dinner on your first night in London. All you wanted was a McDonald's but you thought it would be rude to say so.'

'So you took me to the High Street for a Quarter Pounder with cheese, and then we walked all round Hyde Park very fast to build up an appetite for a second dinner. It was the most exciting evening of my whole life.' She touched the brick wall behind her and Maryam realised that all afternoon she'd been imprinting her hand with different surfaces of the flat. 'One of us is feeling very sad about saying goodbye to this place, anyway.'

It was time to go. They had checked every drawer and cupboard for anything left behind and found no trace of Khan-lives. In a few seconds they would leave, and Maryam would lock the doors and put the keys through the letterbox, never to enter again.

They turned their backs to the street for one final look at the living room, so reduced with all the furniture removed. Their shadows extended across the floor, equal in length, olive leaves shivering around them.

*

Where've you disappeared?
       I think it's time for this to come to an end
Meaning?
          Don't buy that train ticket from Paris
Do I get some explanation?
           I don't want to see you
So we just keep texting?
           I don't want that either
You'll change your mind
          You really don't know me
Time will tell

The exchange brought with it a tiny bit of disappointment, nothing more.

SUMMER

Summer in London, a Pakistan–England Test match under way, and everyone from Zahra's schooldays seemed to be here, at Lord's, a number of them crowded into the Venture Further corporate box, drinking rosé and Pimm's, the men wearing linen and sometimes straw hats too, reflecting their first encounter with a certain kind of Englishness via the BBC adaptation of *Brideshead Revisited* that had done the rounds of Karachi society via pirated video in the early eighties. Some pulled off the look with the breeziness of parody, most seemed dressed for one role while reading from the script of another. The women were more varied in their attire – Zahra had on a halterneck dress that went all the way to her ankles, and Maryam wore the green trousers and white shirt that she always wore to the first day of the Test, her sole act of superstition. She had long been the fulcrum of social activity for the old schoolfriends who flew in from Karachi, Dubai and New York, timing their holidays with the Lord's Test whenever Pakistan was touring. It never ceased to amaze Zahra how much time Maryam had for even the most boorish of the people who hadn't been a regular part of her life since she was fourteen. She extended endless generosity to anyone from the golden days of her childhood who – in Maryam's words, sounding so much like Zeno – 'made an effort', even if that effort was just a text mentioning that someone was going to be in London on these dates and couldn't wait to see Maryam and oh by the way did Maryam know how to get hold of tickets for the sold-out match.

Layla was surprisingly tolerant of it all, but she drew the line at coming to watch a cricket match, so Zahra didn't have her as a buffer against the feeling of outsiderness that never went away among this particular crowd, whose parents and sometimes grandparents had all known each other, and who were fluent in unravelling how one person's second cousin was another person's aunt's sister-in-law. She leaned forward in her chair on the balcony, looking down at the green field and the men in white dotted around it. The stands were full, more white faces than brown, which you wouldn't find at any other match in an England–Pakistan series, but Lord's, with its rules of membership and its ridiculously priced tickets, remained a place apart. It was one of those slower passages of play: the fast bowlers off, no turn in the wicket, the batting pair well set but playing cautiously, mindful of the wickets that had fallen early in the day. With no cover from the midday sun, it was blazingly hot – on-field, the players' shirts clung to their backs with sweat – and most of Maryam's guests were in the air-conditioned indoors section of the box, half-watching the match on a mounted screen, half-catching up with each other. Zahra had been inside herself until a few minutes earlier, when conversation segued from whether or not potatoes were a desirable addition to biryani to the incredible stock-market performance of some company that almost everyone present seemed to have invested in, based on Maryam's advice. Zahra had a limited appetite for conversations in which victory and defeat were measured on the FTSE Index.

Babar came to sit next to her, holding out his hand for the binoculars that she'd been using to watch the bowler's grip, as her father had taught her. She passed them to him without a word, enjoying that feeling of a familiarity that placed their interactions beyond politeness, no need for 'please' or 'of course'; his knee touched hers as he swivelled his body slightly to look at the players' balcony in the Pavilion, and this was without friction or frisson. Babar was an investment banker in New York with a wife and two daughters, and though he and Zahra had seen each other only rarely in the last quarter of a century, there was a sweetly nostalgic intimacy between them, a reminder of childhood crushes and first kisses. Her first kiss at least, on the beach that moonlit night. It was the summer before uni. She hadn't wanted to arrive at Cambridge entirely inexperienced, and Babar was game for a summer romance that meant nothing and everything.

'Couldn't take any more tales of how-my-grandfather-taught-your-grandfather-to-crawl?' she said.

Babar lifted and lowered his shoulders to claim equanimity about all those things that had once bothered him. 'Came out to check you're OK. You seem a bit lost today.'

'It can feel like culture shock to move between my professional life and this lot.' She gestured behind her.

'Hmm. I think I'm "this lot" myself. Kutti!' Babar made his hand into a fist and extended his pinky finger in the schoolyard gesture for 'friendship ended', a hangdog expression on his face.

'Dosti.' Zahra tucked his finger back into its fist and tugged at the index and middle finger, extending them in the 'friendship restored' gesture.

'Phew,' Babar said. Then, 'You can't let politics get in the way of friendship.'

'Other people's lives aren't politics. And anyway, I'm sitting in the Venture Further corporate box – I'm hardly incapable of navigating differences.'

'Look at you two so cosy together.' Saba appeared, and leaned against the balcony railing, phone held up towards the upper tier of the Mound Stand.

'Who you taking pictures of?' Babar asked.

'Everyone,' she said, rotating at the hip, in one direction and then the other, an old-fashioned camera-shutter tone each time she took a photograph. 'Imij is so amazing. Zahra, what username are you hiding under? I can't find you. Ooh! Seven.'

'I'm not hiding, I'm just not there. Seven what?'

'She's tagged seven people in the stands,' Babar said. 'You don't have to be such a Luddite just because tech is Maryam's thing.'

'I'll have you know Maryam is among the chorus of voices instructing me to stay off social media sites. Don't you find this face-tagging thing a bit creepy?'

'I never opted in to it.' He whispered, 'I don't want Saba finding me in a crowded place.'

Saba made an annoying Saba sound that wanted to draw attention. Babar and Zahra ignored her. She made the sound again. Babar tapped Zahra's foot conspiratorially. They continued to ignore her, and she flounced off back inside.

'God, it's hot.' Zahra had been using the Test souvenir magazine as a fan and now opened it to its centre page and placed it, spine up, on her head as a makeshift hat.

Babar caught hold of the edges of the back and front cover of the magazine and curled them upward. 'The traditional Dutch cap is overdue for a fashion revival,' he said, and she swatted his hand away, glad to be so indifferent to looking ridiculous. Maryam's voice rose above everyone else's, and Babar smiled fondly. 'She's unstoppable, isn't she?'

'Always has been.'

'Yeah. I mean, other than you we're all profit-driven assholes in our professional lives, but I think most of us would draw the line at joining – what's it called? Head Table? Top Table?'

'High Table,' Zahra said, after a slight pause in which a rock attached to her heart plummeted, tugging hard.

A truncated gasp from the entire ground as the batsman hit a ball into the air, but it fell well out of the reach of all fielders. It gave Zahra a moment to turn and look at Maryam, unchanged, the same Maryam as always.

'How do you know about the High Table?' Zahra said.

'Guy I knew at Wharton met her at one of their gatherings. Hadn't spoken to him in about a decade, but he called to say could he have her number, she's definitely someone he needs to know when he moves to London. Apparently she pulled Imij out of trouble, got some amazing business ambassador position and fended off a pass from the Prime Minister, all in the space of about thirty seconds.' He leaned forward to watch the game more closely. It was palpable, the shift that said something was about to change; an equilibrium between batsmen and bowlers had been reached, and now someone would do something brilliant or foolish. This was one of the things cricket taught you – equilibrium was always a way station, never an end point.

'Actually, who am I kidding? None of us would draw the line at joining something like that if we could get such high returns from it.' He nudged her shoulder with his, a confidential lean-in to let her know that she could tell him truths she wouldn't otherwise admit. 'If you could write a cheque to the government and in return they'd back down on – what are you campaigning about these days? – state surveillance? – you wouldn't do it?'

'No.' She joined in the applause as a fast bowler returned to the pitch and his first delivery, though wayward, showed venom.

Babar kissed her cheek. 'None of us has changed since we were fourteen, have we? I don't know if it's depressing or reassuring.'

'Fourteen? Try eight.' It was both true, and not. Meeting schoolfriends – Babar, Saba – after a gap of many years was a constant interplay between familiarity and strangeness.

'You know I envy your friendship with Maryam. Always have.' He turned to look towards Maryam, which made Zahra turn as well. She was standing at the boundary of indoors and outdoors, one hand in a pocket, the other hand gesturing as she told a story about taking Zola to the Pakistan Embassy to get her a visa for a trip to Karachi – everyone listening was almost doubled up with laughter at Maryam's recounting of the official's refusal to issue a visa until Maryam produced a father for Zola and a marriage licence for herself; finally, of course, her father had to make a call and the High Commissioner stepped in to sort it out while pretending to have no knowledge whatsoever of the domestic situation that lay behind the problem. There was no shortage of homophobia or racism in this crowd, Zahra was certain, but it didn't touch Maryam, who viewed her own generosity as a sort of *noblesse oblige* that didn't concern itself with the thoughts or opinions of those on whom she bestowed it. It was so easy to imagine her at a High Table gathering, seducing the powerful with her absolute certainty that she belonged among them.

So letting that other bastard walk free to protect this one was all for nothing, Maryam had said when Zahra had told her about Azam. And *Do you think?* when Zahra said she couldn't shake the feeling the Home Office had done it out of spite, directed at her. Even then Zahra hadn't stopped to consider she might see Maryam on the other side of the battlefield if she looked hard enough.

The door to the box opened and Saba walked in, saying, 'Look who I found!', her tone triumphant.

On the field, the batsman struck a boundary – the first in a long while – and the ground broke into loud cheers at the same moment that Hammad entered the box. Zahra removed the magazine from her head. Hammad held up both arms victoriously, a little self-conscious, a little awkward, trying not to appear either. Someone in the box – Saba's brother – stepped forward with enthusiastic words of greeting, and Zahra looked towards Maryam, watching good manners rising like bile in her throat, forcing out the words, 'Hammad, what would you like to drink?'

'Saba said I should come and say hello,' Hammad said. 'Thought I should give you the chance to have the pleasure of throwing me out.'

'One expulsion was enough,' Maryam said, so cool it was possible only Zahra saw the burning fury beneath.

The roar of the crowd signalled an English wicket falling and everyone's attention turned to the TV to watch the replay. Babar hurried inside so he could see it too. Zahra was alone on the balcony for just a moment before Hammad saw her there and stepped out. She registered the physicality of him, not only with her eyes.

He was looking very directly at her even while placing a hand on a chair back and swinging his body over rather than moving a few paces to the side and walking down the aisle that bisected the rows of seats.

'Hello,' she said, to break the incredible tension of waiting for him to come even closer.

'Hello.' He vaulted the next rows of seats, so that there was only one bolted-in seat between them. No linen or straw hat for Hammad; he was in black jeans and a Pakistan cricket shirt from the 2017 Champions Trophy. 'I didn't cancel that train ticket after all.'

'Zahra!' Maryam called out to her. 'Come watch the replay.'

'It seems you need rescuing from me,' Hammad said. He was holding a chilled glass of rosé in his hand and he extended his arm to press it against her neck. The cold of it a sharp pleasure against her overheated skin. He grinned at her, taking in everything the halter dress revealed, unapologetic about the clarity of his intent. She felt the pleasure deepen, a reminder and foretaste of the give and take of desire, too long held at a distance from her life.

*

In the urgency of getting on to the bed, Zahra hadn't closed the slats of the blinds, and this meant there were gaps through which she could watch the willow tree, the shifting patterns of sunlight on its leaves and branches, while Hammad did what Hammad was taking a very long time to do. The foreplay had been exhilarating but too brief, and now there was this.

'Are you close?' he said.

Oh god.

She had said what felt like an eternity ago that this felt nice, but it wasn't the right angle to get her where she needed to go. He'd said, 'All my angles are right angles,' which she understood to mean this was how he liked to do it so she said fine, meaning not everyone's preferences aligned perfectly and he could do other things for her after. Now it was occurring to her that 'All my angles are right angles' was a deeply held belief.

'Very close,' she said, the response drawn from whatever part of her couldn't ever walk out of a theatre during intermission, no matter how awful the play was.

'And that's how it's done,' Hammad said, a little later, propping himself up on one elbow, an arm around her, one leg thrown over hers. The pedestal fan in the corner animated different sections of the bedroom as it rotated – a shiver in the bands of sunlight streaming through the slats, a little dance of tulips on her dressing table, a movement in the bedsheets.

Her phone pinged, not for the first time in the afternoon, with the custom tone that Zola had set so that she could always know when it was Maryam. Hammad hadn't stayed long in the Venture Further box, and Zahra had slipped out a few minutes later, at the lunch interval, when Maryam was busy handing out plates. She'd told Babar she had some work to take care of, and could he let Maryam know. Whatever she might choose to say to Maryam – about Hammad, about the High Table – would come later.

Hammad bent to kiss her breast and she thought, perhaps the next act will be better. But then he straightened again and it was clear the kiss was meant as an end-stop, not a comma.

'Should have had you get in the back seat with me,' he said.

That made no sense. In the back seat of the taxi on the way over, he'd stroked her leg, his hand electrifying through the thin fabric of her dress.

He touched the place above her hip which he'd discovered – more by accident than intuition – to be an erogenous zone. 'I should have known that day about Maryam. What she is.'

'What she is?' Zahra said, realising which back seat he actually meant, suspecting she knew what else he was talking about.

'Yeah,' he said, missing her tone. 'Tell me the truth: has she ever come on to you?'

She sat up, pulled the sheet with her, held it in place just above her breasts. 'Why was I there at all? In Jimmy's car. Why did you ask me to come along?'

'I saw the way you looked at me. I knew there was more going on with Ms Zahra Ali than you wanted to let on. So I thought, let's give her a chance to reveal the panther within.' He laughed, enormously satisfied with himself.

'So I was a treat for Jimmy? How old was he?'

'There's no need to phrase it like that.' His hand was making little circles on her thigh but her body had shut down to him now. 'You girls got lucky that we were both such good guys. The last gentlemen in Karachi.'

'How?' she said, reaching under the sheet and lifting his hand off her. 'In what universe?'

'Oh, come on.' He was the one to sit up now, looking affronted. 'If anyone should hold a grudge about that day it's me. I got expelled. It messed up my university applications. Even now there are people in Karachi who look at me funny because they think I kidnapped two schoolgirls and did all kinds of things with them that maybe they didn't want me to do. When actually the truth is—'

'The truth is, you were terrified. I don't know who scared you more, Jimmy or Maryam.' She saw that find its target, pressed on. If he wasn't going to give her one kind of pleasure she'd seek out another. 'I should have known about you that day. What you are.'

He couldn't help himself. 'And what am I?'

'An absolute waste of time.'

'Fuck you.' He was clearly attempting some kind of dramatic exit from the bed but his feet were tangled in the sheets, and for some satisfyingly long moments he looked very foolish trying to extricate himself.

'Please god, not ever again.'

He slammed not just the bedroom door but the front door too on his way out. She stood up, belted on her dressing gown, raised the blinds and opened the window to let out the smell of him, of them, astonished by her own capacity for idiocy. A new low, this one. Her proclivities had always involved some kind of subterfuge, but they'd never been this sleazy. A judge in her days as a barrister. An old-school gay rights activist who felt his reputation would be ruined if he was outed as bisexual. An MP with an awful voting record. Yes, there were – or used to be – random encounters, those nightclub bathrooms, but you never had to know anything about each other beyond the immediacy of half-clothed sex. She couldn't stop replaying his smile, the self-satisfied way he'd said *last gentlemen in Karachi*. That had crawled right under her skin, was still working its way through her. How often she'd told herself she and Maryam had got lucky that night, but to hear it from him...

Her phone pinged. She picked it up and read through all the afternoon's messages.

Sundays aren't for being at your desk, even I know that (mostly). Are you coming back?

Ugh, Hammad. Thank god he didn't stay long. What was he talking to you about?

It's fantastic carnage out here. Don't miss the highlights.

Babar said he talked to you about the High Table. Is that why you left?

Zahra put the phone on silent, pulled the sheets off the bed and took them to the washing machine. Closing the kitchen door to shut out the noise of the machine, she walked into the living room with a large mug of tea and called the only phone number in the world that she could still dial from memory.

'What a day!' her father greeted her. Sometimes she watched old snippets of *Three Slips and an Ali* online and it was always a little heartbreaking to speak to him afterwards and hear the fissures of age in his voice. 'And you were there!'

'I left at lunch,' she said. Her parents were usually in London in time for the Lord's Test, her father taking particular delight in his continuing welcome at the Media Stand despite having retired from broadcasting in 2010 when the spot-fixing scandal broke his heart. But this year they'd delayed the trip so her mother could recover fully from an ankle injury.

'At lunch?' her father said. 'But the ball had just started to reverse. Why would you leave?'

'Let me hear outside,' she said.

Her parents had long since moved from Sea View to a newer, more upscale block of flats less than a mile further along Clifton Beach. She could hear the needs-oiling sound of the window opening, letting in the outdoor world. The waves broke furiously onshore; the seagulls cried out, nocturnal like the rest of Karachi; a motorcycle gunned past, doubtless leaving its tracks on the grey sand among the plastic and other debris that had been dragged in with the fishermen's nets. The sounds of Zahra's adolescence.

'I was angry at Maryam, so I left,' she said, when her father returned to the phone.

He made a disapproving noise. She could see him clearly, in his favourite chair by the window, the nearly twenty-year-old landline phone with the endless extension cord resting on his belly. 'After you and Tom divorced, your mother and I had a conversation with Maryam. We told her that when one of us dies, the first phone call the other one makes will be to her. Do you know why?'

'Because there's no one else you'd want to break the news to me. What did Maryam say?'

'She said she'd drop everything and book two plane tickets because she wouldn't let you make the journey back alone. She also said she was insulted that it had taken the divorce for us to reach this conclusion – why had we ever thought Tom should take precedence over her in a situation like this?'

She was standing at her bookshelf, looking at a framed photograph of Maryam and herself as children standing under the gul mohar tree in the Khan garden. The exact origins of their friendship were lost in a past that stretched back beyond memory. Had they sat next to each other in those first weeks of kindergarten? Did one drop a school badge on to a hopscotch square and invite the other to play? Her earliest recollection of the two of them was Maryam kneeling down to tie Zahra's shoelaces in the schoolyard before Zahra had learnt to get her fingers or her mind around the looping knottiness of the process.

'No one's dying yet,' her father said, misunderstanding her silence.

'Do you want to know why I was angry with her?'

'No, of course not. I love that girl. So spare me the knowledge of the Patriarch's granddaughter at her worst.'

After the call ended, Zahra looked around her flat – the tree-stump side table beside the gold-and-green chaise longue, Maryam's teenaged painting of a Karachi seascape alongside a chalk-and-charcoal drawing given to Zahra by an admiring artist whose work she couldn't afford, the books all along the length of one wall. Loneliness wasn't something that was part of her experience of life – she was a woman who thought in terms of sanctuary and refuge when she stepped into the quietness of this flat at the end of a day busy with work and friends. And yet, right then, she found herself imagining a day – not soon, but eventually – when loneliness would stalk indoors and refuse to be evicted.

This particular chill breeze had brushed against her a few times before, but she'd always called Maryam as soon as she felt it. 'What you up to?' she'd say, and there'd be something in her voice that would make Maryam invite her over. She'd walk or take the C11 bus to Primrose Hill, tap in the security code to let herself unannounced into Maryam and Layla's house. There'd often be a moment when she'd pause in the reception area that overlooked the lower ground floor. From that vantage point she could smell whatever was cooking on the stove, see Maryam curled on a sofa with her tablet, reading out something amusing or informative to Layla, who moved about the kitchen, chopping and stirring, while Zola came thundering down the stairs to throw her arms around her godmother – the fourth member of her family, as she'd insisted from the time she'd been old enough to draw stick figures and a square-and-triangle house.

She didn't even have to call Maryam. She could call Layla. She could just show up, uninvited. Say nothing about her afternoon. Yell at Maryam about the High Table as though it was just the latest in a series of disagreements that at some point petered out or were brought to an end by Layla's intervention. In the worst moments, they'd left each other's company still cross, and eventually one or the other would send across a clip of George Michael singing, an act of conciliation that couldn't be denied.

Her phone vibrated with a new message from an unknown number. *This is Shaz, Azam's wife. He's been arrested for working illegally. Please help us.*

She rested her head against the wall for a long time.

*

There was so often that one batsman who seemed to be playing in a different match, on a different day, to a different set of bowlers. Majestic, in command, anticipating every turn of the ball. It had been too long since Maryam had played cricket, but she could still remember that feeling of perfect stillness in passages of play when time moved differently for you than for the rest of the world. But no matter how the gods favoured you, when you ran out of partners to bat with it was time to walk off the pitch. Did any other sport allow for the glory of the individual and the necessity of partnership as cricket did?

'When did you turn so philosophical?' Babar said, walking with Maryam across the Nursery Ground of

Lord's. The match had ended a while ago, and the celebratory drinking was carrying on in the Venture Further box, but Maryam was ready to go home and Babar was coming with her. Babar's younger daughter and Zola were passionate friends, though they'd only ever spent a few weeks in each other's company. Theirs was a friendship that largely existed on screens, and it had made Babar a regular fixture in Maryam's household as a background figure waving hello or commenting on some overheard exchange between the two girls. Sometimes he and Maryam would text each other while listening in. Babar: *We were so clueless at their age!* Maryam: *They're clueless too, they just have so many more things to be clueless about.*

'Well played,' said a man with a face red from sun and alcohol, standing up unsteadily from a picnic blanket on the Nursery Ground to extend his hand towards Babar. Maryam was accustomed at Lord's to being treated as though she were just some man's companion, and willing to accept the moment for its graciousness.

'Luck of the toss,' Babar said, shaking the man's hand. 'Anderson would have destroyed us if we'd been batting today.'

'When did you turn into a man of such perfect manners?' Maryam said, looping her arm through Babar's as they wandered on towards the North Gate. 'You were a total hooligan of a boy.'

'But I was always nice beneath it.'

'That's true. For years I hoped you and Zahra would get together again.'

'I don't think I would have handled the brilliance of Zahra any better than poor Tom did.'

'Poor Tom.' She could think fondly of him now that his inadequacy had removed itself from Zahra's life.

Maryam had seen from the start how much of that relationship had been based on a 24-year-old's near-worship of a forty-year-old man, cultured and successful. In the early days, there was rarely a sentence out of Zahra's mouth that didn't start with 'Tom says', but it was always going to be a matter of time before she outgrew him in every way. In truth, the relationship only kept going as long as it did from an excess of the politeness that replaced the early passion; no one wanted to be the one to leave, so they had to wait until Tom was offered a job in New York, which he took so that Zahra could say, 'I think it makes sense for me to stay here,' and both parties were then equally responsible.

'I'm sorry I mentioned the High Table. It didn't occur to me I might know something about your life that Zahra didn't.'

'Stop apologising,' Maryam said. 'It'll be fine. She and Layla will gang up on me next time we're together, and I'll accept all blame, which is the easiest way to end an argument. Yes, you're right, I'm a morally bankrupt person. What do they say then? They're the ones who choose to love a morally bankrupt person.'

At least I'm a grown-up, she wanted to say to Zahra. It was absurd that her best friend should walk out because she didn't like what Maryam did with her money. And on a day when Hammad had re-entered their life. Zahra was the only person she wanted to speak to about how enraging it had felt to have him in her company's box, strutting in with the same swagger that had half-impressed her fourteen-year-old self before she'd seen it for the performance that it was.

'Tell Zahra you're coming to mine for dinner,' she said, exiting Lord's. 'Ask her to join us there. You can witness the ganging up.'

There was a little gap in the heavy traffic on Wellington Road. 'Run!' called Maryam, and they scampered between cars, a pair of hooligans again, waving at the drivers who thumped on horns or yelled something rude out of the windows.

But when they were on the other side, Zahra had written back to say she was already on her way to Chinatown to meet Rose. Rose, whom she saw five days a week at work. What was the need to meet Rose on a Sunday?

Babar laughed. 'We really haven't changed since we were eight.'

When they were eight, best-friendship took up such a vast expanse in their lives. Now, all the space Zahra filled in the world, more of it each year, meant there was less and less of her life for old friends. There was a time when Zahra would spend several evenings a week and most of the weekend with Maryam and, later, Maryam and Layla. Now the Sunday walks – which they'd had to skip today – were a ritual they'd put in place so weeks wouldn't go by without them seeing each other. It was Zahra's hectic life that created the long gaps. Some conference in Brussels, some keynote speech, some gala, some reception, some dinner party with people who all had very long Wikipedia entries. Those places in her mind that the very young Zahra used to go where Maryam could never follow had become real places populated with real people. It had never seriously bothered Maryam, her own life so full. Best-friendship wasn't a vast expanse of time any more; it was being there when it mattered.

But now Hammad had stepped back into their lives and Zahra had walked away and gone to dinner with Rose. How was she to make sense of that?

*

Some kinds of aches disappeared over time, others took up residence. The death of George Michael belonged to the second category, as became clearer each time the eighties playlist sent his voice through the bedroom speakers with a clarity that the CD player of Maryam's adolescence never had. It wasn't just 'Careless Whisper' with its tones of lament but even the frothiness of 'Club Tropicana' that could send her into a tailspin of sorrow.

Maryam sighed, propped up on her pillows. Every other room in the house was teeming with colour and artwork, but the bedroom was greys and white, free of adornment. Lit now by the soft glow of two bedside lamps. The inner sanctum.

'Do the man's memory a favour and listen to the later music,' Layla said, her voice muffled by the shirt she was pulling off, her torso emerging with its slightly thickening waist. One of the surprises of love had been the way it shaped itself around all the signs of ageing; the Maryam of twenty years ago, enraptured by Layla's physical beauty, would have expected to feel some disappointment about the work of time and gravity. But here Layla was, naked and walking towards the shower, not as breathstoppingly perfect as she'd once been, but lovelier than ever.

She opened the message app, held her phone near the speaker and sent Zahra a few seconds of 'Club Tropicana', even though she thought Zahra should be the one doing the apologising for her disappearing act. Then she returned to attacking the day's emails.

'So,' Layla said, emerging from the bathroom, still naked, bringing a scent of citrus with her. 'Zahra found out?'

Layla never said *I told you so*. She just stated facts that would never have come into being if Maryam had listened to her.

'If I told her, that would be saying it's a thing. I don't think it's a thing.' Connor had put it beautifully. Don't complicate matters by thinking of them as the government. They're part of our investment portfolio. We invest in them, we get returns on the investment.

The returns had been magnificent so far. *I'm delighted with how quickly and effectively Imij responded to recent events with an overhaul of their policies towards abuse. This is the spirit of democracy. The users complained, the company changed. There's no need for government to go wading in like a nursemaid determined to strap life jackets on Olympic swimmers.* That video statement had been the Prime Minister's first post on his Imij account. The girl, Tahera, and her father had disappeared completely from the news. The paperwork for the buyout had just been approved by both sides' lawyers.

She pulled back the sheet so Layla could slip beneath it, but Layla remained standing beside the bed, hands on her hips, looking disconcertingly as she did when she knew Zola had done something wrong and was waiting for Zola to realise she knew it.

'You were scared of telling her.'

'Don't be ridiculous. You threw me out of this bedroom for three whole nights when I told you. What could Zahra do that's any worse?'

Layla got into bed but lay down near the edge, as much distance between them as was possible on a queen-size mattress. 'You know I'll throw you out to make myself feel I'm taking a stand, and then I'll let you back in. But you also have to know this isn't your usual profits-before-ethics run-in with Zahra. This government is everything she's spent her professional life fighting.' She picked up the vitamin D bottle from

252

her bedside table, shook two tablets on to her palm, and handed one to Maryam. 'Things like justice and democracy really do matter to her. It's odd how you understand everything about her except that.'

'It's called a Daddy Complex. See, I understand better than you do.' Maryam lifted up the glass on her bedside to show Layla it was empty and put it down, tablet still in her palm. 'But this isn't about that. She acts as if they personally aimed a shit missile into her office from Number 10.'

'Not without reason.'

'She calls them dictators and gets upset when they mind. Am I supposed to let fourteen billion dollars slip away because Zahra's decided to take the government personally? One of us is a professional. Are you really not giving me any of your water?'

'You're sounding very defensive.' Layla finally handed over her glass. 'Keep it. Did Babar also tell her you're soon going to be representing the government with this "Britain's Open for Business" thing?'

'I'm going to be representing the nation.'

'Also, why Bob?'

'Who?'

'Britain's Open for Business. BOB.'

Maryam slid closer to Layla, nudged her with her hip. 'Funny lady.'

'You're going to push me off the bed.'

'I'll catch you if you fall. Always.'

'I know. You think that's all that matters to the people who love you, but it isn't.'

'I can do other things that matter too,' Maryam said, hand on Layla's shower-warm skin.

'Don't push your luck, mate.' Layla turned on to one side and switched off her lamp.

Maryam moved back to her side of the bed and picked up her phone. Zahra had seen her George Michael message, but she hadn't responded.

Soon Layla was asleep, her breath deep and even. Maryam composed a few more emails and checked her messages again. Zahra was online. Still no response.

'Honestly,' she said out loud before turning off her bedside light and wrapping herself around Layla. Who else was she going to talk to about the awfulness of Hammad? Why was Zahra being so irritating?

*

Monday morning and the pedestal fan in Zahra's office was at its highest setting. The ruffling of paper edges around makeshift paperweights formed a soundtrack, not quite white noise but entirely unintrusive for some-one who had grown up with the whirring of fans. Zahra ran her finger down a pile of greeting cards, counting. The cards had been on her desk since yesterday, wait-ing for Zahra to append her signature, and in all too many cases a personalised note, to the preprinted words of thanks for those who'd come to CCL's annual fund-raiser. This duty used to fall to the chair of the board, but a couple of years ago he'd said people wanted to hear from Zahra, not from a crusty old QC.

She slipped the top card off the pile. It was addressed to one of the organisation's most generous donors – a woman with a large amount of inherited wealth who made it clear she expected Zahra's presence at her summer and Christmas parties every year in exchange for her largesse. Years ago, when she was new to England, Zahra had learnt about women like this one from an impossibly sophisticated post-doc from Srinagar: *There's a certain*

*kind of English person who likes to invite people like
you and me to their parties because we can hold a glass
of wine and a conversation at the same time and then
they can feel enlightened in front of their friends without
any risk to the smooth running of the evening.* Zahra
hadn't been a wine drinker, but she took her first sip of
Merlot that same day.

Lovely, as ever, to see you, Zahra wrote. *So looking
forward to the summer party.*

She considered her unhesitating script a moment and
then added an exclamation mark, just so she could tell
herself she was being ironic rather than insincere.

That was about as much as she could manage for now.
She edged the card into its new position at the bottom
of the pile, lifting off the paperweight to aid the process.
The paperweight was a framed photograph that had
accompanied her from desk to desk all through her
working life. It was an old 3x5, colours faded, showing
a Hitachi television set, all bulk, the handwritten lettering on the screen assuring viewers that normal service
would soon resume. Her talisman, a counter-argument
to all brooding over defeat.

She pulled her keyboard closer and went looking for
information about the High Table. There was very little
out there. She widened it to all donors' clubs linked to
the ruling party. That produced a wealth of news articles – cash for access, cash for honours, arms dealers,
the financial industry, Russian oligarchs, government
contracts, tax breaks, secrecy, behind-the-scenes lobby-
ing. 'No links can be proved between the donations
and any government policy' – naturally, that was the
whole point.

No links can be proved between the migrant's
connection to Zahra Ali and the denial of his residency

application. Now that Azam had been detained for working illegally, the most Zahra could do was help get him home to his wife for whatever time remained to them in London. He would almost certainly lose his appeal against the Home Office.

Zahra searched for 'donors' clubs venture capitalists'. She knew she was trying to build a case, but her brain refused to glide shark-like through the material in its accustomed way; instead, a buzzing in her head, hornets, all noise and sting. A bruise on her right shoulder where he'd gripped her as she lay beneath him; she could feel it when she leaned back in her chair.

She was grateful for the distraction when Ray called from reception to say there were two men here to see her, a Mr Najam Hussain and his friend, they said they knew her from Karachi. She had no idea who that was, but usually when people arrived from Karachi saying they knew her it was someone in need of legal help who had a connection with one of her parents, even if the connection was as tentative as a second cousin who had once worked at her mother's school. They almost always had an immigration issue that required a lawyer, but once her parents' names were invoked she had no option but to give them tea and make small talk for a while and send an email or text to the lawyer she was recommending to say Mr or Ms So and So was known to her family. She had initially resented these social obligations in her own days as an immigration lawyer, but the longer you worked with migrants, the more you appreciated informal networks.

'Send them in and ask them how they take their tea,' she said.

Later it occurred to her that the knock on her door should have warned her, presumptuous in its volume and duration. In walked Hammad, with his self-satisfied smile, followed by a second man, markedly different in his manner.

'Hey,' Hammad said, sitting down without waiting to be asked.

The door was ajar and she saw Rose walk past, glancing in as she went. When they'd had dinner together the previous night, Zahra hadn't mentioned any of the events of the day. She'd been too embarrassed by her own poor judgement – the thought encompassed both Hammad and Maryam.

'I have a meeting in five minutes.'

Hammad held out a hand towards the other man, still standing. 'I was having dinner with my friend here last night and he mentioned some legal concerns. I said, I have someone who'll help you.'

'I think you may be confusing me with a solicitor,' she said, determined not to rise to the bait of *I have someone*. 'This is the Centre for Civil Liberties. I'm the Director here.'

'Hammad, let's go,' the other man said. 'I'm sorry, madam, for the trouble.'

He was clutching a briefcase to his chest and his arms were held close to his body. He was wearing a jacket that was much too hot for the London weather, and sweat patches showed at his underarms. He was in his early fifties, she guessed, with thick salt-and-pepper hair and a neatly clipped moustache set in a slim face. Such a Karachi face. The way he was holding the briefcase told her he had important documents in there, and his whole future depended on their safekeeping.

She invited him to take a seat, in her most formal Urdu. 'Tashreef laeeay' – not a phrase that had come out of her mouth in a while, but it seemed necessary to speak to him with an elevated tone of respect to make up for the fact that he had brought the scent of sweat into the office and they both knew it.

'I'm aware it's very stressful dealing with legal issues,' she said, wanting him to know that she didn't hold Hammad against him, she could recognise a man in genuine need.

'Thank you,' the man said. 'Yes, it is.'

Hammad leaned back in his chair, smiling broadly. 'Isn't this a wonderful reunion?'

Zahra and the man looked at each other, and then at Hammad and then at each other, cartoon-like in their synchronised movements.

'Jimmy?' she said.

The man turned to Hammad, one finger pointing at Zahra. 'This is that one?' he said. In that moment, his bony finger pointed at her, she saw him. The man who had rested his finger on her cheek, lightly, because he knew that was all he needed to do to make her obey.

Hammad clapped his hands together, an impresario delighted by what he'd choreographed. 'The two of you! Your faces right now.'

'You brought me here as some kind of joke?' the man – Jimmy, it was Jimmy – said to Hammad.

Hammad shrugged. 'Doesn't feel so nice when you're the one with no control of the situation, does it?'

'You need to leave my office,' Zahra said. Beneath the desk she was gripping her leg.

'You were so much more welcoming yesterday.'

'I'd be happy, delighted, to have Ray at reception throw you out. He used to be a professional boxer.'

'I have a train to catch anyway,' Hammad said, standing up. 'Let's do this again next time I'm back.'

He sauntered out without a glance at Jimmy, who continued to sit in his chair, briefcase still clutched to his chest.

'I didn't know,' he said. 'I saw him yesterday for the first time since that night. Should I also . . . ?' He pointed to the door.

'I'll get us some tea.' Zahra stood up, against his protestations, and walked out of the office, shutting the door behind her. She had no intention of leaning against the wall, breathing deeply, but there she was, doing it, and it seemed the only thing she could do in that moment.

'What's wrong?' Alex, no longer an intern, was walking towards her with three mugs of tea in hand.

Zahra straightened. Rose was down the hall, Ray at the reception desk, Alex standing here looking at her with an expression that said if there was any problem she'd personally drive a stake through its heart. She took two of the mugs, smiled reassuringly at Alex, and walked back into the office, leaving the door wide open.

Jimmy was standing up. 'I thought maybe you were sending the receptionist in to deal with me,' he said, making his hand into a fist and swinging. 'I wouldn't have blamed you.'

She set the tea down on the desk and returned to her chair.

'Thirty years later, and he's still angry with me,' Jimmy said, sitting down, his tone wondering. 'When he got in touch I was so happy – I thought, finally we're old enough that we just remember the good times together.' His smile ingratiating, as if she was part of the good times and he was grateful to her for it.

'What is it you needed?'

259

'You're Habib Ali's daughter,' he said. 'I should have worked it out earlier. I see you on TV, you know, but I never made the connection. So many Alis in the world.' She couldn't quite pin down his manner – his tone was polite, but there was something unpleasant in it, an overfamiliarity. He had placed his briefcase on the floor and was taking up more space in the chair. 'I was such a fan of your father. When I saw him outside your flat that day, when I dropped you home, I felt so bad I had treated Habib Ali's daughter that way. I thought you were just, you know, one of those rich girls. Like that friend of yours.'

He said it as if they shared some understanding about Maryam, the kind of girl she was.

'What was in that bag? The one you picked up from the man near the port.'

He frowned and made a gesture – palms facing upward, wrists turning, fingers curled. The 'who knows?' gesture that said it was just another evening in his life, he couldn't be expected to remember the details of it. 'I would never behave that way today. I want you to know that. Back then, I didn't know how to be with girls.' A subtext she might have imagined to let her know that now he very much did know how to be with girls. 'I didn't know how to say, "Hello, my name is Jimmy, can I take you for a drive?"'

She edged a mug of tea closer to him. 'If you'd said that, I would have answered no.'

'That was your right,' he said, a little too quickly, as if it were a line he'd prepared when she'd left the room and had been waiting to find a place for in the conversation. He sipped the tea, she did the same. Neat soundless sips, both of them. Those hairy knuckles gripping the handle, the lips no longer chapped.

Over the years when some comment of Maryam's had forced her to think of Jimmy, she'd seen his shiny shirt, the thin finger he'd placed on her cheek, the mullet she hadn't then known to describe as such. His face had been lost to her, she'd thought, but it hadn't, all along it had been squatting in some dark fold of her brain and now she could see the twentysomething so clearly in this middle-aged man.

'I'm aware of my rights.' She gestured around the office. 'It's in the job description.'

He stood up, briefcase in hand. 'I'm sorry for taking your time. Obviously you want me to go somewhere else.'

He was almost out of the building before she reached the reception area and called him back. 'You should tell me what you need and I'll let you know if we're the right people to speak to.'

'I'm applying for Indefinite Leave to Remain,' Jimmy said, stepping towards her. 'I know many people are being rejected these days. Hammad said you must have connections with the Home Office, a person in your position. Maybe you can help out a friend of his, put in a good word.'

Hammad, that absolute bastard.

She picked up a flyer from Ray's desk and proffered it to Jimmy. 'If you're concerned about your application, you should get an immigration lawyer. Here's a list.'

He took the flyer between his thumb and forefinger. A little current of energy travelled along the paper before she relinquished her hold on it.

'And if you can't afford a lawyer . . .' she said, switching into English.

His expression carried the offence of a man who had made his way up in the world, and now saw how

261

deliberately she was insulting him in a language the receptionist could understand. 'I can afford ten lawyers.'

'Oh?' she said, glancing at the sweat patches under his arms, knowing enough about the arrows of class to have gauged exactly how that one would land.

He drew his arms tighter into his body. 'Hammad said you'd be happy to help a friend of his. You know, like I said, I've seen you on TV so many times, so—' He straightened his back, shaped his features into an expression of cold authority that made it clear he loathed her, not just for the last few minutes but whenever he'd watched her on television, because of how she looked and how she spoke and the space she occupied in the world. 'And then, yesterday at dinner Hammad told me, I know her! I saw her earlier today. My god, I couldn't believe what he was telling me.' He slowed down the last few words as if recalling, very clearly and in great detail, all the things Hammad had told him. She felt an ancient shame go through her.

'Who are you to humiliate me?' Jimmy said, and the word 'you' was stressed. 'I've said I was sorry for what happened before.'

'You haven't said it, actually.'

She and Jimmy were both speaking in English now and she was aware of Ray looking between the two of them, wondering what was going on.

'I came here because I need help. I have a lawyer. He's looked at my papers. He says they're fine. How can anyone say that these days? Everywhere, people I know being told they have to leave because of some small error, some little fault. Someone with a speeding ticket, rejected. Someone whose accountant made a tax error that was quickly fixed, rejected. These lawyers don't care. They take your money and don't even look properly at your file. I came because Hammad said you would help me.'

'Everything OK?' Rose, from the hallway.

'Rose, do you have a few minutes? I know we don't usually do this, but could you be very thorough in looking through Mr Hussain's immigration file and seeing if there are any red flags? As a personal favour to me.'

For a moment she thought Jimmy would stalk out, but instead he slumped his shoulders, unable to reject the ultimate humiliation of her largesse. Then he followed Rose down the hall without looking back at Zahra.

She returned to her office and left the door wide open, to let the stench of him out. Then she took a tissue from her desk drawer, picked up the mug he'd used, and took it to the kitchenette, where she poured the contents down the sink. She squeezed an excessive amount of dish soap on to the sponge and scrubbed the mug with it. After rinsing the mug, she chucked the sponge in the bin and washed her hands thoroughly. All she could smell now was the lemony pine dishwashing liquid.

She walked quickly down the corridor to Rose's office, opened the door. Rose looked up from the file on her desk; Jimmy turned, anxious, alert for what she might say.

'Everything OK?'

'Fine,' Rose said. 'Everything looks fine so far.'

She went back to her office. The air was still sweat-tinged, Jimmified. She pressed her nose into the crook of her arm, trying to blot him out, but his presence was in her memory. In the car, when he'd rolled up the window, that cologne scent. Musky, spiced, suffocating. How terrifying it had felt to be in her body that night, her heart violent. She rested two fingers against her wrist; her pulse jumped, quick and forceful.

She picked up her phone and sent a message: *How early can you get off work today?*

*

The only remnant of Tom was Zahra's taste for unexpected furniture. Maryam lifted a glass of nimbu pani off the tree stump and settled back on the chaise longue. She had finally come to be fond of this flat, Zahra's place, though for many years it had been hard to rid it of the associations of Zahra's moving-in day – just after Christmas 2007. They'd been unpacking boxes together when Layla called from a café where she'd gone to pick up sandwiches for lunch to say they had to plug in the television, and she was so sorry, so sorry. Benazir had been assassinated.

Maryam made a gesture towards the open window, through which the trapped heat of the day was escaping, as if she could expel the memory. When Zahra had texted to ask her to leave work early – an unheard-of demand – she'd feared it was the kind of awful news that required them to be in a room together. Someone known to both of them dropping dead, a routine medical test revealing something it shouldn't – these were the kinds of events that had entered their lives, a foretaste of the decades ahead. But now that she was here, Zahra was in the shower, leaving her with the nimbu pani and her own curiosity. First the abrupt departure from Lord's and refusal to answer her texts, and now this.

'Sorry,' Zahra said, emerging in a kaftan that the length of her managed to turn into an elegant gown. 'Needed to wash off the day.' She sat down at the foot of the chaise longue, arms hugging her knees close to her chest. 'I have to tell you something about yesterday. I left with Hammad.'

'Why?'

Zahra picked at a loose thread where the fabric of the chaise longue met the frame. When she looked up, there were red blotches on both cheeks. She raised her chin, and it took a moment to work out she was indicating the bedroom door.

Maryam stood up. 'I need whisky.'

'It gives you a hangover. Try the tequila.'

Maryam walked into the kitchen, looked around, saw the wine rack filled only with wine, and walked out. Zahra pointed to the vintage travelling trunk in one corner of the living room – that was new – and Maryam opened it to find a variety of bottles, one of which she recognised as the Calvados she'd brought to flambé something at least five years ago. Longer. Zola had been a toddler, held fast in Layla's arms while Maryam set the – what was it? – aflame. She didn't really need or particularly want whisky, but she didn't know how to respond to Zahra's unexpected – and, as it sank in, grotesque – revelation, so was mimicking the kind of behaviour that people in movies brought to such moments. She lifted out the whisky, placed it back in the trunk and, with a glare that dared Zahra to say anything, reached for the tequila. Then back into the kitchen and out again with two egg cups in the shape of scalped ducklings.

'I do have shot glasses,' Zahra said.

Maryam handed her tequila in an egg cup, filled her own, and remained standing. Zahra downed the tequila in a single gulp, which Maryam hadn't seen her do since her first year at Cambridge, when she'd decided to try everything she'd never tried in Karachi.

'These are creepy,' Maryam said, looking more closely at the duckling waiting for an egg to be placed where a brain should be, only to have it smashed open. Zahra said nothing. 'It was Lord's. You were outnumbered twenty to one by men. You had to pick the sleaziest of the bunch? And how, when? You spoke to him for maybe two minutes before he left.'

Zahra placed the egg cup on the floor, the base precisely covering a knot in the wood. 'He's the guy I was texting in the spring.'

'What?'

'I stopped it because I knew how betrayed you'd feel. But yesterday, well, I felt betrayed by you, so—' She made a gesture with her palms of scales evening out.

'Am I going to be lectured at about the High Table?' Maryam's voice had never been this sharp with her best friend, but the possibility that Zahra was about to vault from such shaky ground on to a moral high horse was maddening.

Zahra shook her head, her expression strange. There was shame in there but something else too. 'What did he do to you?' Maryam said, all her anger swinging towards Hammad.

'Nothing. Nothing like that.' A little smile. 'He really was all hat and no cattle. And not very happy about having that pointed out to him.'

There was some satisfaction in that. 'Well, I can't say I'm surprised or sorry.' Maryam looked again at the bedroom door, looked away. 'Please say you're done with him.'

Zahra still had that strange expression. 'I didn't ever want to see him again. But he came by my office today. With Jimmy.'

'*Jimmy* Jimmy? What? In London?' Maryam felt a little stupid, a little sluggish, as she sat down on the chaise longue. 'What did he want? Why did you even let the two of them in?'

'I didn't know it was them. Some Najam Hussain from Karachi turned up with a friend, saying he knew me. Then in walked those two.' She made a face to express the unbelievability of it all. 'Jimmy didn't know who I was at first, any more than I knew who he was. Hammad ... I don't know. He seemed to think it was funny.'

'Small men like to feel like big men. It's not complicated.'

'The Choreographer of All Things. Yes.'

'And then?'

'Then he left, and it was Jimmy and me. And it became horrible. I don't know if I was the one who was horrible first or if he was.'

'But what did he want?'

'He's applying for ILR, and Hammad told him he had a friend who could put in a good word with the Home Office on his behalf.' She nodded at Maryam's look of disgust and then shifted into one of her Zahra faces. 'I understand his terror of being rejected. Everyone has it these days, unless they're earning six figures. But apparently he's a model citizen-to-be, our Jimmy. I asked Rose, who nosed about his application looking for any snarls. He's some kind of engineer. Moved here from the Gulf with his wife and two daughters. They're divorced now but he pays regular child support. Never even had a parking ticket. Makes charitable donations but not through any of those Islamic organisations that the government might wonder about.'

'Wait, what? He comes in – that man, after what he did – and you send him to your Head of Legal for help? Why didn't you offer him a cup of tea and biscuits while you were at it?'

'Didn't think of the biscuits.'

'Oh come on!' Maryam stood up again, swiftly, her foot hitting Zahra. Zahra cried out, clutched at her ankle, and returned the fierce, angry look Maryam was giving her.

'Why did you give him tea?'

'It's what I do when someone comes to my office. What should I have done?'

'I don't know. But not tea. Throw him out? Call the police?'

'It's no crime to walk into a person's office.'

'And what he did all those years ago? Was there no crime in that?' Maryam frowned. 'Wasn't there? If that were now, if that happened to Zola, what could you charge him with?'

Zahra sat up a little straighter, abstract thinking the element in which she was most at home. 'You could try false imprisonment. Maybe abduction. Certainly danger- ous driving.' Then she raised her shoulders, spread her hands apart. 'Honestly, it's as if that night belongs to a category for which I don't have the language.'

'He terrorised us. He wanted us to know what men can do to women. What's so hard about having the language for that? If your beloved legal system doesn't have the words, there's something wrong with it.'

Zahra cupped her palm against her neck. It had been a very long time since Maryam had seen that gesture of vulnerability.

'You want to know why I gave him a cup of tea? It was so that he wouldn't know he still scares me. Here.' She pointed at her stomach. 'I felt it here. That terror, when you don't know if you'll ever make it home again.'

'Oh, Za.' Maryam sat down, put her arms around her oldest, dearest friend. Zahra leaned into her, forehead pressed against Maryam's shoulder. 'I hated it, hated it.

How he made me feel. And then he looked at me in this way, it was horrible, letting me know that Hammad had told him what we did together, all the details of it, everything.'

'Bastard,' Maryam said, tightening her grip.

'But I don't even know if he really did that or if it was all in my head. Just like that night in his car – I don't know what was him, and what was me. All that shame and fear we carry around from childhood. Do you think someone like Jimmy understands any of it?'

'Why are you trying to talk yourself into saying he did nothing wrong?'

'I was awful to him, Maryam, I was mean and condescending and I wanted to humiliate him. I did humiliate him.'

'Good.'

'It's not good. He came to my office. I had no business behaving that way.'

For a rare moment, Maryam didn't know how to respond. Two men had put Zahra through hell when she was fourteen years old. The next time they met she brought one home and shagged him, she offered legal advice to the other. Sometimes Zahra felt so distant from her it was as though the forty years of friendship between them was just a lesson in the unknowability of other people.

'Why didn't you have him thrown out?'

'Because he came to my place of work needing help. We don't throw anyone out unless they're abusive or violent, and he was neither.'

Maryam pressed her tongue against the top of her mouth and held it there until she was sure she could speak without yelling. 'Does your job really not allow you to have human responses?'

'In this instance, no.'

Maryam had never heard Zahra sound more matter-of-fact. She pivoted so her back was against the wall, and Zahra did the same. They were side by side, shoulders touching, heads leaning towards each other. 'Tell me everything, from the beginning.'

Zahra told her, not in the usual crisp Zahra fashion that started at the beginning and went to the end, but in a circular way, looping back on itself, adding details, that sweaty-coat smell, it had lingered in the office even after he'd left, and did Maryam recall the smell in Jimmy's car, that cologne of his, she'd forgotten it until today, she'd forgotten so many things that now came back, Zahra peeling away from the present into the thing they'd hardly ever talked about – that night, how she'd felt, the absolute terror of it, the certainty that something awful was going to happen which she couldn't put a name to, hadn't wanted to put a name to. Yes, Maryam said, yes.

Eventually, they came to silence. Maryam rested her hand on Zahra's knee. Zahra laid her own hand on top of it. They sat like that for a while, and then Maryam refilled the egg cups with tequila and said, 'I want to see what he looks like.'

It was straightforward enough with Imij. Maryam followed Saba who followed Hammad who had only recently started following a *JimmyHussain*, whose profile picture was a man leaning against a Ferrari. How ordinary he looked, just a middle-aged man, slightly ridiculous with his thumbs-up pose beside a car that clearly wasn't his. She navigated to his page. Picture after picture of Jimmy posing with cars – Jimmy and a Porsche, Jimmy and a Lamborghini, Jimmy and a Tesla. Zahra clicked on a thumbnail image near the bottom of the screen. A grainier picture: Jimmy with a mullet, acned skin, leaning against a Suzuki FX.

It felt unreal, after all these years. FX Jimmy was different from how Maryam remembered him – shorter, so young, his smile friendly. She rubbed her thumb across her finger pads, recalling a line of grease on the car seat; she'd been worried it would get on her favourite pair of jeans.

She navigated all the way down to the bottom of his feed. There was nothing but the car photos.

'Well, he likes cars and he's improved his hairstyle,' Zahra said. 'You're not getting anything more than that.'

'I can get more.'

'Don't,' Zahra said. And then, 'Don't tell me.'

She stood up to walk to the kitchen, as if there was nothing in that sentence that needed to be explained.

'OK,' Maryam said, certain she understood.

*

'He could be a very different man today,' Layla had said, when she came home and told her about Zahra's visitors. 'Hammad sounds like the real arsehole in the situation.'

Layla believed in the improvability of human character, which made her the only real idealist Maryam knew. Zahra didn't fall into that category because Zahra didn't believe people could become better; she just thought she could change the world by the force of her arguments.

Maryam made the call standing beside her study window on the top floor of the house while Layla and Zola kicked a football around the garden in the late-June twilight. Some parts of her life had to take place far out of Layla's hearing. Golden Boy answered on the first ring, calling out Maryam's name with a possibly drug-laced enthusiasm. He was on an island in the Caribbean that he was planning to buy with money from the deal Maryam had shepherded through to its conclusion.

'But how can it be goodbye between us?' he'd said after Maryam's final Imij board meeting. She was glad to be done with the company. There would be more trouble ahead, more Taheras, more pressure on governments to impose fines and criminal charges.

She turned her back to the window so she was facing the far wall with its floor-to-ceiling Pistoletto mirror painting, two nude women dancing together in it, breasts almost grazing, the leaves from a potted ficus tree next to Maryam's desk reflecting on to them. She looked away, towards the blank white door. 'I wondered if you felt like doing me a favour?' she said, her voice dropping slightly.

'I'll give you this island if you want it,' he said. 'But only if you'll let me come and visit you here with no one but the seagulls to see us.'

She laughed, made a joke about all the staff he'd need to clean up the seagulls' mess, told him what she really wanted.

'I've been going crazy trying to work out a parting gift for you,' he shouted down the phone. Definitely drugs.

'And here it is,' she said, trying to match his tone of astonishment at how the universe was showing its favours by giving him exactly what he'd been searching for. He was so delighted by it all he didn't even ask why *JimmyHussain* was of interest to her.

After the call ended, she opened the window, rested her crossed arms on the frame, and watched the two figures at play below. The football spun towards the rosebed off Layla's foot, Zola made a diving stop just inches from the thorny stems. Layla threw herself on top of Zola and the delighted screams that followed told her exactly what Layla was doing to try to get possession of the ball. 'It's a tackle not a tickle!' Maryam called out, and they waved up to her and told her to stop being a work-bore and come and join them.

A download link arrived in her inbox. She blew down a kiss and closed the window before going to sit at her desk with its twenty-seven-inch computer screen. One hundred and seventy-eight images, seventeen videos. The subject line said *Not very popular! Doesn't get out much!*

She knew Layla was wrong about people changing, but even so she was surprised by how quickly she found the proof of it. The video was from last night. A girl, a teenager maybe, looking into a phone's camera saying, 'Look at these pervs.' She turned the camera to face a dance floor – it seemed to be a nightclub – and panned to two men standing to one side, watching a group of very young women in tiny dresses writhing against each other. They weren't saying anything, the two men, Hammad and Jimmy, just watching. Watching with those Jimmy eyes that had watched her in the rear-view mirror all through the car ride. The girl with the camera moved closer to them. 'Hey, perverts,' she yelled. Jimmy turned his back to the camera, the same skinny neck that she'd seen from the back seat, and quickly walked away. Hammad blew the girl a kiss before following. She didn't give up. No girlfear in this one, protected by the camera recording everything the men did. She plunged into the crowd, calling out 'perv, perv', until even Hammad picked up speed and followed Jimmy towards the exit. At the door Jimmy stopped and looked back at the girl as though he was regarding her from the front seat of an FX with tinted windows on Napier Road.

Maryam zoomed in and in on him until he blurred into the nothing that he'd always been. He was the dime on which her life had turned. Not even a gold coin, just a dime. This preener, this poser. He had cost her so much: Karachi, Khan Leather, her grandfather. There would be no justice for that, not in any court of law. But there were older forms of justice. An eye for an eye. She zoomed out, returning with precision his cold, unyielding gaze.

*

The first day of September, and London felt like itself again, late August's barrage of sunshine finally depleted. During the summer there had been endless barbecues in gardens, picnics in parks, al fresco dinners, even, at long last for Maryam, a swim with her daughter in the Hampstead Ladies' Pond which, on a July day of record-breaking heat, finally reached a temperature that a Pakistani body could lower itself into without feeling instantly deracinated. Not a Nigerian body, Layla had said, but in the end even she relented. Everyone had to say repeatedly how glorious it all was. A real summer! Two years in a row! But each weekend approached with a question hanging over it that was increasingly a demand: what will you do to make the most of the weather? Zahra's parents had been visiting from Karachi and her father wanted to know what you could do to make the least of the weather. And now, thank god, it was done, though Shehnaz and Habib Ali had returned home before the weather broke.

It had been cool during Zahra and Maryam's Sunday walk and lunch had been indoors, with the glass doors closed. But now it was mid-afternoon, and just warm enough for everyone to troop out to the deck for coffee, which Zola insisted she was old enough to partake in, though young enough to only want it poured over a scoop of vanilla ice cream. She was offended when Maryam told her that this was already a real dessert, called affogato, and said she didn't want it if the Italians had already thought it up. But a couple of minutes later she was spooning the melting coffee-drenched ice cream into her mouth while perched on the arm of Zahra's chair, telling her of the devastating discovery that her best friend, Mark, who had lived one street away her whole life, was moving to Highgate. When she'd told him he couldn't go, he said she was moving to Lagos for six whole months and would probably find a new best friend there.

'Let me introduce you to the difference in meaning between the words "friendship" and "propinquity",' Zahra said.

Maryam smiled and stretched out on the sofa, her feet in Layla's lap. Layla pressed her thumb against a pressure point on her sole. Zola had spent the previous night at Mark's house, and this morning Maryam had woken to Layla's mouth moving down her spine rather than the usual Zola-singing that announced it was time for breakfast.

The pressure on her sole became more insistent, a signal.

Maryam sat up on her elbows and took a sip of coffee, ignoring Woolf's plaintive look. The dog had once licked up a coffee spill and hadn't since stopped hoping for another taste. 'So there's a thing that's going to be announced soon.'

'Worrying use of passive voice,' Zahra said to Zola, who giggled, having just been introduced to this concept by her godmother.

'There's a campaign to get more investment into Britain. "Britain's Open for Business". BOB, as Layla likes to call it. And I'm one of the people chosen to front it. I'll be a Global Business Envoy.'

'This is a government campaign?' Zahra's tone was neutral, waiting for the response before taking a position.

But Zola was the one to explode when Maryam nodded. The Prime Minister was a sadistic flapjack, an absolute pimple pus-head. Here Zahra Khala was, spending her entire life trying to stop him from drowning people who were escaping from war zones. What was Mama doing getting involved with one of his campaigns? That question wasn't directed at Maryam, but at Zahra.

Zahra looked over at Maryam. After that day in her flat, she hadn't mentioned the High Table again, and Maryam hadn't mentioned Hammad. Neither of them had brought up Jimmy. Zahra gave just the tiniest shake of her head and Maryam extended the palm of her hand towards Zola to say, *Go ahead, then, destroy me.*

'Lots of very good people take government appointments,' Zahra said, wrapping her arm around Zola's waist. 'Children's welfare, the climate crisis, refugees. There are government roles for all these things.' She looked at Maryam when she said, 'The thing to focus on here is, your mama has been asked to do this because no one is better at what she does.'

Only Zahra could make her feel so grateful for a compliment, as grateful as she'd been decades ago when Zahra said she was her only real friend and everyone else was in her life because of propinquity.

'Do you know they call your mama the Czarina of Tech?' Layla said.

'Will she have to be nice to the Prime Minister?' Zola, unrelenting.

Zahra raised her hands to say, *I've done all I can.*

'You know how you're always complaining that Christobel shows off incessantly about her mother's MBE,' Layla said. 'Well, this is a much bigger deal.'

That trumped all other concerns. Zola stood up and did the rooster-walk that was her signature celebration of every goal she scored.

'Do you think the people who call Mama the Czarina of Tech know she still can't put things in the recycling bag properly?'

'Recycling is about as useful as squeezing a lemon into the ocean in the hopes of turning it to lemonade,' Maryam said, relieved that the conversation was moving on to more familiar ground. 'While you all wash out your cans and place them in blue bags, I'm doing two things. One, investing in green tech that might actually save the planet. Two, buying property in New Zealand so if tech fails and the world collapses in flood or drought we can all go and live where we're most likely to survive.'

'Afraid I'll be too busy looking after the climate refugees,' Zahra said. Zola said she'd be doing the same, and Zahra said could her generation please hurry up and take over the world.

'Don't worry, I'll chloroform you both and drag you on to the plane,' said Maryam. Zola looked relieved.

'She really will,' Layla said. 'All of us, if she has to. And Woolf too.'

The wolfhound got to her feet at mention of her name, gracefully climbed up on to the empty garden chair and curled herself into a ball.

'What?' said Zola.

'I think she's decided she's reached the stage in life when she shouldn't have to sleep on the floor any more,' Maryam said. They all laughed at the air of authority with which Woolf had done something she'd been trained out of as a puppy. The feeling of being a family settled on the four of them in the shared humour of this moment, which was constructed of so many moments that came before, stretching back years.

The conversation swerved towards the discontinuation of the number 10 bus route from Hammersmith to King's Cross, which had been such a feature of their twenties. Zola wandered into the garden, having no interest in the discussion beyond declaring that she was going to start taking buses on her own to visit Mark in Highgate. She cartwheeled her way down to Layla's studio and slipped behind it. Her secret place among the blackberry bushes; she'd liked hiding there with her teddy bears as a toddler.

Maryam closed her eyes, lying back once more. Layla and Zahra were talking about a mutual friend from Cambridge, how much she'd changed. She was boring now, a terrible thing to say about someone with no other faults. But it made them not want to meet her though she lived so nearby. And as always happened when they discussed this friend and her terrible dullness (it was nothing new, Maryam had seen it right away twenty years ago), they decided they'd have to meet her for dinner soon because it had been so long, and they didn't want her to think they were avoiding her, though oh god they so wanted to avoid her. Maryam smiled, didn't interrupt. How she loved to hear them together, these two, every timbre of their voices so known that she could see the exact expressions on their faces without looking.

'Mama,' she heard and opened her eyes to see her daughter standing above her with the palms of her hands cupped, their contents hidden. She sat up, placed her own hands beneath Zola's hands, her palm – lifeline, heart-line – against her daughter's skin. She saw Layla turn towards her, heard Zahra stop speaking mid-sentence. Zola smiled gravely at her. It was as though they all felt the same string tug through them, pulling them closer though no one moved.

Zola lifted her palms, separated them with a flourish. Blackberries fell into the hands Maryam raised as though in prayer – ripe-dark, glossy, bittersweet as summer's end.

WINTER

Maryam wondered if her £200,000 donation entitled her to play '(White Man) in Hammersmith Palais' at Chequers on the grand piano that Winston Churchill had loved. Every now and then a Layla thought invaded her brain, and this one felt particularly satisfying, though she'd never act on it – not because of propriety but because it was Layla, not Maryam, who could play the Clash on the piano. Layla who, another two weeks from now, would be in Lagos with Zola.

The Chancellor wafted up to her, his manner emollient since her Business Breakfast with tech leaders in New York had convinced the CEO of a leading internet company to keep his European headquarters in London after Brexit. In truth, the CEO had never seriously thought about moving out of London, but he'd known Maryam a long time, owed something of his early success to her investment, and was happy to overplay the significance of the breakfast to the Chancellor.

'First time at Chequers?' the Chancellor said.

'What would Churchill make of the two of us in the Great Hall?'

He didn't like that, neither the suggestion that she was his equal nor the reminder that they were both anomalies here, and did his usual thing of making eye contact over her head at someone else in the room. Maryam moved away, towards the Russian oligarch's wife whom she had befriended over the course of several High Table events. They'd discovered the pleasure of turning the country's most influential men into awkward schoolboys every time they wandered off from the rest of the pompous gatherings with the explanation 'women's matters', which covered a range of possible issues from saturated tampons to hooks that wouldn't stay fastened to an unwillingness to walk down long corridors to a loo unaccompanied. Now she hoped that invoking 'women's matters' would allow them to leave the wood-panelled Great Hall with its oppressive paintings crammed on to the walls to wander through the rest of the Prime Minister's country home. But the Prime Minister intercepted her along the way.

'Let me tell you how to detect when a man in this room can't be trusted,' he said, taking her by the elbow and leading her to a corner away from everyone else. A painting was mounted at eye level directly on to the wood panelling. A self-satisfied man looked back at them. Remarkable, how little the ruling class in England had changed over the centuries. Or perhaps power carried its particular stamp – there was nothing in the man's expression that was unknown to her from her own upbringing. 'This was painted by a lady artist and every man who wants to convince a woman of his sensitivity to the achievements of her sex brings her over and talks about it.'

He smiled; she smiled in return to show she understood the joke and thought him clever and charming.

'I should know more about art after all the years I've been with Layla. That's my partner – she's an artist.'

If anything, his hold on her elbow tightened. 'What I really want to know is how you did it.'

'It?'

'Found exactly what you needed to use against that man. Of course I also want to know why.'

'I found it the very old-fashioned way,' she said. 'I hired private investigators. How else would I have done it?'

'How else indeed?' He dropped his hand. 'You must have remarkable private investigators to find that needle in a haystack you owned until recently.'

'Yes, wasn't that a funny coincidence.'

The wife of the Russian oligarch swished up to them in her noisy silk dress with enormous sleeves, alerted by the earlobe-touching signal that Maryam had been sending her way.

'The Chancellor was talking to me about this pasty fellow,' she said, smiling at the Prime Minister. The PM's veneer dropped to reveal the ugliness of a man who can't bear any form of insult. 'Apparently the painter was a woman.'

'Oh, ha. Yes,' the Prime Minister said. He winked at Maryam, conspiratorial.

'It's lovely here,' Maryam said, moving towards the window that looked out on to the vast manicured grounds. It was far too cold, the heating set for men in black ties rather than women in cocktail dresses. 'But I'm sure you'll want to escape to the sun at some point this winter.' He was known for his fondness for holidays by the sea. She said a friend of hers had a stunning island home, which is to say he owned the entire island. She knew he'd love for the Prime Minister to stay there. She showed him some pictures on her phone. The Prime Minister said god, that looked like heaven. Conversation glided forward.

*

'Smile,' the man said, and Zahra moved her mouth into a rictus that no one could mistake for happiness.

'Call that a smile,' he said, but she continued to look at the camera with that frozen grin and deliberately deadened eyes. You took what forms of subversion you could get away with in a place like this. She'd heard about this guard from a colleague in Legal who'd recently visited the detention centre – you'll know him by the tattoo of Van Gogh surrounded by sunflowers on his arm, her colleague had said. He made everyone smile for the photographs that he slipped into lanyards for ID purposes, even people coming to say goodbye to loved ones they might never see again.

He handed her the lanyard, the vein on a bicep cutting through Van Gogh's cheek, and placed a band that said VISITOR around her wrist. She walked the few paces to the desk where she had to hand in the book she'd brought. The guard at the desk was dressed as all the others were – big black boots, black trousers and black shirt emblazoned with the logo of the private security company that ran the detention centre – but her smile was friendly, and then turned genuinely regretful as she weighed the book and said it was over the limit.

When Zahra picked the book she hadn't considered the weight limit of personal items that each detainee was allowed. *Britain's Best Bakes* tipped Azam's scales over the cut-off point.

'But only by seventy grams,' the woman said. Surely that was a figure low enough to be forgiven but, no, she reached into a desk drawer and pulled out a pair of scissors. Zahra and the guard looked at the table of contents, trying to work out what was dispensable. Scones? Buns? Fancy biscuits? In the end, Zahra cut out the introduction and soufflés and fruit cakes, and the woman bagged the book and said the detainee would get it after it had been inspected to make sure it wasn't hiding any contraband.

The December cold assailed her as she exited the structure, leaving behind its Disney murals and Christmas tree and the perverse CHECK-IN sign above its desk as though this detention centre was just another terminal of the airport beside which it had been constructed. As she crossed the car park, Zahra could see the runway through a wire fence, a British Airways aeroplane taxiing along it, taking people on holidays or business trips or to long-awaited reunions. She felt the shame of being part of that world, so unthinking about the luxury of coming and going.

She walked up to the warehouse-like building towards which she'd been directed, and used her shoulder to push open the heavy door marked VISITS. It should have been a relief to get out of the cutting wind, but indoors felt more oppressive than outdoors. There was one room after another, one guard after another, checking her visitor number, checking her lanyard, sending her through a scanner that didn't beep but still was followed by a complete pat-down. Her mouth inspected, the skin behind her ears inspected, hair lifted off her neck even though it barely covered her neck. You felt criminal simply for being here. Through another door, another door, a waiting room, another door and finally into the detention block. The door to the block opened with a high-pitched scream as though the building were an animal in fear or rage, and then the door closed and the silence within was absolute. No birdsong, no planes, nothing of life beyond this space. More doors, stairs, guards, checks and finally she was in the visitors' room with its low ceiling and one drooping potted plant. The guard at the far end instructed her to

287

sit at that table there, next to the window, although there was no one else here and no reason why she shouldn't be allowed to choose where to sit.

The window overlooked a yard. This was where the vans brought detainees it had rounded up; and this was where it filled up vans to take them to charter flights that would fly them back to the countries they had left, often fled. The door through which the detainees came and went from these vans had a sign over it saying, WE ARE ONE HAPPY FAMILY NO MATTER WHO WE ARE. What kind of mind would think to put up a sign like that? The cruelty of this place made her set aside all the usual words – *immoral, unfeeling, playing politics with people's lives* – and land instead on *evil*.

'Thank you for coming,' she heard, and looked up to see a man in a tracksuit and flip-flops. Azam, so altered. He'd lost a great deal of weight, his eyes shadowed with exhaustion, and the smile he gave her was weak, as though he was too out of practice with smiling to know how to do it properly any more.

She handed him the cup of coffee she'd bought at the vending machine outside this room, using the £5 she'd been allowed to bring through for this purpose – all her other belongings were in a locker in CHECK-IN.

He opened the lid, sniffed it luxuriously. 'Who needs a double macchiato with oat milk?' he said, and briefly he was familiar again.

'I bought you the book you asked for,' she said. 'But it was too heavy so I had to cut out soufflés and fruit cakes and . . . something else, what was it?'

'Not eclairs, I hope?'

'Azam, I'm not an animal.'

'You are an angel.' She saw him glance at her wrist and take in the bracelet he'd given her.

'I'm going to set up a bakery,' he said. 'In Kabul. They've never eaten such things. Chocolate tart with candied lemon. Fondants filled with salted caramel. I'll be a millionaire. The BBC will come to interview me. I'll say, your country sent removal vans for me – like I was a piece of old furniture.' He leaned back and closed his eyes, as if that burst of optimism had taken everything out of him.

The judge who had heard his appeal had said she would have ruled that he could stay if that one punch had been the only reason for refusal. But then he'd gone and worked illegally, leaving her no choice but to uphold the Home Office's decision. His lawyer was trying every avenue of further appeal, but Zahra had spoken to the lawyer and knew there was no real hope of reprieve.

'I'm sorry,' Azam said to her. 'I know I let you down.'

She shook her head, unable to say anything.

'All this because I was working in a kitchen for six pounds an hour. If I hadn't, I would be at the bakery right now, waiting for Mr Bose to come in for his afternoon coffee and lemon drizzle cake. Texting Ray across the road about the footie. Thinking about what the missus and I were going to do for dinner.' He raised his empty hands and lowered them, indicating the impossibility of it all now, the ordinary details of his life a miracle he'd never experience again. Zahra remembered dinners in her adolescence, passing her father a salt shaker and wondering if it would be the last time, if tomorrow someone might come to take him away.

'How long will they keep me here? I'm going mad.'

'I wish I knew,' Zahra said. There was no time limit on detention. It could be days or weeks or months. She'd heard of cases where it was years. CCL had been trying for ages to change the laws. 'Are the conditions they're keeping you in very bad?'

'Six of us in a cell. With a toilet. And no privacy. Why can't they put a screen around the toilet, why can't they do that? They want us to know we're animals to them, nothing better than animals.'

He was looking across the courtyard as he spoke, towards the two footballs stuck in the razor wire above the boundary wall. Zahra thought she knew what went on in places like this, but no one had ever mentioned the toilets without privacy. Perhaps it was a new indignity, perhaps there were so many indignities that went on here that no one could bear to list them all.

'She's going to stay here, isn't she?'

He meant his wife, Shaz. She knew Kabul only as the place her parents had risked so much to flee. Her family was in London – her parents, siblings, nephews and nieces. All her friends, every known thing in the world was here. Everything but Azam.

'She thinks I don't know. She's not going to tell me while I'm in here. People keep trying to kill themselves, sometimes they succeed.' Azam sat up, rubbed his eyes with the heel of his palm. 'I'm sorry, this isn't why I asked you to come. There was a man here. He said he knew you. He said things about you I didn't like. I almost hit him, but then I thought you don't want me hitting another person. Do you know someone called Jimmy?'

'Jimmy's here?' She looked up at the door, half-expecting him to walk through it.

'Not any more. They put him on a plane back to Pakistan. But he was saying ridiculous things about you. That you work with the Home Office to get people deported from England. He told me that you must have

290

told them to reject my application because his rejection was exactly the same reason – bad character and conduct – and he knew you were behind that.'

'That's absurd,' she said automatically. 'There must have been a specific reason for his rejection.'

'Yes, he said it was something he'd done years ago.'

She raised the heels of her boots off the floor and pressed the soles of her feet hard against the carpet to absorb the energy running quick through her. 'How many years?' her voice a little breathless.

'When he first came here. Five, six years? He didn't pay a bill. Less than ten pounds it was, and for that they threw him out of the country.'

Her relief was enormous.

'I don't work with the Home Office, Azam.'

'You don't think I believed him! I just thought you should hear about it. He said he knows who your father is and he's going to tell him what you did.'

I'll tell your father. That was all he had in his arsenal, like a flailing schoolboy who knows there's no way to fend off the punch coming at him. She almost found it in her to feel sorry for him. A £10 bill!

Azam hadn't liked Jimmy. Jimmy said anyone who tried to appeal their cases was a chutiya – Azam apologised for using the term of abuse, but that was what Jimmy had said. He said the appeal system was rigged. It would drag on for years, forcing you into some kind of crime like Azam had committed and in the meantime all your savings would go to lawyers. He said Azam was a double chutiya for sitting in here thinking his lawyer was going to find a way to get him out before the government got round to finding a chartered flight to put him on. Jimmy hadn't appealed his case, but he also hadn't bought himself a ticket back to Karachi when his leave to remain was denied. His daughters were in London, living with his ex-wife. He knew she wasn't going to send his daughters to visit him in Pakistan.

So Jimmy had ignored the notices telling him to leave the country until armed men broke down his door in the middle of the night and brought him here. Every weekend his daughters came to visit him in the detention centre. Immigration officials also came to see him. They knew he had the money to buy a plane ticket; if he did that, they would let him walk on to a PIA flight and leave respectably. But no, he wanted those weekend visits with his daughters, as many as he could get.

Zahra looked across the room. One other table was taken now. A man dressed like Azam was seated on one side, another man in a three-piece suit, very dapper, across from him. They were both in their sixties, maybe even their seventies. The first man had his arms wrapped around his body, the second man was sitting on his own hands. They were both silent, looking at each other in a way that anyone who had ever been in love would recognise. The first man's chest rose, and a long sigh left him. The second man bent his head. The first man extended his palm and caught his lover's tear, brought it to his lips.

'Seven weeks,' Azam said. 'Jimmy was here seven weeks. Could you do that?'

Could she endure seven weeks in a place like this for the sake of one visit per week with anyone? Who would that anyone even be?

'I didn't like him,' Azam said again. 'But he didn't deserve this. None of us deserve this.' It had been eleven days, and he was broken already. Seven weeks.

She turned her face away from Azam to look at the footballs impaled on wire, and then at the blue sky above;

a plane cut through the expanse, its tail fin unfamiliar. She imagined the men and women in window seats seeing England for the last time, and then she imagined the ones who kept their eyes locked straight ahead, not wanting to look at the lives lost to them forever.

*

The Christmas tree was beginning to droop, a scattering of pine needles on the floor near the glass door that led into the garden. Maryam slid Christmas ornaments off the branches, tossed the robust ones into a polar-bear-patterned backpack, handed the fragile ones to Zahra to wrap. Nusrat Fateh Ali sang about intoxication through speakers so small their power was astonishing, which was not a thing anyone had ever said about that great mountain of a singer. It was the final evening of the year. Zola and Layla had been gone three very long days. Maryam took down a wolfhound ornament, looked across the living area to Woolf, snoring on her pillow bed.

'She'll be lonely when you're in the office,' Zahra said, following the direction of her gaze.

'She's already getting so much love from the neighbours. They have a group chat set up to coordinate who'll visit her every mid-afternoon when she's used to Zola and Layla coming home from school. My dog is more popular than me.'

'There there, pup. I like you.' Zahra patted Maryam's head.

It had been years since they'd spent New Year's Eve together. Zahra was usually out with Rose and that crowd, Maryam at home with Layla and Zola and Mark and his family. But this year Zahra had started talking

293

about what they'd cook together for their New Year's meal, as if it had already been decided that it would be just the two of them. Now the scent of lamb biryani was beginning to permeate the room, a subtle under-note to the jasmine candles that were arranged all round, on counters and tables and even the floor, making it unnecessary to turn on any lights but the ones on the Christmas tree.

Zahra placed a wrapped crystal bauble back in its box, picked up her glass of red wine and sniffed at its wide bowl. She raised her eyebrows at Maryam – you didn't have to be a connoisseur to know this wasn't the usual £12 Côtes-du-Rhône that was Maryam and Layla's house wine. Probably closer to £1,000, though Maryam wasn't about to mention that. A Christmas gift from Margaret Wright, unusually lavish, in recognition of the windfall from the Imij sale. Layla had refused to drink it – the pressure of doing it justice with her appreciation was too high, she'd said.

'Jimmy's residency was refused,' Zahra said. She'd walked over to the glass sliding door, standing where Maryam couldn't see her.

'Oh?' Maryam was unwinding the loop of a cassette-tape ornament that had tangled on pine needles.

'He ended up at the same detention centre as Azam before they flew him out. He was claiming I got the Home Office to reject him.'

Maryam glanced over her shoulder at Zahra. Zahra was looking at something in the sky. It wouldn't be midnight for a while, but Londoners from all the surrounding neighbourhoods must already be gathering on Primrose Hill to get into the prime position for seeing the fireworks over the Thames. Perhaps someone had started to release sky lanterns, red on black, floating high.

'I'm not sure what's happening here,' Maryam said, tapping on her phone to turn down the volume of the music.

'Happening where?'

'Are you telling me something or asking me something?'

'What would I be asking you?'

'OK,' Maryam said, turning back to the tree.

A few moments later: 'If I were asking you something, then?'

'Then I'd tell you not to worry. I kept your name entirely out of it.'

Maryam tossed the wooden cassette tape into the bag, looked wearily at how many ornaments remained. She and Layla were always careful not to spoil Zola; her life was ridiculous enough already compared to her friends at state school – Layla's insistence, the state school – but the Christmas tree was an exception. Ten feet high, its branches laden; they'd need a stepladder to get to the top of it. Why wasn't Zahra helping?

'He was rejected over an unpaid bill. A ten pound bill.' Zahra had turned towards Maryam now, was frowning a little as if irritated by something she felt she should be able to work out, but couldn't.

'Telling or asking?'

'Asking.'

She opened the Imij app, entered *Hentucky Fried Chicken* in the search bar, clicked the 'history' option and moved the date sliders to the position she wanted. Zahra remained standing where she was, so Maryam went over to her and held the phone up so they could both watch the CCTV video that had been posted five years ago. It had been the last video in the folder Golden Boy had sent her, and she'd clicked on it drained of hope that she'd find anything she could use. A man leering at girls in a nightclub wouldn't be enough, she knew.

And then she'd seen this: a man in a Hentucky Fried Chicken-branded shirt put a rectangle of paper on a Formica-topped table, talking amiably to two customers. He walked away, and a few seconds later one of the men – Jimmy – inclined his head towards the door and the two men stood and ran out.

FREE HFC SUPER-MEAL FOR ANYONE WHO CAN IDENTIFY THESE MEN the post said.

'Engineer's salary and he won't pay for fried chicken,' Maryam said. 'Such a colossal loser.'

Zahra pressed Play and the scene repeated itself. She rubbed her hand over her face, clearly forgetting about the eyeliner she'd worn to make the evening feel festive.

'How did you find this?'

'Can't possibly say.'

'And, what? You write to the Home Office and say there's a man who appears to be running out of a restaurant without paying for fried chicken—'

'Appears to be?'

'There's no footage of the food. Maybe it was raw? He has the right to leave without paying if the food isn't up to standard.'

'Seriously?'

'I can't believe even this Home Office would think this clip is proof of anything.'

Zahra sounded a little peevish, as if she thought she was the one who knew everything about how the Home Office worked, and how dare Maryam upturn her expectations. Zahra took another sip, looked outside again. Maryam looked with her. A sky lantern seemed caught in the branches of the neighbour's tree, but that was just a trick of perspective. It was beginning its descent, the moment when what was beautiful revealed itself as dangerous, an open flame at the heart of it.

'You went through the High Table.' Zahra's voice soft, almost as if she was speaking to herself.

'I may have asked some people to make sure this was directed to the right officials at the Home Office.' *It's very good of you to convey this important information about someone seeking to settle here*, the Prime Minister's Special Adviser had said. *Of course we can't influence decisions.* The Prime Minister, standing behind the Special Adviser, had winked at Maryam.

'And you weren't planning to tell me any of this?'

'You said don't tell you.'

'I said what?'

'You said, don't tell me. In your flat. The day Jimmy came to your office.'

'I meant don't tell me what you find out about him.' She took a step back. 'Maryam, for god's sake. I didn't want to have to think about him any more. Plus, I didn't want information neither of us was entitled to know.'

Maryam rolled her eyes and walked across to the utility room to fetch the stepladder. 'It's you and me. There's no need for the pretence,' she called out on her way. She hooked the ladder on to her shoulder and carried it to the tree.

'What pretence?'

It was only then that she understood Zahra wasn't going to thank her, or even to acknowledge what she'd done for both of them, but was accusing her. That face of hers, all sanctimony and outrage.

She leaned the ladder on to the wall, walked back to Zahra. 'You haven't changed, have you? You want something to happen, and you don't want to take any responsibility for it happening, so it all shifts on to me. That was Zahra then and it's Zahra now.'

'A man was thrown out of this country,' Zahra said. 'Seven weeks in a detention centre and then put on a plane and made to leave his children.'

As if Maryam hadn't even spoken. As if what she said was nothing.

'I was thrown out of a country. And it was a lot longer than seven weeks in that prison of a boarding school.'

'I can't believe even you would make that comparison.'

'You just stood there, first with our parents and then with the headmistress – twice – listening to everyone say what a wonderful friend you are, how lucky I was to have you looking out for me, how stupid and selfish and irresponsible I was.' That got to her, Maryam could sense the internal squirm. 'And the thing is, I didn't mind. I really didn't. I knew how much it mattered to you to be seen as the responsible one. The good one. If you hadn't become Head Girl, your world would have ended. I never wanted what you did, never understood why all those stupid things were so important, but I wanted you to have everything that mattered to you.' An old question came back. 'Why did you even insist on getting in the car?'

Zahra looked away, at the world outside, at her own candlelit reflection. 'I don't know.'

'You must know. I kept trying to go back inside. I could tell Jimmy was all wrong. You hadn't the faintest idea.' A movement along the muscles of Zahra's face. 'Or did you? Oh god. Please don't tell me your proclivities started with Jimmy.'

'Not Jimmy.' She put her hand to her hair, pushed it back, tucked some strands behind her ear. 'Hammad.'

At first Maryam thought that for some reason Zahra was talking about the last few months, the recent entanglement. But the look of shame on Zahra's face made everything suddenly very clear. 'That's why you got in the car? That's why everything happened? Because you fancied my boyfriend?'

'He wasn't really.'

'You kept warning me off him. I thought that was friendship. It was the opposite of friendship.'

Zahra's fingers white on the bowl of the wine glass. It would break with the pressure if she didn't let up. 'No. I knew he was bad news. I was trying to protect you.'

Now came rage. 'Protect me? I've put everything on Jimmy. All that I lost. Jimmy's fault. Jimmy made my grandfather turn on me, Jimmy made my parents send me away. But you're the one who opened the car door. You're the one who stepped inside. I could say no to Hammad, I could say no to Jimmy. But I couldn't say no to you, not when saying no would have meant leaving you alone with them. You're the reason. You're why I lost everything.' She swept her hand in a gesture to take in *everything* and it knocked the glass out of Zahra's hand, an arc of wine leaping in the air, the glass shattering on the floor, Woolf raising her head to bark.

Maryam moved to quiet the dog, while Zahra strode briskly towards the kitchen, in search of clean-up equipment and to switch on the overhead lights so she could see all the broken glass. Maryam went from candle to candle, blowing them out, giving her time before she had to look at Zahra again. When Maryam circled back to the scene of the crime, there were sodden red pieces of paper on the floor, and Zahra's hand directed her to keep away from the area where tiny shards of crystal still glinted before pointing at the ceiling, where some of the wine had ended up. Maryam brought round the step-ladder, climbed to the top rung, and sprayed the bottle

Zahra handed to her. Wiped away the stains. The dust-pan glimmered as if piled with diamonds.

It was a little more work to triple-bag the crystal shards, throw away the paper towels, secure the rubbish bag that everything went in and place it near the bottom of the stairs so that she'd remember to take it out to the bins in the morning. All of this done in silence. Then Maryam poured wine in a tumbler, and slid it across the kitchen counter to Zahra. Walked towards the Christmas tree, and picked her own glass off the floor. They drank, looking at each other for the first time since the glass shattered, a distance of several feet between them.

'You really don't know, do you?' Zahra said. 'There's only one person who made your parents send you away. It's you, Maryam. You wanted some thug to do I don't know what to Jimmy – break his legs? Worse?'

'No! I didn't want Billoo to touch him. Like he hadn't touched us. I wanted him afraid. I wanted him to imagine all the things Billoo could do to him.'

'What kind of things? Torture? Murder? Rape? Only a monster would want someone to imagine all that. Your parents must have seen you were a monster. That's why they had to get you away from a place where you could call on a Billoo.'

Maryam pressed a hand against her stomach. 'All these years, you've carried this around. This belief that I'm a monster.'

'Did Layla ever tell you, in your early days together, when she first recognised the side of you that can snuff out a dream and call it profit, she came to me and said, *Will I lose myself completely if I allow this to continue?*'

'Keep Layla out of this conversation.' It was bright in the room with all the lights on, too bright. With the heel of her shoe she pressed down on a button and the Christmas tree went dark.

'There was a part of me that wanted to say yes. That part was Layla's friend. But then I said no. That was your friend speaking. I thought she could keep the monster quiet, maybe even send it away.'

'Don't you try and tell me you regret that. She and I are happy in ways you'll never have.' It was so easy, too easy, for each of them to draw blood; they knew all the exposed places, the armour-chinks and the softness of the belly beneath.

'At what price?' Zahra walked across to the display cabinet, lifted out the nude sculpture and held it in both hands. 'What happened to the woman who made this? She was a blaze of light when I first met her.' She put the statue down again, swivelled it around so that everything revealing was hidden from view, only the long bundled hair, the back and arms visible. 'She capitulated. That's what you made her do. That's what you did to her.' She gestured towards the Christmas tree. 'You put out her light.'

War, then. 'If I'm a monster, what does that make you? The pristine goddess who lets slip her monster to savage those who cross her.'

'Oh, come on. Are we really still pretending I wanted you to go after Jimmy?'

'Why else did you call me over and tell me all those things – Najam Hussain, applying for ILR. An engineer, arrived from the Gulf. Every identifying detail. You'd already told me about Azam, how he was being sent away because of "character and conduct". The Home Office will get rid of anyone on the flimsiest excuse, you said.'

Zahra laughed, a fake laugh, how would they ever share a joke again? 'Who else would I call over? You were the only one who was there. The only one who knew.'

'The only one who knows you. The only one who knows your subtexts. I know all the dark places that you try so hard to hide from everyone, maybe even from yourself, maybe especially from yourself. You try so hard to be a good person, Za, I've never seen anyone try anything so hard.'

'What better to try for than that?' Even now, so fucking superior.

'It shouldn't take so much trying. Look at Layla, does she try? No, it just comes to her. It's who she is – kind, generous, loving. You look at that and you call it capitulation because it's so many galaxies away from who you are that you can't even see it.'

'Stop it.'

Maryam walked closer to Zahra, advancing on her. 'You try to be good and you fail. There is always that other Zahra lurking. The one who didn't like any boys until one of them liked me. The one who made me get into that car and then stood there innocent while everyone said I was so lucky to have a friend like her. The one who never wanted love from a man when she could get lies and deception and secrecy. The one who places a halo on her own head so we can all look at its shiny glow and ...' She stalled, unable to know where to take that sentence and saw Zahra recognise her hesitation, saw Zahra think smugly that she herself had never started a sentence she didn't know how to finish. 'And not notice all the darkness inside you. Well, I see you.'

'You see some of me.' It sounded like a concession, which meant it was a wind-up to an attack. 'There are other parts you don't see because – there's a good phrase

I heard recently – it's so many galaxies away from you that you just can't.'

'Are we going to talk about your steadfast belief in justice and democracy and the moral character of a nation? Does Good Zahra want to be acknowledged?'

Zahra stepped forward. Now there was very little distance between them. 'Not long ago you said the scariest thing that happened in our lives was Jimmy. That wasn't even the scariest thing that happened in that year. I thought someone was going to take my father away and throw him in a prison or whip him at a post. I told you about the Brigadier's visit but I didn't tell you how it felt. Isn't that strange? We told each other so many things, but even then I must have known that you wouldn't understand it. In your world, a man getting arrested for drug smuggling was a social dilemma. You lived as if the world we were in didn't touch you. You had no idea about the absolute terror of powerlessness.' She held up a hand. A new thought had come to her. 'Only Jimmy made you feel it, and that's why you hated Jimmy. But here's the difference between us: feeling that powerlessness made me think, I don't want that in the world. I don't want it. No one should know that kind of terror. And it made you think, I'll be the terroriser, not the terrorised.'

Maryam put her glass on the floor so she could applaud. The music had stopped a while ago and the sound echoed, made Woolf climb off her bed and come to see what was happening. 'I concede. Madam Lawyer, that was an excellent closing argument, I'm sure the jury will be convinced.' She leaned forward, dropped her voice. 'Because the jury doesn't know you. Remember how you felt when Jimmy sat in your office? Remember how you felt in that car? That's what you brought to me, your loyal monster of the High Table, when you said "Najam Hussain, engineer, applying for ILR".' A new expression on Zahra's face: uncertainty. And then she went very pale.

One of us will hit the other, Maryam thought. One of us, both of us. We'll make it hurt. And then I'll have to explain it to Layla.

'I'm taking Woolf out,' she said, leaning back on her heels, widening the distance between them. She slapped her hand against her thigh, and Woolf followed her across the living area and up the stairs.

The night was sharp with cold, clear enough for stars. From Primrose Hill she could hear the burbling chatter and singing of the crowds keeping themselves warm with alcohol. Her head was full of noise, accusations and counter-accusations echoing. 'Fucking superior,' she shouted, and the women in front of her crossed over to the other side of the road. She and Woolf walked to the park entrance nearest them, far enough from the crest of the hill that the only people here were those entering to make their way up to the vantage point that would show them London's light-studded skyline beside the dark snake of the river. Once, Woolf used to love to tear across the park and had to be kept on a leash for these night walks. But now she had barely placed four paws on the grass before she bent her back legs, emptied her bladder and turned to leave.

'Why isn't Layla here?' Maryam said, one hand brushing against the fur of the animal's back as they walked home. 'I'm not a monster, am I, Woolf?' The dog looked up at her name, made a consoling sound. The short distance to home seemed very long. Maryam was cold and exhausted, every muscle painfully tight. She couldn't do another round of that – she shivered –

horribleness. God, it had been horrible. They'd both been horrible.

When she walked back down to the living area, Zahra wasn't there. She didn't know if she felt relieved or sad about that. Then she saw the figure moving about outside, Zahra in the garden talking on her phone. She'd turned the oven off – of course, no drama would allow Zahra to let the biryani overcook. That made Maryam smile. There was some way back, there must be. They'd find it. She took the biryani out of the oven, lifted the foil. Perfect.

The door slid open, the chill of outdoors rushed in, Zahra followed with an unreadable expression.

'Who were you talking to?'

'The Chair of CCL.'

'At this hour on New Year's Eve? What for?' She carried the biryani to the table, already set, raita prepared in its earthenware bowl.

Zahra walked as far as the breakfast bar, halfway across the living area, which had the dining table at one end and the sliding door at the other. She pressed her finger on a red dot of wine that they'd missed in the earlier clean-up and rubbed it absent-mindedly on her white silk sleeve. 'A man came to CCL asking for help with his immigration case and I gave his information to someone who had him booted out of the country. He was someone I had an old grudge against. And I gave the information to a person who shared my ill-feeling for him, and who has powerful government connections and no morals. It seems that there's a possibility I acted as I did knowing exactly what she would do. Either way, a man was torn away from his family and his life because I betrayed client confidentiality. I'm not fit to be Director of CCL.'

'Don't be ridiculous. No one but us knows what happened, no one ever will.'

'Jimmy knows. Not the details, but he knows it started with me and ended with the Home Office. One conversation with Hammad will be all it takes to work out the missing piece – Maryam Khan, Prime Minister's Global Business Envoy.'

'Stop imagining crazy things. There isn't a shred of evidence. Who in this world will care about Jimmy and Hammad's conspiracy theories?'

'You believe what matters is getting away with things, nothing else.'

'Oh, I see, you want to prove you're so different.' She kept her tone light, determined not to be dragged into a mud fight again. 'You're not proving it because you didn't really say any of that. Not to the Chair. If you were going to confess, you'd find a priest – I'm sure the Catholics would have you, anyone would, you're a national treasure after all. Now come and eat. The wine on an empty stomach isn't helping anything.'

'I wasn't confessing. I was resigning.'

It had been a night full of small detonations, but Maryam hadn't imagined there was a self-destruct button.

'They won't accept your resignation.'

'I've put the organisation's reputation at intolerable risk. My resignation is accepted. It's over.' Zahra frowned, and said, in the same tone with which she'd earlier asked how many black and how many green cardamom pods to put in the biryani, 'What will I do now?'

'Zahra.'

Zahra steadied herself against the breakfast bar. 'Oh god,' she said, as if only just comprehending.

Maryam walked over swiftly, gripped Zahra's wrist. 'We'll make this OK. We'll fix it.'

Zahra leaned forward, her cheek against Maryam's. Maryam put her arms around Zahra, felt the comfort of their togetherness, the unchanging truth of their friendship through everything the world could throw at them, through everything they could throw at each other.

Zahra whispered in Maryam's ear: 'A part of me has always hated you.'

She stepped away, and walked across the living area. Near the stairs she stopped, went down on one knee and took Woolf's face in her hands. She fondled the animal's ears and Woolf made a whimpering sound, full of sorrow.

Then Zahra stood and walked up the stairs, straight-backed. When she came to the top, she reached for her coat hanging on the rack, and Maryam saw the slump of her shoulders. Everything was in that slump – the disgrace that lay ahead, the empty days, the shame-filled nights, the end of the whole life she had so carefully planned for herself.

'Za!' she called out, but Zahra didn't look back. She opened the door and walked out, into the sound of revelry.

The phone played a happy tune. It was Layla, calling to see how the evening was going. She would be listening to the ringing phone, imagining Zahra and Maryam sipping wine, laughing, swapping stories of childhood, the meal they'd cooked waiting to be devoured, the ornaments put away until they brought them back out next year for another Christmas together, much like the one before and the one before that. Maryam let the phone ring and ring, elbows braced on the breakfast bar, head in her hands. A monster.

LONDON
2020

SPRING

The trees were abundant with leaf once more, the dogs frolicked as though it were any other spring. People walked, purposeful, veering away from each other and nodding in thanks for this new act of courtesy. The dogs were considered safe by some, so several hands reached out, hoping to brush against silken fur. The rarity of touch. A tall woman was walking swiftly down the path that cut from north to south; a smaller woman made more languid progress along the east-to-west path. They arrived at the same moment where the two paths met.

It had been months since they'd last seen each other but neither acknowledged the other. The east-to-west path had come to an end so it only made sense for the second woman to turn on to the north-to-south one. Strides adjusted. The path was broad enough for two women to walk alongside each other while still staying apart. And so they walked. Through Primrose Hill, across the street, along the zoo enclosure where the giraffe house was closed and down through Regent's Park.

Ambulances wailed, clouds drifted past the sun, the cricket pitches were deserted. A child fell and bloodied her knee; her mother implored passers-by not to stop and help. They walked and they kept on walking. Out of the park, along Park Crescent, down the eerie emptiness of Regent Street, and past Eros's statue where two lovers kissed in defiance of everything, in celebration of everything, and further on they went towards the bronze lions of Trafalgar Square and beyond they would keep going, beyond to the Thames itself, and perhaps then they would turn, perhaps, or else not. All the while they kept looking ahead and didn't speak. There was nothing to say, and nowhere else to be.

ACKNOWLEDGEMENTS

Alexandra Pringle, for the magic of the last twenty-eight years.

Victoria Hobbs, Faiza S. Khan, Rebecca Saletan and everyone at Bloomsbury, Riverhead and A. M. Heath who has played a role in the life of this book.

Lynn Akashi, Tahmima Anam, Therese Chehade, Asad Haider, Suzy Hansen, Maha Khan-Phillips, Zain Mustafa, Dermot O'Flynn, Anna Pincus, Elizabeth Porto, Gillian Slovo, Pam Thompson, Karachi Twitter, Alex von Tunzelmann.

And all my childhood friends.

A NOTE ON THE AUTHOR

KAMILA SHAMSIE was born and grew up in Karachi, Pakistan. Her most recent novel *Home Fire* won the Women's Prize for Fiction in 2018. It was also longlisted for the Man Booker Prize 2017, shortlisted for the Costa Best Novel Award, and won the London Hellenic Prize. She is the author of six previous novels including *Burnt Shadows*, shortlisted for the Orange Prize, and *A God in Every Stone*, shortlisted for the Women's Bailey's Prize and the Walter Scott Prize. Her work has been translated into over 25 languages. Kamila Shamsie is a Fellow of the Royal Society of Literature and was named a Granta Best of Young British Novelist in 2013. She is professor of creative writing at the University of Manchester and lives in London.

@kamilashamsie

A NOTE ON THE TYPE

The text of this book is set in Linotype Sabon, a typeface named after the type founder Jacques Sabon. It was designed by Jan Tschichold and jointly developed by Linotype, Monotype and Stempel in response to a need for a typeface to be available in identical form for mechanical hot metal composition and hand composition using foundry type.

Tschichold based his design for Sabon roman on a font engraved by Garamond, and Sabon italic on a font by Granjon. It was first used in 1966 and has proved an enduring modern classic.